BLIND MOON ALLEY

ALSO BY JOHN FLORIO

Sugar Pop Moon

A Jersey Leo Novel

BLIND MOON ALLEY

John Florio

SEVENTH STREET BOOKS®
AN IMPRINT OF PROMETHEUS BOOKS
59 JOHN GLENN DRIVE • AMHERST, NY 14228
www.seventhstreetbooks.com

Published 2014 by Seventh Street Books®, an imprint of Prometheus Books

Cover image © Bernice Abbott, Changing New York series 1936.
Photography Collection, Miriam and Ira D. Wallach Division of Art,
Print and Photographs, the New York Public Library, Astor, Lenox,
and Tilden Foundations

Cover design by Nicole Sommer-Lecht

Inquiries should be addressed to
Seventh Street Books
59 John Glenn Drive
Amherst, New York 14228
VOICE: 716–691–0133 • FAX: 716–691–0137
WWW.SEVENTHSTREETBOOKS.COM

18 17 16 15 14 • 5 4 3 2 1

Library of Congress Cataloging-in-Publication Data

Florio, John, 1960–
    Blind Moon Alley : a Jersey Leo novel / John Florio.
        pages cm
    ISBN 978-1-61614-887-4 (paperback)
    ISBN 978-1-61614-888-1 (ebook)
    1. Bartenders—Fiction. 2. Bars (Drinking establishments)—Fiction.
3. Prohibition—Fiction. 4. Criminal investigation—Fiction. I. Title.

PS3606.L665B55 2014
813'.6—dc23

                                                        2014006858

Printed in the United States of America

For the outsiders.

1931

CHAPTER 1

Newspapers create heroes. Six months ago, they created me. On Christmas, the *Inquirer* turned me—a twenty-four-year-old albino with chalk-white skin, kinky yellow hair, and fluttering green eyes—into the toast of Philadelphia. It took all of eight words to undo a lifetime of insults. *Son of Former Boxing Champ Saves Kidnapped Boy*. That headline, along with two columns of ink and a three-inch shot of my glorious mug, filled the upper-right corner of the broadsheet, pushing Aaron Garvey's date with the electric chair down below the fold. It was a snowy morning, but every newsboy in the city had that paper hoisted over his head. Now it hangs on the wall behind me as I work the bar at a speakeasy the locals call the Ink Well.

I'm Jersey Leo, a genetic milkshake with one too many scoops of vanilla, a piano keyboard with no sharps or flats, a punch line to an inside joke that I've never been in on. Despite what you might have read in the *Inquirer*, I'm no hero, at least not the kind you want your children to be. Ask any one of the cops who've come to me for a spiked beer or a stuffed envelope; he'll tell you I'm breaking the law every time I fill their glasses. No, I'm not out to rid our streets of crime and corruption. All I want to do is pour some moon, make a little dough, and if the stars align, spend a bit of time with a certain five-foot-two-inch coat checker whose eyes haven't seen enough of the real world to stop sparkling. The only reason I made the front page was because I found myself standing at the wrong end of a gun barrel and made sure it wouldn't happen again—to me or anybody like me.

A trail of blue cigarette smoke snakes its way over the bar as the radio plays "Little White Lies." Aside from those little lies and this bleached bartender, there's nothing else white in the place. The Ink Well is a colored joint, a tiny hole tucked away in the narrow basement of a nondescript brownstone on Juniper and Vine. It's an easy target for the uniformed bulls of the sixth precinct—at least a half-dozen of them show up every week to drink our booze and take our cash. The good news is that the Feds don't even know it's here. You've got to go around the building's main entrance and down five stone steps just to find the front door. Once you're inside, the place is no bigger than a tenement flat. The front room fits only three candlelit iron tables. Pass through it and you'll reach four booths sitting opposite a polished oak bar that runs along the brick wall in the back. Find the bar and you'll find me.

I like the place for the same reason as the folks who come here. The Ink Well is cozy and dark; the kind of joint that softens the edges of a hardened city. Just walking through the door helps me forget the bread lines that are waiting around the corner. There aren't many places an albino can call home. This is one.

Tonight, chattering voices and clinking glasses fill the air that's normally as quiet as the bell on the owner Doolie's cash register. Doolie can thank Homer, a longshoreman I met two years ago while I was hijacking rum at the Philly Navy Yard for my boss back in New York. Homer's no Einstein—the cops call him a retard—but he's popular enough to convince eight of his friends from the dock to join him for a drink in the middle of a hundred-degree heat wave.

He's standing at his usual place at the back end of the bar, talking with a barrel-chested old-timer with two chins, a round gut, and bags the size of chestnuts under his eyes. I recognize the lug as Doolie's childhood friend, a factory worker named Calvin I met here a couple of weeks ago.

I empty what's left of the bourbon into Homer's glass, but I leave his and Calvin's money on the bar, untouched. Homer's a day laborer; Calvin lost his job at Baldwin Locomotive about a month back. I just can't see taking the last of their dough.

"He done it for sure. He let that cop bleed," Homer is saying, no doubt referring to Aaron Garvey. Beads of sweat roll down his angular forehead as he speaks. "Man had a right to do it. Took guts, it did."

Homer usually swings his head up and points his puffy eyes at the ceiling when he speaks, but when he mentions Garvey, he looks down at his shoes. His sloped shoulders seem to drop even lower and his long neck seems to bend like clay. He slowly shakes his head.

"They gonna fry 'im for sure," he says, his right hand in his pants pocket and his left holding his bourbon. "Yes sir, they gonna fry 'im. Damn shame."

Homer is right—Garvey has no hope with Governor Pinchot—but he's the only one in Philly who seems to care. Everybody else still remembers what happened three years ago at the Red Canary. Garvey took down a bull—he put a slug in the cop's brainstem and then refused to testify at his own trial. Most of the locals would pull the lever themselves.

Me, I was tight with Garvey in grade school and still can't get used to the idea that my childhood buddy is a cold-blooded killer.

"I knew Garvey growing up in Hoboken," I say but let it rest. If I tell Homer that Garvey was my only friend back then, I'll have to talk about how many times he took beatings for me, how many times he fought off the teachers who'd whip my pale ass just to watch it turn red. Garvey didn't speak about it then, and I'm not about to bring it up now.

"Used to be a good Joe," is all I say.

Calvin hoists his glass and takes a slug. He's either drinking to Garvey, good Joes, or free booze.

Homer wants to hear more about Garvey—the look on his thin, creased face is that of a kid about to meet Jack Dempsey. But I'm going to disappoint him.

"I haven't seen him since the sixth grade," I say, shrugging it off.

"Those bulls done pushed him, they did," Homer says, his eyes rolling back to their usual upward position. "You'd a done the same."

As I toss the empty bourbon bottle into the trash, I spot Angela greeting a regular named Wallace. She takes his hat and hangs it up. I picture myself following her into the coatroom, my hair slicked back, as straight and shiny as John Gilbert's, my skin as clear and smooth as Valentino's. I imagine us sitting at Monte's on Broad Street. Her hair's done up and her nails are painted. I'm wearing my Sunday best. We share a salad. We sip tea and tell stories about growing up; we tell each other what scares us in the dark. We keep on talking as they sweep the floors around us.

Doolie's in the kitchen and yells to me that he needs a fresh bottle of brandy. I've only got a couple of fingers' worth up here, so I lift the mat behind the bar, open the trapdoor, and make my way down the spiral staircase into the sub-basement. I step into the familiar scent of moist dirt as I pull the chain on the light that hangs from the ceiling. The room is cool and dank. Beer kegs line the stone wall on my left. Eighty cases of whiskey and moon are stacked across from them, blocking the hatch that leads out to the dirt road Doolie calls Blind Moon Alley. As far as I know, the only time that alley is used is when the Ink Well gets a delivery. I've got to admit it's a pretty good setup.

I open a case of brandy, grab a bottle, and head back upstairs. When my head emerges from behind the bar, I see Doolie and Angela in front of the kitchen, staring at me. A group of silver-haired Joes across from them are drinking martinis and laughing as they sing "Walking My Baby Back Home," but my friends' faces tell me we've got trouble.

Doolie's eyes are wide open as he nods toward the phone booth next to the kitchen. The receiver is dangling on its wire.

I walk over to him and he whispers to me.

"State pen," he says.

"For who?" I ask.

When he doesn't say anything, I have my answer.

I can't blame him for being worried; the only legal thing we've served tonight is a martini olive. But I've been around a while and I've never heard of a warden arresting anybody. Then again, I've also never heard of a prison warden calling a speakeasy. I step into the phone booth, grab the receiver, and slide the door shut.

"Hello?"

"Mr. Leo?" the operator asks.

"Depends who's calling."

"One moment, please."

There's a clicking sound as the call is patched through and I hear a man's voice. It's raspy and weak.

"Hiya, Snowball," he says.

I was hoping I'd heard the last of that name once I left New York; it only reminds me of what I am outside of Philly. My father always said that some things can't be shaken.

"Snowball?" he asks again.

This time it hits me who's on the other end.

"Garv?" I say. The phone booth is stifling, but I'm not about to open it now.

"Damn, it's good to hear your voice," he says. "What you doin' in Philly? Saw your picture. Fuckin' hero."

I have no idea how he got his hands on the *Inquirer*, but at least that explains how he knew I was in Philly. He must have spent the past six months tracking me down until somebody gave him this number. Not an easy task, considering the location of his office.

"Don't believe everything you read," I tell him, surprised at how easily we're falling into our old rhythm after twelve years.

"Bullshit," he says. His voice is cracking and I wish I could pour him a beer. Then he says: "Y'know, they're fryin' me in a couple of days."

I tell him that I heard about it on the radio.

"Asked me what I want for my last meal," he says. "As if it's a fancy occasion, right? Just like a regular restaurant, except the chair at the head of the table has fuckin' cables attached to it. I told them to go screw their mothers."

There's nothing to say, so I stay quiet. Before he says anything else, the call clicks back to the operator. She tells me to report to Eastern State Penitentiary, Tuesday night, seven o'clock.

I'm not following and I tell her so.

"Mr. Garvey's last meal," she says. "He's allowed one guest, and he's requested you."

The tone in her voice says she assumes any friend of Aaron Garvey's is a criminal. I'd feel better about myself if she were wrong.

She spills a bunch of details and I jot them down on the back of Doolie's yellow pages.

I wipe my sweat from the receiver with my shirtsleeve, hang up the phone, and step out of the booth. The older guys are still singing in the corner. I tell Doolie and Angela that everything's fine, then take my place behind the bar and splash some bourbon over ice for Homer. I don't mention that I'll be meeting my old friend Aaron Garvey just in time to watch him die.

I put a smile on my face and rinse a batch of highball glasses. I'm trying to wash Garvey off my mind, but I can't stop wondering why, if the guy could share his last meal with one person, he picked me.

CHAPTER 2

My apartment is two flights up from the Ink Well. One of the windows in the parlor is painted shut and the plaster on the ceiling is cracked and peeling. I'm not complaining; it's a decent place and Doolie cut me a square deal. The guy doesn't have deep pockets—the Ink Well is getting squeezed just like every other joint in town—but as long as I'm running the bar, I don't have to pay a dime in rent. If he hadn't hired me, I might be back in New York, sleeping on a park bench or fighting for a bed in a church basement.

A gust of wind rattles the window and I look outside before pulling down the shades. There's still some light in the sky, but the air is muggy and a thunderstorm is baptizing the Philly locals. Two blondes are across the street, huddled under the awning at Ronnie's Luncheonette, smoking cigarettes and laughing, oblivious to the fact that Aaron Garvey will get smacked with a thousand volts of juice later tonight, right here in the City of Brotherly Love.

I've got the radio on. Rudy Vallee's singing "You're Driving Me Crazy," and the music brings me closer to another world—one without speakeasies, electric chairs, or albinos. Listening to Rudy Vallee makes me feel white. Normal white. As he croons, I picture myself on a beach, free of blisters and prescription creams. My mirror hangs directly over the radio, so I turn the other way, toward the kitchen. I sing along with Rudy and promise myself I'll smear some of the doc's ointment on my face as soon as the song is over.

I reach into my pocket, pull out thirty bucks—my week's pay—and shove it into an envelope. Then I sit at my desk, which has nothing on it other than a typewriter, a stack of blank paper, and a framed photo of my father during his younger days in the ring. I scrawl his name—Ernie Leo—on the envelope and address it to the Hy-Hat, the Harlem social club I started visiting when we moved to New York eleven years ago. Now I own the place and the champ runs it. From what he tells me, things are going well. The Hy-Hat has more members than ever before and he's giving late-night boxing lessons to the older kids; even some of the girls have been hitting the dummy bag. He says I should quit breaking the law and work with him, but it doesn't seem to cross his mind that the Hy-Hat would be an empty storefront if I weren't sending an envelope his way on the first of every month. And I need a bar in front of me to do that.

Hunching over the Underwood he bought me before I dropped out of City College, I hammer out a note. I tell him about Garvey's invitation to dinner, and I ask him if he remembers how the girls in Hoboken used to call Garvey "Adonis" because of his massive shoulders and bright white teeth.

My sweaty index fingers dampen the metal keys as I thank him for taking care of the Hy-Hat. I tell him that I'll quit bartending and join him at the club as soon as I find a job back in New York. But then I reread the note, rip it out of the typewriter, and toss it in the trash. I don't want to let the champ down again. The truth is that I won't be walking away from the Ink Well any time soon. New York isn't doing any better than Philly—its classifieds are thinner than my shaving razor. For now, the cash I send will have to speak for me.

I seal the envelope and jam it into my pocket. Then I reach into the closet and put a five-dollar bill into the Zealandia shoebox I use for Angela's high-school fund. She wants to go back to school—she dropped out so she could help her uncle, Doolie, run the Ink Well when his wife died. The problem is that she can't afford to leave her job. Doolie covers her apartment over on But-tonwood just like he does for me in this place. By this time next year, though, I just might have a surprise for her.

I close the box, throw on my raincoat, and head out the door. Dinner's at seven and I don't want to keep my friend waiting.

❦

I pull the Auburn to the curb and kill the wipers, lights, and engine. Eastern State Penitentiary might as well be a military fortress, right down to the filth on its walls and guards at its iron gates. It's hard to believe I'm in Fairmount, not even two miles north of the Ink Well.

The rain is tap-dancing on the roof of the car. I don't have time to wait it out; dinner starts in half an hour. I yank my fedora down low on my forehead, pull the lapels of my raincoat over my neck, and trot across the avenue. The shower is blowing sideways; it's stinging my cheeks like a plague of warm needles.

Turrets reach up and pierce the sky to my right and left. I'm sure each one houses a marksman with a loaded Springfield, steady trigger finger, and little time for Aaron Garvey's friends. The prison stretches more than five city blocks. I make it under the granite arch that marks the main entrance and shake the rain from my hat and oxfords. A red-haired guard in a blue uniform and tan cap struts out of the gatehouse. The badge on his chest says his name is Milmo.

I start to tell him why I've come, but before I can get a word out, he sees my face and winces. The rain is still prickling my skin and the blotches on my face are probably the color of a candied apple.

"You're here for what?" His eyes meet mine, and he stares me down. Maybe he doesn't like albinos. He should only know what I think of prison guards.

"I'm here to see Aaron Garvey."

He straightens up when he hears the name. It hits me that I'm still relying on Garvey to be taken seriously.

Milmo tells me he has to pat me down.

"I'm not stupid enough to show up here packing heat," I tell him as I unbutton my raincoat. "But you're gonna find a flask in my back pocket."

He's bigger than I am but that's not saying much. I'm barely six feet tall and weigh a buck-sixty-five. My midsection is soft and my shoulders are so bony they look as if a miner could use them to chisel stone.

He frisks me. Once he's satisfied I'm clean, he reaches around my waist and pulls out my flask. Then he opens it and takes a sniff of Doolie's best whiskey.

"Smells illegal," he tells me.

"It is," I tell him. "But I was invited to dinner and didn't want to show up empty-handed."

He takes a healthy slug and screws the top back on as his cheeks flush. Then he slips the flask back into my pocket. For a cheap shamus, he's sure got the swagger of a real cop.

He ushers me into the gatehouse, where three other guards are sitting on folding chairs and listening to Eddie Cantor on the radio. I turn away from the bright lamps they've got burning, but it's no use, my eyes shimmy. Milmo stares at me with the same confused expression I get from the rumrunners who say I'm too white to be colored, and too colored to be trusted. I could save him four years of medical school by telling him that albino eyes go haywire every once in a while, but I skip it.

"If you don't pick up the pace," I tell him, "I'm going to miss the appetizers."

He grabs a stack of papers on his desk and has me sign one that says I'm Jersey Leo. Then he gets a short, bald guard named

Flanagan to join us on our walk to cellblock one. They open an iron gate and we make our way through the empty, fenced-in grounds. It's a desolate, flooded square, even starker than the schoolyard Garvey and I played in back in Hoboken.

I follow them down a dim, muggy corridor lined on both sides with matching doors. The doors are solid wood—no windows—and I wonder how many guys have childhood friends locked up here and don't even know it. We stop at a door marked forty-two. Milmo and Flanagan draw their nightsticks and stand on opposite sides, Milmo on the left and Flanagan on the right. Milmo reaches over and slowly unlatches the door, then motions with his head for me to go on in.

For the first time since I arrived, I wonder if I'm about to see the warm eyes of my old friend or the cold glare of a ruthless killer. Milmo's waiting at the door and I won't give him the satisfaction of seeing me blink. My throat goes dry and my ears go hot, but I walk into the cell without breaking stride.

The cramped room has a high arched ceiling with a small hole exposing a patch of gray sky. Rain spits into the cell, sprinkling the back wall. In the center of the space is a square table with two meals waiting; on the far side of it sits my old buddy Aaron Garvey. When he sees me, he flashes one of his schoolboy grins and I'm immediately back at Elementary School Four.

"Hiya, Snowball," he says, standing up and shaking my hand.

His lopsided smile is tainted by a mouthful of yellow teeth; a front tooth is broken and nearly as brown as his skin. He looks weaker than I'd imagined—Adonis's chest is now at least three inches smaller than his stomach—and when he shakes my hand, his bony grip manages only a light squeeze before it relaxes. People think Garvey is losing his life tonight, but it's been getting sucked out of him since he walked in here three years ago.

"Look at you," he says as he gives me a pat on the back. "Y'look just like in the paper."

I don't bother to comment that newspapers print in black and gray. "Thanks," I say.

He shakes his head in disbelief. "Hard to believe it's been so long." When his last couple of words pass that broken tooth they're accompanied by a faint whistle.

Garvey sits back down and the spirit drains from his face. His dark cheeks are drawn, but in his reddish-brown eyes I spot a glimmer of the twelve-year-old kid who fought for me. That kid needs help, and I'm sorry I can't be the one to give it to him.

Milmo stands in the corner of the cell, his nightstick at his side, and I hear the door shut behind me. I realize that he'll be with us until I leave, which means Garvey and I won't be talking about a number of things during dinner—including him.

"Have a seat," Garvey tells me, pointing to the open folding chair as if he were sitting in a real dining room. I throw my coat and jacket over the back of the chair and sit down. The chair is uneven—it rocks from leg to leg. The air is saturated and my shirt collar clings to the back of my neck. I try my best to look comfortable.

"I brought you something," I say as I pull out my flask.

"Hopin' you would," he says. The grateful tone in his voice is as much a part of my old friend as the way he rubs his ear with his thumb.

There are two empty coffee cups sitting on the table, so I fill each one halfway. He lifts his.

"Old friends," he says and downs his whiskey.

Milmo coughs and I know why. He's not about to watch us finish off the booze without getting a taste. I hand him my cup; for this meal, I'll be drinking straight from the flask.

Satisfied, Milmo walks behind Garvey to the back of the cell, where he sits on the corner of the cot and sips his hooch.

I refill Garvey's cup and then down a slug.

"Glad y'showed up," my friend tells me. "I'm on my own here. I might be alone later tonight, too."

He must know that the execution is open only to the press and immediate family, so I don't bother explaining why I'll be back at the Ink Well when he says his final good-byes.

"It'll be fine," he says with a sarcastic chuckle. "What could go wrong?"

"Nothing," Milmo says from behind Garvey.

Garvey's shoulders stiffen and he flips his thumb toward Milmo. "Thinks I'm a fuckin' butcher."

I'm wondering if Milmo is wrong, but I won't put my friend on the spot, especially since he's only got a few hours left to live. I must be wearing a troubled expression, though, because he volunteers an answer.

"Oh, I done it," he says, tugging on the cuffs of his gray prison garb. "But I ain't what they think."

Then he wipes his forehead with the crook of his arm and starts talking about the old days. I let him talk, but I'm missing half of what he's saying. We must be closing in on seven-thirty. That gives Garvey thirty minutes before he's driven over to Rockview and strapped to Old Smokey. As he rattles on, I pick at the dinner he ordered for each of us: a boneless steak, two fried eggs, a baked potato, a wedge of lettuce with blue cheese dressing, a slice of cheesecake, and a chocolate milkshake.

I'm sawing away at my steak with one of the state's butter knives when Garvey asks me if I remember playing hooky to watch the Giants at the Polo Grounds. He's wasting time. I wouldn't care, except he's fidgeting in his seat like a twelve-year-old itching for recess.

"Hey, Milmo," I say.

"Yeah?" the guard says, not bothering to stand up or turn his head my way.

"Don't you need to check on your buddy outside?"

"I've got a job to do," Milmo says. "And it's to watch the two of you."

I saw this coming from the minute Milmo took my hooch. Reaching into my overcoat, I pull out the envelope with my father's name scratched across it. A pang of guilt bites at me as I picture the champ trying to meet the Hy-Hat's rent with nothing but a cashbox filled with IOUs.

I rip open the envelope, pull out a pair of sawbucks, and jam the rest into my pants pocket. Then I walk over to Milmo and extend the bills between my index and middle finger. "I'll bet you twenty dollars nobody will ever know if you were here or not."

It's a fat offer, but Milmo doesn't budge. Maybe he gets greased more often than I thought.

A grin twists the side of his mouth. "In here freaks pay double."

I stare him down. "In here I'm not the freak."

Garvey gets up from the table. "Damn right."

My friend is a bit shaky when he walks—I wonder what kind of beating he took before dinner tonight—but the loose skin under his eyes has gone tight. For a split second, I see the kid who stood up to those heartless teachers back in Hoboken—and the man who squeezed that trigger at the Red Canary.

"It's okay, Garv," I tell him, motioning him back to his chair. He doesn't sit down, but at least he stays quiet.

Milmo looks up at me. "Well?"

The clock is ticking, so I reach back into my pocket for the ripped envelope. I pull out the last of the money I'd earmarked for the Hy-Hat.

"Thirty bucks," I tell Milmo as I hold out my entire week's pay. "Split it with your boy outside, however you like."

"Sold," he says and takes the cash. He slips it into his breast pocket, underneath his badge.

Before he leaves, he finishes off his booze and puts the empty coffee cup on the table. Then he leans in front of Garvey and takes the flask, passing it under Garvey's nose before heading for the door.

I block his way. "You can't take it all, Milmo. Christ, even a Fed would leave a taste."

Milmo chuckles and splashes some of the brown into the two coffee cups, making a point to spill a bit of Garvey's onto the table. Then he tells us, "You've got three minutes."

Finally, he disappears, shutting the door behind him and leaving me alone with my friend.

I sit back down, my neck soaked with sweat. It's hot as Doolie's kitchen in here and dealing with Milmo hasn't exactly cooled me down.

"Owe you one," Garvey says.

"Not the way I see it," I say. "You saved my ass more times than I can count."

"Not true," he says. "But I'm glad you think so." Then he leans forward and whispers as if Milmo were still sitting behind him. "'Cuz I need a favor."

I nod, figuring I can handle pretty much anything he asks.

"You remember Myra Banks?" he asks me.

"Sure do," I tell him.

Myra and I were the two misfits of Elementary School Four. She was a sad, quiet kid; she took a lot of guff because she had a club right foot and dreamt of being a Ziegfeld girl. She'd spend most of her time alone in the school library, her face buried in *Photoplay* magazine. She was my first crush, my first kiss, and, I suppose you could say, the only girlfriend I've ever had. We ran into each other in New York five years ago. It was late November, a week after Thanksgiving, and snow was coming down in lazy flurries. She didn't have a penny, but she'd come to see the Ziegfeld Follies on Broadway. I was making decent money rolling kegs in Hell's Kitchen—I'd just dropped out of City College but I told her I was still studying there—and I bought her dinner on the West Side. We ate pot roast at a place called Rosie's; then we took the A train up to the Hotel Theresa and escaped into each other's arms. We spent the night under a quilt, doing things we'd never heard about in elementary school. She'd grown into quite a looker; her skin was a light tan, her eyes the shape of large almonds, and her wavy hair as long and loose as Mary Pickford's. But what I remember most was her foot—how it looked out of its shoe—twisted and mangled, with a red bony bump sticking out where the instep should be. Looking back, it makes sense we found each other.

"What's become of her?" I ask Garvey, my mind flashing dusty images of her crooked front tooth, soft pink nipples, and tender red ankle.

"You won't believe it," he says with a light chuckle. "She owns a piece of the Red Canary."

"Are you joking with me?"

Garvey doesn't say anything, but his lack of response is answer enough.

"How the hell did that happen?" I say.

It just doesn't fit. The Red Canary is where Garvey gunned down that cop. The owner is Otto Gorsky, a twisted killer who goes by the name of Mr. Lovely. I don't know a lot about him, other than he's connected to Chicago mobsters and has a chauffeur drive him around in a burgundy Packard town car that's dressed up with fat whitewalls and has a gleaming serpent on the hood. But the details don't matter. A guy like Lovely isn't about to partner with a Negro dame who's broke and crippled, I don't care how good she looks. I've heard the rumors that he's near death, that he's got some kind of weird disease, but word on the street is that he's still the same cold-blooded reptilian bastard he's always been. He'll make you rich if you do him right, but he'll butcher you like an animal if things go wrong. Just last week, he supposedly sat in an armchair, laughing and munching on jelly beans as his triggermen sliced up a two-timing rumrunner named Floyd Rumson with an ice hook and a pair of rusty hedge clippers.

Myra can't stand up to that kind of depravity. I remember the bullies riding her; they laughed at her clumsy black shoe, her limp, and the way her thick upper lip trembled when she was frightened. They called her a gimp. They threw stones at her. They stole her shoe right off her foot and loaded it up with a fresh, steaming pile of horseshit. She was an easy target. And she took it all without fighting back.

Garvey's looking at me. "I know what you're thinking," he says. "But it's true, she owns a chunk of the place. Why else would I have been there?"

"Okay," I say, still having trouble putting the broken girl with the quivering lip and oversized tears in the same room as Lovely. "I guess I'll buy it. Myra owns a piece of the Canary. And?"

He leans forward and lowers his voice. "And she bought it with my money. Twenty large."

"You gave her twenty thousand?"

"Loaned her," he corrects me, still in his hoarse whisper. "She was supposed to pay me back."

"Forget it, Garv." I'm not about to yank twenty grand from a woman who was naked and moaning that she loved me the last time I saw her. "Let Myra have her piece."

His jaw is tight. "You're not getting it. The money's gone—Myra used it to buy into the Canary. The problem is the dead cop's partner, Reeger. Since I landed here, he's been on her back, raiding the joint, locking her up for weeks, really swinging his hammer—all because she knows me. If I were on the outside, I'd take care of this myself."

His eyes go so cold they send a chill up my spine. I put my elbows on the table, leaning forward so my armpits can breathe. I want to help my friend, and there's no question I owe him, but he's desperate and I'm not exactly sure what he's asking.

"What do you want me to do, Garv?"

"He's sending me a message," he says. "I want you to send one back."

Garvey's got to realize that Reeger isn't going to walk away because a bleached bartender shows up in the name of a dead man. The only way to end this is to plug Reeger, and I'm not about to gun down a cop, I don't care how long I've known Garvey. My friend must know somebody with bloodier hands than mine.

"Why me?" I say.

"You always cared about Myra. And from what I've read, you're the man for the job."

"I'm not. And I haven't seen Myra since the sixth grade."

I'm lying and I'm not sure why—it's not as if Garvey will be around long enough to sing. But I remember Myra asking me not to give her up; she was worried about a guy she called Jonesy, the latest in her list of soul-sucking cretins. This one had moved into her place, promising his love but delivering nothing other than a left hook and fractured cheekbone. I still wonder if it was her fear of Jonesy that pushed her to crawl under the blanket for one more go-round with me that night.

"Let's leave and never come back," she said when we'd finished, picking up a *Life* magazine and pointing to the photo of the Hollywoodland sign on its cover. Her hazel eyes were alive with possibilities, but all I did was sit there wondering which one Jonesy had blackened. "We can get on a train right now," she said.

It wasn't the first time she'd brought it up—she'd talked about running off to Hollywood for as long as I could remember. But that night her dream was raging. Had I said okay, I just may have found myself tending bar on a beach in Santa Monica. But reality has a way of taking the fun out of life. I had kegs to roll and rum to run, so I said no. I didn't realize what I'd done to Myra until she buried her face in her hands, hiding the shame of another rejection behind her shiny, wet fingers. I wanted to add that I'd never felt more at home than when we were under those hotel sheets, but I stayed mute, and still curse myself for doing so. She deserved to hear it. As things turned out, we never spoke again after that weekend, although I did send my thoughts her way that Christmas. They arrived in the form of two local triggermen asking for Jonesy. I doubt the bastard ever touched her again. If he did, it was with ten broken fingers and a shattered kneecap.

Garvey is still waiting on my answer, no doubt hoping I'm softening. "You'd be pulling Myra out of the fire," he says. "She might even toss you a few bucks."

I'm sure the Hy-Hat could use the dough, but if my father doesn't like taking the cash I earn bartending, he's certainly not going to want any money I boost from a speakeasy.

"Sorry, Garv."

"You'd be helping the Canary, too," Garvey says. "Reeger keeps showing up, making a scene, can't be good for customers. Charge the joint in hooch," he says. "Or women."

The door opens and Garvey stops talking. He takes another bite of cheesecake and motions for me to do the same.

I spear a forkful as Milmo hands me back my flask, now empty.

"Back so soon?" I ask.

He shrugs his shoulders and wisecracks, "I missed you guys." Then he sits back down on Garvey's cot.

Garvey's looking at me, no doubt hoping for a sign that I'll wrap up his unfinished business.

"I'll think about it," is all I say.

"All I'm askin'," he says before picking up his cup and taking a slug of brown.

Then we finish what's left of our meal without saying a word. We both know I'll have to leave soon, and talking just seems to speed up the clock. I grab my whiskey, hoping it will help me shake the fact that I'm not able to save the only kid who ever stood up for me.

Garvey taps his cup against mine and we sit in silence, nursing our final drops of hooch.

⬦⬦

The clock at the end of the bar reads just shy of midnight. The Ink Well is empty except for Homer and me, so I pour him a shot of moon and match it with one of my own. I'm drinking to Garvey, who'll be saying his final words when the minute hand strikes twelve. The radio is playing "Please Don't Talk about Me When I'm Gone" and I promise Garvey that I won't.

"Sure sounds like Garvey's a good Joe," Homer says. He runs his hand over his nappy black hair and gazes upward again. If I didn't know better, I'd expect him to order some of the whiskey glittering on the top shelf behind me.

"Doesn't matter," I say. "It won't help him now."

"I don't blame him none for what he done," he says, his fist clenched around his shot glass. "No, I don't."

"I don't either," I tell him, even though I'm not sure what I think. I'd like to believe Garvey was set up, but he never addressed it when I visited the pen, and the folks who were at the Red Canary that night said he shot the bull in cold blood.

I refill Homer's glass when a broad-shouldered palooka in a baggy blue raincoat and dark fedora walks through the door.

Normally, I wouldn't look twice except he's white. He's not a local bull—I already know all of their faces. He must be some kind of thug, maybe a stickup artist. For the first time since I left New York, I miss bartending at the Pour House. At least Diego had my back, working the door and frisking for metal.

As the guy makes his way to the bar, beads of sweat coat his creased forehead. A scar on his left cheek resembles a blood-red caterpillar, and he's got a bulb at the end of his nose that looks as if it's gone a couple of rounds with a knitting needle.

"Whiskey," he says in a scratchy voice and lights up a ciggy. "A double, rocks."

"Coming up," I say. I throw four cubes into a glass and drown them.

I slide his drink across the bar and he's careful not to touch my hand when he grabs it. I'm used to it; everybody's afraid to catch what I've got.

He downs his whiskey and slides his glass back at me. I fill it again, same ice.

Homer looks confused. He gazes at the oaf and then steals a glance at me. I suppose he's thinking I should do something, but I'm not being dealt much of a hand.

The oaf looks at the front page of the *Inquirer* hanging behind the bar. "You must be that albino," he says, nodding toward the paper.

"You must be a genius," I say, wondering why my tongue is always a half-step in front of my brain.

He's got a few inches on me, so I put him at six-two. I curse myself for not having my gun tucked under my apron; it's sitting with my brass knuckles behind the ice bin, doing me no good.

Homer slips his right hand under his gut and into his pocket. I don't know what he's packing, and I'm hoping things stay calm enough that I never have to find out.

"That'll be two bucks," I say.

The guy's lips stretch into a smug smile and he plunges his hand into his pocket. I'm expecting to see a gun, but he pulls out a badge.

"Jack Reeger," he says, flashing the metal at Homer and me. "But you boys can call me Sarge."

So this is Reeger. He's not about to tell me he'll let up on Myra, so I wait for him to tell me why he's here. And what it will cost me to get him to leave.

He takes a drag on his smoke and blows a cloud between us, where an implied threat hangs in the air.

"Where's Garvey?" he says, with a tone as light as a friend asking for a dime.

I look at the clock. It's five past midnight.

"Dead," I tell him. Then I add, "Sarge."

Reeger's face crunches. He leans on the bar, his cigarette bouncing on the corner of his lips when he speaks. "You were there tonight, right? There can't be two of you."

"There can't be two of anybody," I snap back. "And yes, I was there. Now I'm here." I nod at his hooch. "You owe me two bucks."

My heart's dancing fast enough to headline at the Cotton Club.

Reeger pounds his fist on the bar. "He's not going to walk away," he shouts, the corner of his upper lip twisting as he barks. "Now tell me where he is, you white-bleached jigaboo freak whatever the fuck you are."

He reaches into his jacket and this time I'm sure a gun is coming out. Homer doesn't wait to find out. He pulls a utility knife from his pocket and presses the steel blade to Reeger's neck, right under his jaw. I clench my fingers against the smooth brass rail that wraps the bar. I'm convinced the Sarge's windpipe is about to start hissing like a steam whistle.

"You best pay," Homer says, his eyes aiming straight up

toward the ceiling and the vein on the side of his neck bulging. "Fork over the two bucks."

"Calm down, Homer," I say, but the look in my slow friend's eyes says he wants to cut Reeger to the floor, badge or no badge.

Reeger's lids narrow. He reaches into his breast pocket, making a show that he's not pulling a gun. As he pulls out his bill-fold, he swings his elbow directly into Homer's throat. Homer's blade clangs to the floor and he's gasping for air.

I go for my gun, but Reeger lunges over the bar and grabs my collar with both hands. Homer's on the floor across from the bar, croaking.

Reeger pulls my face so close to his that I can see a hair shooting out of the scar on his cheek. "I'll take a look around if you don't mind."

Then he wraps his right hand behind my head and slams my nose against the brass railing in front of the bar. I feel like I've been hit by a speeding subway train. I lift my head up; my temples are pounding and I smell blood trickling out of my nostrils.

The room is spinning, but I can tell Reeger has a gun and he's pointing it between my eyes.

He says, "You screw with me, I won't only drop the hammer on Garvey, I'll nail you and the retard."

He walks to the back of the joint and looks into the kitchen before poking his head under the tables in each of the booths. He must be satisfied we're alone, because he crosses the barroom and walks over to Homer, who has crawled in front of a table in the front room. Homer is on his knees, clutching his Adam's apple.

Reeger pushes his gun behind Homer's ear. "Nighty-night, Retard."

I'll never get over the bar in time to stop Reeger from pulling the trigger. Homer must realize the same thing, because he looks at me and starts bawling.

"My name is Homer," he rasps through his sobs before shutting his eyes and waiting for the bullet.

I can't turn away—I feel as though somebody has to watch Homer when he dies to prove he was ever here at all. My teeth are clenched and I'm ready for the pop of Reeger's pistol. Instead, all I hear is the click of an empty chamber.

Reeger chuckles. "You've got more luck than brains," he tells Homer.

Then he kicks Homer in the rib cage and walks to the door, leaving the poor guy curled up on the floor, clutching his side. When Reeger grabs the doorknob, he stops and turns to me.

"Send Garvey my love," he says. "Snowball." He walks out, leaving the door open behind him.

Homer hobbles through the front room, shuts the door, and slides the deadbolt.

Blood is leaking into the back of my mouth; I'm trying to stem the flow by pressing my nose with the bottom of my apron. Homer stumbles behind the bar, throws a dishrag around a couple of fistfuls of ice and gives it to me. The look in his eyes tells me I'm in bad shape.

I hold the rag to my face as I tilt my head back and stare at the water pipe that runs the length of the tin ceiling. The music on the radio cuts out and an announcer reports that death-row inmate Aaron Garvey escaped as he was being driven to the electric chair at Rockview Penitentiary. According to the newsflash, Garvey made it past two armed guards. One, James Milmo, is in the hospital.

Under the dishrag, as blood tickles my throat, my lips stretch into a smile.

CHAPTER 3

Angela comes out of my kitchen with two tall glasses of fresh iced tea.

"Where's the sugar?" she asks, her voice soft as the hum of the small table fan on top of my radio.

"There isn't any," I say. "I'm running low on everything. I'll stock the kitchen tomorrow."

She looks at me like I'm kidding, but I mean it. I'm not bad with a skillet in my hands; I used to do a lot of cooking for the kids at the Hy-Hat. I'm about to ask her to come back for dinner next week, but my eyes start shimmying. I block her view by pressing the bag of ice to the bridge of my nose.

I've spent most of the last two days in the same position: stretched out on the couch with my head on a pillow and my nose on ice. I know the risk that comes with hospital paperwork, so I asked Doolie to track down a Philadelphia doctor willing to do a house call at a juice joint. The best he could come up with was a trainer from a boxing gym in South Philly. The guy knocked on the back door of the Ink Well right after I locked up last night. He was no doctor, but that didn't slow him down. He tilted my head back, pinched my nose between his fingers, and popped the bone back into place. He said it was a clean break and that I'd be as good as new once I heal. That doesn't help me as I sit here, in front of Angela, with a pair of purple half-moons hanging under my eyes and two sticks of cotton plugging up my nostrils. Every time I sneeze, I feel like I've been shot through the temples.

Angela waits as I sit up. I put the bag of ice on the floor and try not to stare at the green cotton skirt clinging to her hips. It's the same skirt she wore the day she convinced Doolie to hire me, showing him the *Inquirer*, telling him how I'd rescued that kid from Port Richmond, and warning him about a couple of roughnecks who'd been at the bar the previous week looking for trouble. She thought the joint needed some protection and convinced Doolie that I was the man for the job. I hope she doesn't think less of me now. She believed in me, and when you're missing a chromosome or two, that feels more special than it should.

"Your sugarless tea, sir," she says and hands me my glass.

I take a swig, and even though I can't taste much, the chilled liquid feels good rolling down my throat.

"Mmm, good," I tell her.

"You're going to need some food," she says before taking a seat across from me in my armchair. She crosses her ankles and cradles her glass between her palms. "I'll bring some dinner up later."

We sip our tea in silence. I know she's hoping I'll tell her more about my busted nose, but I've got to keep handing her the same line I've been giving Doolie: a fight broke out at the bar and some guy, an ex-boxer with a cauliflower ear, came at me. He broke my nose but I managed to wrestle him out the door. I'm not sure Doolie believes me but I'm sticking to the story. I even covered my tracks by swearing Homer to secrecy. I can't tell the gang at the Ink Well that Reeger is targeting me because he thinks I'm hiding a convicted cop killer. That would put everybody in constant fear of Reeger. And Garvey. And me.

"You still worried?" I ask her.

"Of course I am. Look at you, Jersey. You look awful."

I'm glad the name Snowball has vanished along with Garvey, but hearing Angela talk about my ugly mug hurts in a place far deeper than the bridge of my nose.

"What if that man comes back looking for you?" she asks me. "What will you do then?"

I can't tell her the truth. And I can't tell her that I know how to handle myself, not while I'm holding an ice bag against my busted nose.

"He'll never find me," I say. "Because I'll be here, drinking iced tea with you."

A smile crosses her face but it doesn't stick.

I try a second time.

"I promise I'll call Doolie if the guy shows up again," I tell her, hoping my tone is soothing enough to stop her from digging for more. "Really, I'll be fine."

She goes into the kitchen to refill the ice bag, so I don't have a chance to ask her if she's still considering going back to school. We used to talk for hours about my year at City College, why I quit, and why saving the Hy-Hat was more important to me than earning a degree. She treated me like some kind of professor because I'd walked into a college classroom. I didn't deserve it, but I'd sure like to see that look on her face again.

I get up and peel back the shade on the window that faces Vine Street. The bench in front of Ronnie's Luncheonette hasn't been empty since Reeger rearranged my nose. This morning, a guy with a mustache sat there, eating breakfast. Now an old dame is in his place—she's got a Bible in her lap but she's not reading it. I wasn't born yesterday. It's ninety degrees out there and Ronnie didn't get this kind of business in the heart of spring.

Angela comes back with a fresh bag of ice and I take it.

"You might be right," I say, holding the sack against my face as I return to the couch. "Maybe we should get a second man at the Ink Well, just until I'm back on my feet."

I can see the relief wash over her. "You're not as dumb as you look," she says, smiling.

If that impressed her, she'd be really dazzled to know that I've already got the man for the job. He's eager, trustworthy, and strong—and he can't stand bulls. I just have to be sure he won't go crazy and press a utility knife up against anybody's throat. Again.

❈

It's Friday night at the Ink Well. The joint is dimly lit and fully stocked; the radio is playing softly behind me. Things are returning to normal: we've already served the wave of factory workers who come here to revive their souls after spending eight hours on an assembly line.

So far, the only interruption to the room's chatter was a radio update on Garvey. The state police think he's moving west—a woman says she saw him on a bread line in Harrisburg. Everybody at the bar stopped to listen before doubling down on whiskey and calling Garvey a scumsucking murderer. The only one in his corner was Homer; he kept punching his thigh and asking me how Garvey might dodge the cops and make it out of the country. I didn't have an answer. I'm wondering if Garvey does.

Doolie took the night off, so I'm closing the joint with Angela. Homer's on the door and I've got my snubnose under my apron, tucked into the waistband of my pants.

I gave last call at two a.m., but Angela's friend Wallace is dawdling with some friends at a table in the dining room; they're dissecting the Scottsboro case over the last of their sandwiches and beer. Calvin's still here, too. He saddled up to the bar around eight and has been asking me about the bar fight. I can't blame him for being curious. After all, he's here as often as I am and has no interest in running into a ginned-up Jack Dempsey wannabe.

"I never thought that kind of stuff would happen here," he's saying.

Again, I hate myself for lying, for telling Calvin he's not safe here, that there's an unlocked window in our underground refuge.

"Times are changing," I say and shrug my shoulders.

"Sure are," he says and downs the last drops of his Rob Roy.

The poor lug's still out of work. He's been doing everything he can to make his grocery money go farther—baking his own bread, cooking his own jam, canning his own tomatoes—but there isn't a trick in the book that can stretch a paycheck of zero. He makes a couple of bucks singing with his quartet at a barbershop here in Center City, but the shop just got a radio and he'll soon be losing that money, too. He's not as worried about himself as he is about his wife, Rose. The night he lost his job, he went through half a bottle of King's Ransom before he mustered up the courage to go home and tell her that he had nothing to show for eighteen years at the Baldwin plant other than a handshake and a pink slip.

He's got three bucks sitting on the bar and I can only hope he's got more in his pocket. His tab is close to ten dollars, but I take only one and leave him two. If I don't help him out, he'll be busted by month's end. He nods in gratitude, pockets his bills, and heads for the door. I follow him and tell Homer to take the rest of the night off.

"You sure, Jersey?" Homer says. I can see he's disappointed that Reeger hasn't shown up. He's itching for another crack at the guy.

"Go home," I tell him. "I'll keep the door locked until the place empties out. See you tomorrow."

He pulls his flat cap from his pocket and tugs it onto his head. Then he leaves with Calvin, bending the poor guy's ear about how he'd have done the same thing as Garvey if he were ever thrown in the pen.

Angela comes out of the kitchen as I'm shutting the door behind the two of them. She's no cook, but she volunteered to fill in for Doolie on his night off. A gob of ketchup smears her apron and sweat stains the pink cotton under her arms. My guess is that she'll think twice about manning that stove again anytime soon. Doolie is the only one of us who can stand that kind of heat for an entire shift.

She's fingering her hair with her right hand—she's had a bald spot about the size of a poker chip ever since she was burned as a kid and I can tell she's trying to cover the small patch of exposed pink scalp. She hands the check to Wallace; he gives her a couple of bills and tells her to keep the change.

When Wallace's crew is ready to leave, I open the door, let them out, and slide the deadbolt back into place. Angela and I are alone but I'm not sure she notices. She cleans the table and gets ready to leave for the night as Nat Shilkret's orchestra plays "You Can't Stop Me from Loving You" on the radio. I wonder if she hears the song quite the same way I do.

I open the trapdoor and make my way down the spiral stairway—the cool, dark air feels good against my damp neck. It's late, but if I can restock the bar quickly enough, I'll walk Angela home. I pull the chain and light the room. I nearly trip off the final step when I see I'm not alone.

"Hiya, Snowball."

Sitting on a stack of liquor boxes is Garvey. He gives me a weary grin but then spots the metal plate guarding my nose and winces. "Jesus."

I don't stop to explain—I just run to the hatch to make sure it's locked. It is.

Garvey is dirty and banged up. The acrid smell of his sweat reaches all the way across the room. His prison duds are so soiled they look more like a grease monkey's outfit than a state-issued jumpsuit. He's got an unruly beard, a swollen lip, and a crusty purple scab along the top edge of his left ear.

"How the hell did you get here?" I ask him in a hoarse whisper.

"Easy," he says, flashing one of his old schoolyard grins. "That whiskey you gave Milmo really got him going. After you left, he ransacked the cellblock looking for more. He found a bottle of rye—I think he took it off some bank robber—and polished it off with Flanagan in my cell. Those boys were sloshed. In the back of the wagon, I palmed Milmo's keys right off his belt, then undid my cuffs while the two of them sat there yakkin' about the good ol' days. The minute the truck slowed down, I made a break for it. Flanagan was already out cold, but Milmo still had an eye open. He went for his gun, but one punch put him down. I made it out of the truck and the driver never even knew I'd slipped out."

"But how'd you find the Ink Well? It's not as if we've got a sign hanging outside," I say, still keeping my voice down in case Angela gets too close to the bar. Then I add, "I thought you were in Harrisburg."

"Harrisburg?" he whispers, a faint whistle coming from that broken brown tooth. "Is that what they're sayin'?"

I nod. "That's the word on the radio."

"Not true," he says, shaking his head. "I ran at night, covered my duds with grease, and asked an old hobo if he knew an albino bartender. Y'know, there aren't many. It didn't take all that long to find the place."

He smiles but I can't do the same. My mind is racing and all I'm seeing are bad endings.

"So what now?" I say. "You can't stay here. You want to know what happened to my nose? Reeger came here with a bunch of questions and didn't like my answers."

"Reeger," Garvey says, his voice no louder than the rustle of a leaf. "I'll handle him."

"That's not gonna be as easy as you think. He's got a whole squad out looking for you. His boys are tailing me day and night."

Angela calls my name. I motion for Garvey to be quiet. She opens the trapdoor and I pray I don't hear the click of her heels on the hard wooden steps.

"G'night, Jersey," she shouts down.

"G'night," I say, hoping Garvey's sweaty smell doesn't make it all the way up the stairs. "Remember to lock the door behind you."

I hold my breath, braced for the worst.

"Okay, see you tomorrow," she says. She shuts the trapdoor and I let out a sigh of relief. Then I put my finger in the air to keep Garvey from speaking until I'm sure Angela is well out of earshot. When I hear the front door close, I turn back to him.

"Tell me you have a plan," I say.

"Who's she?" he asks.

"Never mind her. Start talking."

"Do you have anything to eat?"

I must look annoyed because he says: "Please, Snow. I'm starving."

I can't turn him down, so I bring him upstairs into the kitchen and make him a cold meatloaf sandwich. He eats it like the starving man he claims to be—taking big bites and barely chewing. I pour him a glass of milk but can see he'd like something stronger, so I spike it with a shot of scotch. Then I make him another sandwich and tell him to slow down, that I'm not kicking him out.

Leaning on the fridge, I watch him eat and wait for him to fill up. Halfway into the second sandwich, he starts to talk.

"I need the money," he tells me, his cheek bulging from a lump of meatloaf.

"The money?"

"The twenty large. I need Myra to pay me back."

"I thought you said she gave it to Lovely."

"She did," he says, nodding. "But now I need her to pay it

back. How else'm I supposed to live? If I'm gonna run, I'm gonna need that dough."

I'd like to tell him he's wrong, but he's not.

He takes a slug of the spiked milk. "What'd she say about Reeger?" he says. "He still on her back?"

"I never met with her, Garv," I say, shaking my head. "And I never said I would."

He looks disappointed in me; as if they'd fried him up at Rockview and he came back to find out I hadn't fought for his honor. I try not to let it eat at me.

He's still looking around the kitchen so I toss him an apple. It's barely in his hand when he bites into it.

"I'm gonna have to get out of the country," he says as he chews. "Got no choice."

He's right. He can't fight that murder charge. He's already lost his appeals, and that was when he was given a chance to speak. Now he's a marked man, a breathing bull's-eye.

I can't send him back out on the streets; everybody in Philadelphia wants him dead. He'll be gunned down within days. Or, if he's lucky, the cops will bring him in alive and fry him before the week is out. But what he wants—my help in dodging a state-wide dragnet—could land me in the chair next to his.

I look at my old friend as he munches on the apple. I want to give him a bushel of fruit, and sandwiches, and dinners. And I'd like to see him get the hell out of the country. But if I'm going to help, there are some things I have a right to know.

"Garv," I say.

He looks up at me, his right hand holding the apple and poised in midair. I speak slowly, as if that makes the question any easier to say, or to hear.

"What exactly happened that night?" I ask him. "At the Canary?"

"You think I'm a killer, too?" He looks down toward his feet, which are bare, bruised, and swollen. The nails are caked with dirt and dried blood. I can't imagine how he ran on them all the way from Eastern State.

"It's not about what I believe," I say. "I just need to know the truth."

He nods as if he understands, and starts talking, slowly.

"The whole thing started long before you read about it in the papers," he says. "Myra chased some guy here from New York—a thug, small-time stickup artist, did some time in Pittsburgh over at West Pen. Anyway, she came here for him but wound up at the Red Canary. She's a singer—y'know, a nightclub act—at least she is now. Gorsky, I mean, Lovely, liked her, so he sold her a piece of the place."

"So how'd it wind up with you shooting a bull?"

His eyes go cold and the corners of his lips turn downward. "Joe Connor," he says. "Reeger's partner."

He's staring at the oven door as if he's watching the scene play out in front of him.

"I had an arrangement with Myra. I gave her the money, and she was gonna give me a hundred bucks a week until it was paid off."

I imagine he charged Myra some kind of vig, but that's not the point. "And?"

"And Connor wanted Myra to start paying him instead of me. He'd been badgering me for months, bringing me in, arresting me, but I always told him the same thing—he could jam his badge up his ass, I wouldn't let him or anybody else muscle in on me. Well, his boys came down on me, Snow, and they came down hard. I gave as good as I got, but that night at the Canary I couldn't keep up with them. They banged me up all over. I couldn't even stand up on my own. Connor, he puts one live round in his cylinder, spins it, and jams it in my mouth. He sticks the fuckin' barrel so hard down my throat he breaks my tooth. Then he puts my hand on the trigger and tells me to squeeze. And all the time he's laughing, telling me he's the law, he's the boss, how if I don't like it I could call the cops. I'm tasting metal, Snow, and his boys got their guns on me, and I'm so damned scared I peed my pants. I prayed dear God for my life, not for the one I'd lived, for the one I'd never had. I prayed for the wife I never found, for the boy I never raised."

Garvey stops talking for a moment. He stares into the musty air in front of him and his eyes well up.

"He made me pull that fucking trigger, Snow, but the chamber was empty. And God help me, he made me pull it a second time. And the chamber was empty again. So I took the fucking thing out of my mouth and aimed it at Connor—and pulled the trigger a third time. I got lucky. I nailed him right under his jaw, and goddammit, it felt good. It felt great. That bullet was meant for me, Snow, but it hit him. His boys were on me right away, but they couldn't do nothin'. The place was flooded with cops—clean ones—right after the shot went off."

"Jesus, Garv."

"If I didn't nail him, I'd a blown my own head off."

"So why didn't you say that in court?"

Garvey gives me a look that says the courts are as corrupt as the cops, and I know he's right. "They brought in two witnesses," he says. "Reeger and Myra. Reeger nailed me. Big surprise. Myra was so damned scared she barely opened her mouth. They'd a killed her if she talked."

He says it as if cold-blooded murder is logical and I suppose, in some worlds, it is.

I look at my old friend, a small-time crook caught in a street war with hardened bulls. I'm in debt to the guy he used to be and the best I can do is pay back the man he has become. No, I can't get the cops off his back, but with a little luck, I can get him out of the country before Reeger or the state police nail him.

"I figured something like that happened," I tell him. "That you had no choice."

His tired eyes wake up. "So you're in?"

"Damn straight," I say. "I can't let you out there alone. Not like this."

"Swell," he says and breathes a sigh of relief. Then he adds, "You know I'll have to stay here."

I shake my head. "Can't do that," I say. "But I've got a place where you can lay low. You'll hide out there while I sort the money stuff out with Myra. We'll need to get you cleaned up, some new clothes."

"Snowball," he says. "Thanks."

I think that's the first time I ever heard Garvey thank me, probably because he's never owed me anything before.

"Glad to help," I say and I mean it. How many people get a chance to save the Joe who fought for them as kids? Not many, I'd imagine.

There is a difference, though, and I'm sure Garvey realizes it. At Elementary School Four, he was fending off a bunch of wise-cracking sixth-graders. Me, I'm about to take on a city's worth of bloodthirsty, law-bending cops.

CHAPTER 4

*I*t's the Fourth of July and I'm celebrating Independence Day by helping my old buddy find freedom. It's a scorcher; the sun is coming through the Auburn window and toasting the side of my neck. I slip on a pair of dark glasses—those rays are murder on albino eyes—but the damned things make it even harder for me to see the road in front of me.

I haven't been back to New York since I drove to Philly months ago. The night I left, I walked out of a speakeasy overrun with gangsters and packed my things for what I thought would be a quieter life at the Ink Well. But now, as I cruise up New York's West Side, it hits me that my life hasn't changed at all. I'm on the run, I'm ducking the cops, and to make matters worse, I've got an escaped convict crouching behind me in the backseat.

"Almost there," I tell Garvey as we pass 86th Street.

"Swell," he says. He's sitting on the floor with his knees to his chin. His legs must be cramping up, but if he lived through two years at Eastern State, he'll make it through this.

We left Philly just before dawn. I snuck Garvey into the Auburn on Blind Moon Alley; we couldn't have been in the open air for more than fifteen seconds. He still needs a bath, but at least he's out of his prison grays. He's wearing some of my old clothes. They're far from tailored—the pants are too short and the shirt collar is too tight—but they'll have to do until I find him something better.

My plan is to set him up in the back room of the Hy-Hat, where he'll have food and a place to sleep. While he's hiding out,

I'll head back to Philly and get in touch with Myra—maybe she can give Garvey some of his money back. The only question is my father. The champ has no idea I'm coming, and considering how he feels about me bartending at a juice joint, he might have a problem helping out a convicted cop killer.

I drive through Harlem and turn onto 127th Street. As I approach the Hy-Hat, I can see something's not right. Three teenaged boys are standing outside the club clutching pool cues and looking toward Seventh Avenue. They seem rattled, as if the town bully just spotted them on their way home from school. I toss the sunglasses onto the passenger seat to get a better look. A young girl is leaning against a fire hydrant; she can't be more than twelve. All four kids are colored, but the young girl's skin is as light as a coffee with two creams. Her dress is a size too big and her kinky hair is gunked up with grease; it looks like she tried to wax it into Shirley Temple ringlets but quit before finishing. She's bawling and rubbing her eyes with her knuckles.

The closer I get, the more obvious it becomes that these kids are in trouble. And the champ is nowhere in sight.

"Stay down," I tell Garvey.

He doesn't answer, but I hear rustling in the back. I gave him an old cotton blanket as a cover; he's probably pulling it over his back.

I guide the Auburn to the curb in front of the Hy-Hat and park. Then I duck down and grab my pistol from under the seat. I slip it into the back waistband of my pants and loosen my shirt so it drapes over the metal.

When I walk toward the teens, they don't greet me with the usual handshakes and pats on the back. They seem frozen in fear. The young girl has stopped crying and is gawking at my nose guard and raccoon eyes.

"I'm Jersey," I say and extend my hand.

She's never met me before, but all the kids at the Hy-Hat know who covers them when they can't meet their dues. The fear leaves her face and she shakes my hand with her tear-moistened fingers.

I recognize the tall, gangly boy. He's Billy Walker, a big-hearted fifteen-year-old who has been coming here for years. I'm about to ask him what's going on, but the girl grabs my wrist and starts jabbering. The top of her head barely reaches my chest.

"We called the police," she says, her round cheeks glistening. She points inside. "It's Mr. Leo."

I don't know what I expected but this isn't it. I run into the Hy-Hat and find my father slumped on the floor at the far end of the game room. I rush over to him. He's leaning on the wall; he's got a cut above his eyebrow and another along the cleft of his chin. His starched white shirt is ripped across his left shoulder and he has a nasty scratch along his collarbone. If I didn't know better, I'd think a tiger jumped him to get at his meaty brown neck.

He looks at my black eyes and bandaged nose. "What the hell happened?"

"Let's start with you." I say, nodding toward the room. One of the ping-pong tables has been smashed in two. There's a broken bottle of pickles at my feet and a tray's worth of sandwiches strewn across the room.

"Some thugs showed up lookin' for Aaron Garvey," he says. "Why in God's name would they think he was here?"

The answer is sitting on my tongue—*Because he's right outside, Champ*—but the words won't leave my lips.

My father looks around the room, at the old ping-pong table we'd spent so long repairing, at the empty booths usually filled with kids. "I'm sorry," he says.

I guess he thinks he let me down, that he failed at protecting the club even though the kids are all still standing. I know failure, and this isn't it.

"They started badmouthin' you, too," he says. "That's when I went at 'em. Busted my hand and my knee." He holds up his calloused right hand and shows me a row of puffy, swollen knuckles.

There are a dozen kids standing in a circle around us. I'm hoping they're too young to read the papers. If they do, they're bound to recognize Garvey.

"There's a man in the car out front," I say to a shirtless boy sitting on his knees next to me, crying. The kid's got purple jam on his chin and smells of grapes.

"Tell him Snowball says to get in here right away."

As the kid runs off, I loosen my father's tie and unbutton his collar. I try to help him to his feet, but I can't lift him.

"In here," I call out, hoping Garvey can hear me.

Instead of my friend's raspy voice, I hear a young girl's high-pitched sobs coming from a few feet behind me. It's the kid with the Shirley Temple curls.

"He had a gun," she says, her bawling now coming in bursts. She sounds more like she's hiccupping than crying.

"A gun?" I ask the champ.

My father's got his arm around my back. He leans toward my ear and keeps his voice low. "Two thugs. One roscoe."

I curse myself for not coming here sooner, and for not bringing Homer with me. It also occurs to me that I've got to get Garvey a pistol.

The girl starts talking through her sobs again—she's speaking at top speed, as if she needs to get the whole story out in a single breath. "They came in here and were arguing with Mr. Leo in the game room and he beat them up and then one of them took out a gun and Mr. Leo kept punching but they hit him on the head with the gun and he fell on the floor."

She finally takes a breath.

"That's when we called the police," she says.

I don't tell her the cops are the ones who did this.

"Did one of them have a scar on his cheek?" I ask.

She says yes, one had a scar, and the man with the gun had a mustache. Any doubts I had regarding Reeger's connection to the surge in business at Ronnie's Luncheonette just disappeared.

"What's going on, Son?" my father says. The look in his eye says he's afraid of the answer.

Before I can start, Garvey walks into the room. He's dirty and smelly—and looks far from an Adonis in his ill-fitting clothes.

The champ's cheeks sag when he sees what's become of his old charge. I can only imagine how he'd have felt if he saw Garvey in his prison uniform.

"Well, I'll be damned," he says, his voice trailing off.

Garvey nods his head to acknowledge the conversation they're not having. Then he says, "It's been too long, Champ." He looks around the ransacked game room and adds, "We gotta get a move on."

My father turns to me. "You gonna tell me what's goin' on?"

"It's a long story," I say.

The champ's jaw tightens. "Start at the beginnin'."

"You're gonna have to trust me," I tell him. "It's not what you've been hearing on the radio."

He doesn't say anything; he's waiting for more. I know my father, and he's not going to budge until I tell him something he wants to hear.

"Trust me, Champ," I say. "It's not what it seems."

He must buy it because he looks at Garvey and shakes his head. "Son, there's only so fast you can run."

"That's why we're driving," I say, and then ask Garvey to help me with my father.

We get the champ to his feet and start walking slowly toward the door. The champ is still muttering questions, most of which are directed at me.

"Who you running from exactly? Just the cops? Hoods?"

I say they're the same thing.

"Cops don't bust noses," he says, eyeing the guard taped to my face.

"Sure feels like they do," I say.

When we get to the front door, the kids are still right behind us and I'm gripping the champ by the back of his torn shirt. I can hear police sirens blaring—they can't be more than five blocks away.

"So who was the guy who showed up here?" the champ asks me.

I tell him I'll answer all of his questions later, but right now he's got to move more quickly.

The sirens are getting louder and Garvey doesn't need any prodding. He's got my father's right arm around his neck and is pulling him forward. The champ's trying to keep up but his leg is dragging.

We make it to the Auburn; I open the passenger door and drop him into the front seat. He slowly bends his knee to get his leg under the dash. Garvey squeezes into the back and I trot around to the driver's door.

The kids gather by the Hy-Hat entrance, waiting to hear something that will right things.

Instead, I say, "Don't tell the police we were here."

I get behind the wheel and curse myself for sucking a gang of milk-drinking, ping-pong-playing outcasts into my mess. They have no idea what hit them, let alone what to tell the cops.

The Auburn's rear wheels screech as I pull away from the littered curb, leaving the kids to talk their way out of trouble. I can't bring myself to look behind me as I speed away from the one place that I've always managed to keep clean. Until now.

Doc Anders soaks a tray of bandages in a dish of slushy plaster and wraps my father's hand in a cast. I've known the doc for years; he spent a lot of time in front of me when I tended bar here in New York. He's an oddball but I trust him—he knows what he's doing and he keeps his mouth shut.

When we got here, the first thing he did was lock the door and draw the shades. I sat in the dark catching my father up on the basics—how Garvey got railroaded, how he showed up at the Ink Well—as the doc examined the champ's knuckles.

"It looks as though the radiocarpal joint needs more support," he says and nods, as if he's agreeing with himself. Then he slides his brown horn-rimmed glasses up his nose with his gloved index finger and goes back to work.

The champ keeps his arm extended in front of him so the doc can continue wrapping his hand, the busted tool of his former trade. I feel responsible.

"I'm sorry you got sucked into this, Champ," I say to the man who raised me after my mother left, the man who loved me without regard to the freakish pallor of my skin. He's getting older now—he's fifty-one—but I remember him long ago, taking me to the Polo Grounds, buying me strawberry ice cream at the Jersey City Carnival, telling me I was the same as everybody around me, that I could be anything I wanted to be. Had I listened to him and stuck with college, none of this would have happened. I'd never have been in the *Inquirer* and Garvey wouldn't have found me. The champ would be back at the Hy-Hat showing Billy Walker how to throw a left hook; and Angela would be in the Ink Well coatroom, hanging jackets without looking over her shoulder. If I could go back in time and redo things, I'd be sure to make the champ proud this time around. When I see the plaster on his hand, my throat closes and my eyes well up. The skin cream I put on my lids rolls into my eyes and burns like gasoline.

"This ain't your fault," he says. "You're tryin' to do the right thing, I s'pose. I'm just not sure that young man should be runnin'. And now you're runnin' with him. You're breaking the law . . . again. Why do you always have to get mixed up in these things?"

"What else can I do?" I say. "He's got nowhere else to go."

"S'pose not."

My father looks as if he's at a wake, mourning the death of the Aaron Garvey he used to know. He wants to find a way for Garvey to get out of this mess, but he wants to do it by the book. I'm no lawyer, but I'm pretty sure the book says that convicted cop killers fry.

I leave him and the doc and go to check on Garvey, who's keeping watch in the waiting area. The place is even stuffier than the exam room. I'd give anything for the luxury of breathing through my nose.

I find Garvey pulling a window shade away from the glass and peeking at the street outside. A slice of sunshine crosses his soiled face as his eyes dart from left to right and back again. We're on the ground floor—he can't be seeing much more than a few feet of the chipped sidewalk and the leafy branches of the maple tree. I look at his frail, beaten body and realize that after his stint at the penitentiary, he might as well be taking in the Grand Canyon.

"Where's Reeger gonna show up next?" I say.

Garvey finally turns his gaze away from the street. "Wherever you are," he says with a chuckle, even though he's not joking.

I picture the Sarge showing up at the Ink Well looking for me—and dropping the hammer on Angela and Doolie instead.

"I've got to get back to Philly," I say.

"The city might be safer when you're not there," Garvey says, crossing the room to the right window. He checks the street again, drumming his fingers on the gray marble windowsill. I almost wish Reeger would show up just so my friend would have something to do with his energy.

"I'm going back anyway," I say. I couldn't live with myself if I didn't do all I could to protect Angela. Her only crime has been hanging coats in a speakeasy.

By the time Garvey and I get back to the exam room, the champ's hand is wrapped in a hard white cast and he's got his torn seersucker jacket slung over his arm. His suit is about four years out of style, but I'm sure he'll try to get another season or two out of it. I'd buy him a new one, but he'd never wear it. Taking my money, he says, is the same as breaking the law with me.

The doc tells me he wants to take a look at my nose. I can't wait to get these cotton rods out of my nostrils, so I jump up on his exam table. He shines his tiny flashlight at my cheeks, peers at my skin through his horn-rims, and mutters under his breath. Then he removes the metal guard from my nose, and with a skinny gripper that looks like a miniature pair of pliers, he carefully tugs the long, bloody cotton sticks out of my nostrils. Breathing never felt so good.

"Your nose is doing fine, healing nicely. Just leave the guard on for another week or so," he says.

Then he thumbs my right eyelid and angles my head toward the overhead lamp. I tell him I don't have time for a checkup. I know I'm an albino.

"Your skin concerns me, though," he says, ignoring me. "You've got to stay out of the sun." He sounds as if he's afraid of disappointing me, as if I were planning a second career as a lifeguard.

"Okay, no daylight." I'm cracking wise, but the doc's not listening. He's clucking his tongue and examining the burnt rims of my ears. He's a funny old coot. He'll lecture you on how your blood carries oxygen to the brain and then forget where he left his office keys.

I'm itching to get back to Philly, but the doc has me wait while he opens his bottom desk drawer and rummages through a bin of vials and bottles. After a couple of digs, he pulls out a new tube of cream and hands it to me. He tells me to lather up generously when I'm in the sun. I nod and slide the tube into my pants pocket.

"Ready?" Garvey asks.

"Yep," I tell him.

I turn to the champ. "We'll drop you at the Hy-Hat on our way back to the Ink Well."

"I'm comin' with you," he says. "None of us'll be safe until this gets cleared up."

I'm surprised that he wants to come along. I'm also worried that he's going to nag us about breaking the law.

"Champ, they need you at the Hy-Hat," I say.

He doesn't have time to answer before Garvey pipes in. "Whatever we do, we better do it now," he says. "We gotta keep on the move."

"Then let's go," the champ says, pointing toward the door.

I can tell he's not taking no for an answer.

"You sure you want in?" I ask. "This could get really ugly."

"That's why I'm comin'," he says. "To stop that from happenin'."

He has no idea how bad things can turn, but I nod and give him a pat on the back. "Okay," I say. "Then let's go."

It feels good to have him with me.

We thank the doc and walk to the Auburn, which is parked on 88th Street. I take the wheel, my father sits in the passenger seat, and Garvey slumps down in the back.

"So what don't I know?" my father asks me. "Sometimes you got a way of leavin' stuff out."

"I told you everything," I say, and I did. He knows about Reeger, Garvey, even Myra and Lovely.

"Then Reeger's coming back," the champ says. "And you're gonna need somebody at the Ink Well with you. You got room for another pair of hands?"

He'd never work at a juice joint, so I know he's thinking of his old friend, Johalis. It's a smart move. Johalis spent years working the grift in Philly. The guy knows the local streets like I know sunburn. He's got friends everywhere—in the speakeasies, at the stationhouse, even in City Hall. Johalis always talks about how the champ saved him from a couple of overenthusiastic bagmen back in the day; now he'll have a chance to even the score. I'd have called him already, but there are some favors you can't ask anybody but your closest friends—and hiding a convicted killer is one of them.

I pull onto Riverside Drive and a smile crosses my lips. I'm battered, bruised, and banged-up. But at least I'm not alone.

⊰⊱

Like most grifters, Johalis lives in a place that's nearly impossible to find. For starters, his place is on Ludlow Street, but not the one that runs five miles across town. He's on a different Ludlow: a tiny, one-block hideaway that's tucked away east of Center City. And finding the street doesn't help much, because even the mailman can't tell one row house from the next. All eight have matching stone steps leading up to square wooden doors and, next to the front stairways, street-level basement apartments with black metal doors. I remember Johalis lived below a trumpet teacher, so it isn't until I hear a screechy scale blare out of a second-story window that I think I've found his place. I tap the diamond-shaped glass window on the apartment door and wait to see Johalis's wrinkled lids peer out from behind the yellowed lace curtain.

The night air is soggy—it's wrapping my body like an invisible, moist blanket. My nose guard is burning my skin; it feels as though it just popped out of Doolie's toaster. I'm dying to take the damn thing off for a few minutes but know I shouldn't. Instead, I take off my fedora and give my forehead a wipe with the crook of my arm.

The champ is standing curbside—he's got his eye on the Auburn, which is parked down by South Fifth. Garvey's still crouched down in the back; he'll need to stretch his legs soon, but we're waiting to make sure the coast is clear of Reeger's boys.

"You sure you've got the right door?" my father asks me. He's never been here, so he's even more in the dark than I am. I shrug my shoulders.

The champ's suit pants are dirty and ripped. His lower lip is swollen and tinged with blue. His right eyebrow has a crust of dried blood, and his shirt is ripped up to the elbow to make room for the cast. I want to offer him and Garvey a bath, a meal, and some clothes, but if Johalis isn't home, I'm not sure where to bring them. It can't be to my place, not while half the precinct is dining on the fine food at Ronnie's Luncheonette.

Johalis would have some ideas, but the curtain doesn't move. There are hundreds of places he could be, one of which is at the bottom of the Schuylkill in pajamas made of cement. The trumpet upstairs scratches out a kindergartener's nursery rhyme, and I wonder if a slow round of taps would be more appropriate.

"Forget it," my father says from the curb.

Maybe the champ doesn't realize it, but we're running out of options. I knock harder, as if slamming my knuckles against the glazed glass could somehow force Johalis to appear.

"Let's go," the champ says again, already halfway back to the car.

I knock again, but when the curtain doesn't budge, I give

up and walk down Ludlow to join my father and Garvey in the Auburn.

I'm nearly at South Fifth when a steel blade kisses the back of my neck. The thug who's holding it doesn't need to speak; I'm sure it's Reeger, or somebody on his payroll. He yanks my arm behind my back and pulls me one step into an alley. Pain shoots up my shoulder and I'm afraid to make a move, much less turn around. I've got my snubnose in my pocket, but it might as well be at the Ink Well. I put my hands where he can see them.

A deep voice fills my right ear. "Jesus Christ, Jersey. What the hell are you doing here?"

Johalis looks like he tumbled out of bed. His black hair is greasy and hanging loosely over his ears; his long chin is covered by moss-like stubble.

"Looking for you," I say, my voice shaky.

He lets go of my arm and I shake it in the air a few times, trying to regain feeling.

Johalis has an inch on me, but he's in no better condition than I am. His stomach is the size of a basketball and pops out over his belt; his shoulders might be even bonier than mine. But the guy knows his way around a street fight. Put him in a boxing ring with Reeger, and there's little doubt the Sarge would walk away with the title. Put them in an alleyway, and my money's on Johalis.

I jerk my thumb toward his shiv.

"Expecting somebody?" I ask.

"No, but when somebody shows up with tape covering their face, I get careful. Sorry." He smiles and his crow's feet crinkle.

My father is making his way back up Ludlow. He's biting at his upper lip, but when he sees Johalis, he relaxes. I wonder if he realizes that his friend makes a living by bending the law, that the tools of Johalis's trade are no more elaborate than a nose for opportunity and a barrel of street-smarts. Knowing the champ, he chooses not to see it.

"There you are," he says to his friend.

Johalis doesn't comment on my father's cast or banged-up face, nor does he ask about my nose guard. Instead, he pats the champ on the back and launches into stories about the times they lugged bricks at a construction site by the Hudson River. If I didn't know better, I'd think they enjoyed pushing two-hundred-pound wheelbarrows for a living.

I'm sure he's biding his time, waiting for my father to get to the reason we're here, and his wait isn't long. The champ tells him everything: how Garvey called me, how Reeger showed up at the Ink Well and then again at the Hy-Hat. He even tells Johalis how Garvey needs to get his money back from Myra to flee the country. Johalis listens poker-faced, but when the champ throws in that he wants to help me without breaking any more laws, Johalis lets out a long, slow whistle.

Fireworks go off over the Schuylkill and I remember it's the Fourth of July. My father keeps on talking, but I gaze up at the glittering display. For a brief second, I'm sitting on the roof of the Ink Well with Angela, watching the Philadelphia sky light up in red, white, and blue. I wonder how I can get there from where I am now: plotting to save my pal from the electric chair.

"I keep telling Jersey to quit the bar," the champ tells Johalis.

I can't let it go without explaining my side. Neither of them understands what the Ink Well means to me.

"I can't quit, not now," I say. "Reeger will drop a hammer on the joint."

"But you can't protect the place on your own," my father says.

"Sure I can."

Johalis glances at my nose, probably doubting my ability to protect anything. Thankfully, he changes the subject.

"Slow down," he tells us. His voice is as rich as cocoa and as thick as a malted. I'm telling you he could woo a Rottweiler out of a butcher shop. "I've got to clear some things up," he says. "From the little you told me about Garvey, I'm assuming he had good reason to kill that cop. Am I right?"

"If I didn't think so," the champ says, "I wouldn't be here."

I nod in agreement, although I doubt my father would feel the same had he first met Garvey at Eastern State and not at Elementary School Four.

"I figured as much," Johalis says. "So let's worry about him first."

"So you're in?" I say.

Johalis flips his thumb toward my father. "If it weren't for him I might not be standing here," he says. "Yeah, I'm in."

The champ smiles and starts to say thank you, but Johalis cuts him off. "Jersey," he says, "Get your buddy off the street and bring him inside."

I run over to the Auburn as the fireworks rumble overhead. While I'm leaning into the car, I give Garvey my snubnose and tell him to keep it strapped to his ankle from now on. I also tell him to clam up on where he got it; I can only imagine what the champ would have to say if he found out I wasn't only hiding Garvey but arming him. Then I grab a bottle of sugar pop moon from under the seat and tell Garvey to follow me.

We race up Ludlow to Johalis's place and duck inside. The apartment isn't big, but it's comfortable. There's a kitchen and a parlor in the front; Johalis says he's got two bedrooms and a bathroom in the back. The place is filled with carved wooden furniture, and I'd bet my bottom dollar the warehouse doesn't even know it's missing.

Johalis tells Garvey to go on back and take a shower, and then clears a space in the parlor so the three of us can sit around the marble coffee table. Over Johalis's shoulder is a wooden grand-father clock, and next to that, a beveled mirror on the far wall. I avoid the mirror—I can just imagine what a day in the sun has done to my cheeks.

I put the bottle of moon on the table and Johalis goes to the kitchen for some glasses. When he comes back he's got a pack of Lucky Strikes in one hand and four shot glasses in the other.

"None for me," my father says. Apparently, he's okay with helping a convicted cop killer flee the country but thinks downing an illegal shot of moonshine is going too far.

Garvey comes back into the room, toweling his beard and wearing nothing but his unwashed boxers. His legs are as bony as his chest.

"I'll get you some clothes in a minute," Johalis tells Garvey and motions for him to sit. Then he pours three shots of moon-shine, lights a Lucky, and tosses the rest of the pack to Garvey.

"Thanks," Garvey says. "For the smokes, and for the cover."

Johalis lets out one of his warm belly laughs. "We haven't covered anything yet. But we'll try."

"Just for the record, I didn't gun down that bull, at least not the way they said I did," Garvey says to Johalis. "You're helping me, so I want you to know that."

"Accepted and agreed," Johalis says and clinks his shot glass with Garvey's.

I join the two of them in the toast and we down the moon. As it heats my chest, I try to push Angela out of my mind.

"If we can hide Garv," I say, "we've got a chance."

Johalis nods, but not with any kind of confidence.

He turns to my father. "You'll take the second bedroom, Ernie."

I can see my father doesn't want to intrude, but he's got no other choice.

"I'll make it up to you," the champ says.

Johalis dismisses him with a wave of his hand. "I'll also pick up your clothes from New York. You're gonna need them."

"Where's Garv going to hole up?" I say. "It can't be at the Ink Well. Reeger is on it day and night. We were lucky to get out."

"That's why you shouldn't go back," my father says.

I wish the champ could understand that this is more important than my safety or his concept of a legit day's pay. "Those people are depending on me," I say.

"Jersey's right," Johalis says, "He's got to go back. Otherwise Reeger will start looking for him, track him here, and we'll all get nailed. Let Reeger stay focused on Jersey and the Ink Well. We'll put Garvey somewhere else."

He's obviously got a plan and I have no idea what it is. Maybe it's better that way. All I can do is hope that Johalis is as sure-handed as that smooth voice makes him out to be.

We pour another round of moon, and the liquid oils our spirits. Garvey starts talking about elementary school; he shares with the champ and Johalis a bunch of stories that haven't crossed my mind in years. The four of us laugh the night away, and for the first time since I visited my old friend at Eastern State, we're free of the specter of guns, badges, and electric chairs. I sip another shot of moon and let the shine coat my tongue. The fireworks crackle overhead, and I wonder if Angela is there to see them.

CHAPTER 5

I rang the bell for last call a half-hour ago. It feels strange to close the bar at one o'clock, but it's a weeknight and Doolie wants me to cut back on the late hours. He's worried I can't protect the place, but I'm not going to let him down again. I've got Johalis working the bar with me on weeknights and Homer manning the door on weekends. And we've got backup: the champ is only ten minutes away at Johalis's place. I'd hate to call him while his right hand is in a cast, but he'd only need his left to take down half the sixth precinct.

As for the Hy-Hat, I've put Calvin in charge until further notice. I even let him and Rose live out of a room in the back of the club. Of course, I couldn't let him take the job without telling him the truth about Reeger.

"You're a savior," he said, his unshaven cheeks creasing as he smiled. "I'll return the favor someday."

"Just keep the place going," I told him. "And that means steering clear of Reeger, so be careful."

"Don't worry," he said, downing his Rob Roy so he could run home to tell Rose of their good fortune. The look on his face made the bags under his eyes seem pounds lighter, as if I'd erased eighteen years of clock punching with a single paycheck.

I tell myself I gave Calvin the job as a favor to Doolie, but the truth is I did it for myself. I filled an empty pocket and it felt good.

Of course, nothing will be back to normal until Garvey is off my hands—and out of the country. For now, we have him stashed with Madame Curio, a hooker who doubles as a palm reader in a shop about a mile from Wanamaker's department store. I'm ashamed to say I know her place. Yeah, there were times I was low enough to lose myself in her gin-soaked whispers. Thinking about those nights makes me want to scrub myself with soap, but I muscle through my shame by reminding myself that the Madame is helping me save Garvey's life—which makes her one of us. Besides, her shop is a perfect hideout. It's in a desolate area—every storefront on the block is boarded up—and the Madame has never, ever sung to a bull.

I sweep the floor while Johalis mixes a whiskey sour for Wallace. Our usual late-night straggler has spent most of the evening sitting alone, reading *The Maltese Falcon*. He's a student at Penn and already has the look of a professor: nappy hair, wire-rimmed glasses, and a prominent Adam's apple that juts out over a navy-blue necktie. He spends the summer months shuttling files at City Hall, but the day will come when he'll be making headlines. Any Negro they let into Penn is bound to do a lot more than tend bar.

"A last splash for the soul," he announces as he stands by the bar and watches Johalis drain a shaker into his rock-filled cocktail glass. I want to ask him about the *Falcon*—why he's reading it, if it's good—but I'd be too embarrassed to admit that I haven't picked up a book since I left school five years ago. I've often told my father that leaving college put a roll of cash in my pocket, but I've never admitted to losing my soul in the process. I promise myself that I'll go back someday. But I know it's a lie.

Wallace drops his money on the bar, takes the drink, and goes back to his table.

Johalis grabs the coins and dumps them into Doolie's register. "You off to the Red Canary?" he asks me as he stacks the shakers and locks up the register.

"That's the plan," I say.

Angela spent the evening waiting tables; she hangs her apron on one of the hooks behind the bar and as she reaches up, her dress rises toward her knee. I'm tempted to ask her if she'd like a ride home—I'm heading toward her place anyway—but I decide to wait until the tape is off my nose.

"'Night, Jersey," she calls out. When she says my name, there's a lilt in her voice that's as sweet as a violin.

My eyes start jiggling again, so I lean toward the cash register and straighten a stack of coasters.

"'Night," I say.

She heads to the front room and I see she's got some books under her arm; she must have started prepping for the high school entrance exam. She and Wallace leave the place together, strolling with the kind of four-legged gait that only comes with practice. I try convincing myself that a bookworm like Wallace wouldn't be interested in an uneducated speakeasy coat checker, but my heart knows otherwise.

I wish Angela were a cheap flapper so I could hate her, but she's not and I don't. She's no floozy and Wallace is a good-enough Joe. My throat goes tight and I swallow hard. When I look up, Johalis is staring at me. He knows why I'm quiet, but he's too nice a guy to say it.

"Closing time," he says.

"Yep."

"You sure you don't want backup?"

He's afraid I'll run into trouble at the Canary, but he doesn't know my history with Myra.

"Yeah, I'm fine," I say.

We lock up the bar and Johalis heads down Vine. I walk up Juniper as visions of Angela and Wallace burn my soul. When I get in the Auburn, I peel the tape off my nose guard even though my face still hurts like hell and large yellow-purple stains linger around my eyes. Fuck it.

I start the engine and pat my shoulder holster to feel the six cylinders of security that are lodged within it. It's not my rod—Garvey has my snubnose—but Johalis got me this one and he swears it's accurate, powerful, and untraceable. I can't imagine Reeger will be waiting at the Canary, but I'm still not about to walk in there cold.

❧

The Red Canary is only a couple of miles from the Ink Well, but it might as well be in another universe. The joint fills the upper half of a brick building off Rittenhouse Square on Pine Street. It's two floors of gambling, music, booze, and women—right in the swankiest part of town. Still, if you didn't know it was there, you'd never find it. Heavy burgundy drapes keep the Feds from seeing through the windows, and thick plaster walls stop the music and laughter from hitting the street. The place never did well as a restaurant, but it's been pulling in big bucks ever since Lovely turned it into a speakeasy.

The entrance is an unmarked fire exit in the back service alley, which is something I didn't realize until I saw a pair of drunken lovebirds sneak out the door. I slipped inside after they left and ventured up the metal service stairs to the top floor.

Now I'm sitting at a table for two; I've got my back to a cream-colored plaster wall that's so smooth it shines like glass. In the middle of the room is a square bar manned by three tenders and surrounded by suits, rummies, and platinum blondes. Across from the bar, in the far corner to my right, a piano player is pounding out a folk song I remember the champ singing to me when I was a kid.

A leggy waitress with red hair and a snug blouse asks me what I'd like. It doesn't take Sherlock Holmes to know that she's on the menu. She's smart to choose me—I'm alone, banged up, and an albino—any hooker worth her weight in salt would be trying to close this deal. But tonight, there's only one woman who can mend the cut I'm nursing, and she's on the other side of town with a whiskey-sour-drinking bookworm.

I tell the redhead I'll take a double shot of her best gin as I scan the place for Myra.

"Sugar, I hope you're not here to even some kind of score," she says, nodding toward my nose.

"I would," I say, "but Dempsey's too scared to show up."

She rolls her eyes and starts to walk away, but I call her back and ask her if she knows Myra Banks.

"She's on in a few minutes, Sugar."

"The name's Jersey," I say. I can see she doesn't care; names have no place in her line of work. She's already heading off to another table, her hips rocking from side to side.

I spot five suits sharing a bottle of whiskey at the bar. Judging by their narrow lapels, they're cops. Under normal circumstances, I'd write them off as garden-variety street bulls, but Reeger's got me nervous. I eye them for a while, but they don't seem interested in detecting anything but another round of scotch.

The piano player finishes his tune with a flourish and calls out for Myra to join him. A woman sitting at the bar stands up, downs the rest of her champagne, and walks through a roomful of diners to the piano.

So this is what's become of Myra Banks. It's only been five years, but she sure has changed. The first thing I notice is her foot. She must have left that special shoe of hers in an operating room, because she's wearing a pair of open-toed silver pumps and her gait is steady and strong. A hip-hugging sequined dress covers one of her shoulders but leaves the other exposed—smooth, brown, and inviting. Her hazel almond-shaped eyes are working overtime, twinkling under the muted chandeliers.

The lights dim even more as Myra glides into the circular glow of a small stage lamp. She begins singing "Hello, My Lover, Goodbye," and the piano player accompanies her with soft, rolling chords. Now I understand how she got twenty grand out of Garvey, and how she became part-owner of the joint. Her voice is as lush and warm as cashmere, and that dress is as curvy as a mountain stream.

The rummies have gone quiet; all eyes are on Myra. As I watch her sing, I remember how much she cared about me, how she, more than anybody else, understood how it felt to be different. I think of how we skipped civics class and snuck down to the pier, sat under an overhang, and planned our Hollywood getaway until the sun was long gone from the sky.

But I'm not here to fall in love again. I force myself to turn away, to take inventory of the joint, to picture the night Garvey came here and gunned down his freedom.

The redhead brings me my gin and I down a slug as Myra finishes the last song of her set. She's not just singing, she's flirting with the crowd—smiling, teasing, toying—and the light-headed Joes are eating it up. When the lights go back up, I swear the temperature in the place is at least ten degrees higher. I wait for the applause to die down; I figure I'll get her once she's back on her stool. But instead of walking to the bar, she comes over to my table and takes the seat opposite me.

"Jersey Leo," she says and gives me a smile right off a movie still. Her teeth are now lined up straight, and she's got a new beauty mark on her right cheek. If she sees the bruises on my face, she doesn't show it.

"Myra Banks," I say as the piano player launches into an uptempo rag. "You've got some voice."

"I may have the voice, but you're the front-page story."

"Pure bullshit," I say.

She dismisses me with a light chuckle. Then she taps a cigarette into a long, slender holder and lights up. The stem of the holder looks like it's made of ivory and I wonder how much of Garvey's money it took to buy it.

"You look wonderful," I tell her.

Her face takes on a bored expression that says she's heard those words so often they've lost their meaning. But I recognize the truth that's hiding behind her eyes; I see it every morning in the shaving mirror. There's no compliment big enough—and no stage grand enough—to undo the abuse she took as a kid.

"So what brings you around?" she says. "Another kidnapping?"

I can see by the way she's waiting for an answer that she hopes it's true. I guess she's gone numb to the lights and sounds of Lovely's speakeasy.

I lower my voice and tell her we need to talk about Garvey. "He needs our help," I say.

She takes a quick look across the bar, but the cops are so deep into their bottle they're not hearing any voices outside of it.

"Follow me," she says.

She motions to the tender that she'll be back, then takes me around the far end of the dining room past the piano. We duck into a small hallway; I follow her past two small changing rooms and into a large dressing room on the far right.

The space smells of makeup and cheap perfume. A shiny silver mirror sits on the desk in the corner. Next to the desk, a row of dresses, feather boas, corsets, and a pile of fishnet stockings hang from a wooden rack. We all have places we go to hide the bruises we were dealt as kids. Me? I run behind a bar. Myra must come here.

She locks the door behind us, takes a bottle of gin off the

bookcase that lines the left wall, and pours a splash into two juice glasses. She opens an ice bucket next to the bottle, plops a cube into each drink, and gives both glasses a swirl with a twist of her wrists. Through the door, I hear the sounds of shouting voices, tinkling piano keys, and a spinning roulette wheel.

"So whatever happened to that guy in New York?" I say and toss my fedora onto the red velvet couch next to the door. "Y'know, Joe Toughguy?"

She shrugs. "Disappeared with the rest of them."

"Really?" I say. "It's hard to believe they *all* disappear."

"I'm talking about the ones worth keeping."

"So am I," I say.

She shrugs again. "What can I tell you?" she says. "They leave."

"Well, in his case, you're better off," I say.

"S'pose so," she says.

I'm glad she doesn't follow with a similar line of questioning for me. Instead, she hands me one of the glasses and raises hers.

"To old friends," she says.

"Old friends," I say, then clink her glass and take a shot. This gin is cold and refreshing. I tell her so and she says not to thank her, to thank Lovely.

"Not anytime soon," I say.

She laughs. "I don't blame you," she says as she drops another cube in her glass. "So what's the story? Garvey's on the run, right?"

"That's the short version," I say. "The long version includes the part that says it takes money to run, and he doesn't have any."

"So how can I help?"

If she knows where this is heading, she's as smooth as the booze she's pouring.

"He needs the dough back," I say. "The twenty grand."

She gives me a troubled nod. "Makes sense," she says. "But I don't have it anymore. I used it to buy into this place. And when you do business with Lovely, you don't buy out."

"But you were going to pay Garvey back, right? Where were you going to get that money?"

She stares into her glass as if she's about to read tea leaves but doesn't come back with an answer. There's more to this story, and getting her to open up will be about as easy as shucking a clam with a dollar bill.

"Hey, I'm in this, too," I say. "I ran into a cop named Reeger. He's out for Garvey and he doesn't care who he mows down to get at him."

She's barely listening. She's looking out the window at the blinking lights on Rittenhouse. I'm not sure how I wound up here—grilling Myra about Garvey's money—and my guess is that she's wondering the same thing. I down the drink. It burns my chest and I enjoy it.

She doesn't bother turning her head when she speaks. Normally, that would get my goat, but in this case, I'm grateful that she's talking at all.

"I did something really stupid."

"Who hasn't?" I say.

A crash comes from the bar. People are shouting and glass is breaking. I've been around speakeasies long enough to know these sounds. It's a raid. I'd like to meet the cop who decided to drop a hammer on Lovely. The bull must have nuts the size of cantaloupes.

A voice yells from the barroom. "I'm looking for Aaron Garvey and a white nigger freak called Snowball."

Myra turns to me, her eyes wide open. "That's Reeger," she says.

Could Reeger have followed me here? I hear him working his way through the joint, shaking down the waiters for the skinny on Garvey. I pull out my gun and wait by the door. I'm no triggerman, but if Reeger comes at me I'm going to plug his sinuses. I'm about to open the door, but it hits me that Garvey wound up on death row for doing the same thing I'm thinking of doing now. I re-holster the rod and look for a way out.

I motion toward the window. "Where does that fire escape lead?"

"The back alley," she says. "But Reeger's probably got a guy down there."

I slip out the window, but my eyes start shaking as they adjust to the darkness.

Myra leans out of the building behind me. "I'm coming, too."

She kicks off her pumps and follows me down the fire escape—she's so close I can smell her perfume. The humidity has slickened the iron rungs, and the leather soles of my oxfords are slipping with every step. When we reach the bottom landing, I take a look around. There's not a bull in sight, so we drop down into the alleyway and scoot back to the Auburn. She jumps into the seat I had reserved for Angela.

We pull away, leaving Reeger back at the Red Canary. I've got my eyes peeled for cops, but Myra's laughing like a kid who just bolted out of the school cafeteria doors for summer recess.

⁂

Myra's leaning on the Ink Well bar as I scoop some ice into a shaker. I thought about bringing her to Madame Curio's so she could settle things with Garvey, but I couldn't risk being tailed. I snaked through side streets, circled City Hall, and snuck into the bar through Blind Moon Alley. We're here for the night. I'd let her sleep at my place, but we'd have to step outside to go upstairs. And I'm not unlocking that door until sunrise.

It's my first time inside the Ink Well after closing time, and I like it more than ever. Rudy Vallee is on the radio—"If I Had You"—and the flickering candles on the front tables bathe the place in a soft glow. There must be fifty guys back at the Canary who'd want to trade places with me right now, tucked away down here, alone with Myra. And yet all I can think about is how much I wish it were Angela sitting behind that martini glass.

Myra nods toward the newspaper that put my face on Philadelphia's doorstep. "I'm not surprised," she says. "You always had it in you."

I forgot how nice it felt to impress a woman—and I'm glad it's Myra. "Thanks," I tell her.

She walks through the joint as I pour two fresh martinis. She's still in her sequined dress, shoeless, and I wish I had some comfortable clothes to offer her. I wonder what she's thinking as she takes in the place. It's a far cry from the Red Canary, which buzzes with gamblers, dancers, and spenders until the wee hours. Me, I prefer this.

I drop an olive into each glass. "So Garv needs money," I say. "Badly."

"I know," she says with her back to me. She's examining the glossies of Duke Ellington, Jack Johnson, and Ethel Waters hanging over the booths across from the bar. She's a silhouette in the subdued light; her dress shimmers along her hip. "And I do owe him the twenty grand."

"At least we all agree on that," I say. I bring the martinis to the booth closest to the front room, nearest the fan, and she joins me.

We sit across from each other; she leans her back to the wall and raises her legs onto the padded bench.

I raise my glass. "To Elementary School Four?"

"To never going back," she counters.

We clink glasses and sip our martinis. They're ice cold, but not frigid enough to cut the heat down here.

"So can you get it?" I say. "The twenty grand?" This is the third time I'm trying—I asked in the Auburn, too—and I'm getting tired of the half-answers.

"Like I said, I gave it to Lovely for a piece of the place—not that I've ever gotten anything for it aside from a bunch of free drinks. He's got the money and I can tell you he's not about to give it back. It's not like I bought stock or something."

"So that's what you meant when you said you did something stupid?"

She leans her head against the wall and looks up, sighing.

"Well?" I say.

I guess she realizes no raid is going to cut her off again, because this time she keeps talking.

"I was going to pay Garvey back in installments," she says. "A hundred a week."

"He told me," I say.

She lets out a bitter chuckle. "Everybody wanted those payments. Connor wound up dying for them."

"He told me that, too," I say.

"Well, now Reeger's muscled in. He's taking them—and he bumped them to one-twenty-five. And I've been stupid enough to pay him. But what am I supposed to do? Call the cops?"

Garvey said Reeger was coming down on Myra, but he didn't know how bad things had gotten. The Sarge is doing more than evening a score, he's generating a revenue stream. And I've got to give him credit—he's doing it without squaring off against Lovely.

Myra takes another belt of gin, but there's no drink strong enough to get her out of this mess.

"Garv doesn't need all twenty grand," I say. "Can't you get some cash off Lovely, maybe five or six grand, so Garv can get out of the country?"

Even I hear how ridiculous I sound. Lovely would dismember a penny-ante crook who crossed him for fifty cents. I remember Doolie telling me about a gambler who was into Lovely for eight grand. The poor bastard left the hospital missing his left ear and bottom lip.

Myra answers me with a smirk.

"I'm just trying to help Garv," I say. "Are you forgetting how many times he saved our butts?"

"I like Garvey as much as you do," she says. "But the only place I can get that kind of money is off Lovely. Even if he gave it to me—which he won't—I'd be left paying him and Reeger. I'd be dead in no time."

She's right. Sooner or later she'd miss a payment to one of them, and either way, she'd make up for it with her life.

The radio begins playing "Every Day Away from You" and it reminds me of the gang up at the Hy-Hat, playing ping-pong, listening to the music box. It's only been a few days since the champ was up there, but it feels like ages ago.

Myra sits up and looks at me. "I'll pay you instead of Reeger," she says, her eyes brightening. "And you can get the money to Garvey, one payment at a time."

She shimmies out of the booth and paces the floor in a wide circle; she's got the look of a scientist stumbling upon the secret of eternal youth. Her words pick up speed as the idea forms in her head.

"It's perfect," she says. "Garvey will get the money and you can keep Reeger off my back. You're the only one who can do it."

The gin is softening my senses and I want to be the guy she thinks I am. I want to step up and protect her the way Garvey did for me. But I can picture how Reeger would react if he found out I started taking the payments, and I don't like the way the story ends.

"I'm the wrong guy," I tell her.

"No you're not," she says. "I know you; you'll figure something out."

I shake my head. "I'm sorry, Myra. There's a reason I've got the door locked. We're talking about Reeger."

She leans over and kisses me on the mouth, slipping her tongue between my teeth. I can smell the pomade in her hair and a tangy, perfumed sweetness coming from her bare shoulder.

My first thought is that she needs help and will do anything to get it. My second thought is that I don't care. I put my arm around her as our tongues dance a slow tango and I pull her closer. I see my hand against her shoulder: my skin, pale and raw, against hers, smooth and brown, radiant and soothing.

She traces her tongue across my face and over the bridge of my nose; she breathes lightly on my scab and I feel my face flush. Her hair teases my forehead as she palms the side of my face and then drags a fingertip along the rim of my ear. I'm intoxicated by the taste of her lips, the smell of her skin, and from thinking that it's possible she still wants me the way she did at the Hotel Theresa.

She guides me out of the booth, leans back on the table, and pulls me on top of her. I turn away from the kitchen, away from the soiled apron that hangs there waiting for the coat checker with the tiny bald spot. Then I look into Myra's hazel eyes and wonder if I'm really the only one who can undo the years of scorn that still haunt her.

She used to say that we'd find peace—that we'd run away to a place where we'd be free of bullies. Maybe she was right, and maybe this is it. Maybe the Ink Well—this dark, shuttered, two-bit colored speakeasy—is our refuge. Maybe we've found Santa Monica.

Or maybe she just wants someone to stand between her and Reeger.

CHAPTER 6

An early morning rain cooled the city streets, but now the sun is back—it's baking the asphalt dry and pushing the temperature up over a hundred. I'm riding on Market, heading to Madame Curio's, and the Wanamaker building towers over me.

A radio report says the manhunt for Garvey is moving down the Susquehanna from Harrisburg to York, but some state cops are still lingering here in Philly. It's hard to miss their blue coats, brass buttons, and bobby hats. I just passed two in front of Broad Street Station; there were four more near the Excelsior Hotel. Unless they're planning on driving over to Filbert Street and having their palms read, they won't be bumping into Garvey any time soon.

It's been two weeks since Myra and I revisited our childhood vow at the Ink Well table, and neither one of us has spoken with Garvey. We're probably better off staying clear of him, not because of the state cops—they have no interest in Myra or me—but because of Reeger and his boys. There's no telling how many eyes are on us.

But the Madame called Johalis in the middle of the night, rattling on about needing to see me right away. She should have tried calling me at the Red Canary. She would have found me in the back dressing room, sharing a shaker of gin with my old classmate. She also would have found the classmate asking me to take Reeger's payments again, and me saying no, again.

When I reach the stoplight at Bowers, I tighten up when I

see four city bulls clustered around a streetlamp. I quickly realize they're not part of the stakeout; they're at a crime scene. A dead man's legs extend beyond a row of hedges; a squirrel crawls along his shin and stops to lick at his exposed ankle. The bulls are looking down at the corpse, their faces twisted in disgust. The tall, skinny one turns away—he takes off his hat, leans over a blood-splattered garbage can, and heaves his guts up. My guess is that Lovely left his signature on that corpse—only his kind of twisted sadism can prompt a reaction like that one. When the light turns green, I pull away and don't look back.

I continue down Market, then turn onto Filbert, a desolate, two-block stretch of abandoned shops and aborted dreams. I pull up to Madame Curio's, a hole-in-the-wall that was a candy store before the market crashed, and park next to a gumball machine that won't see a kid, or a gumball, as long as the Madame is running the operation.

I check to be sure that mine is the only heart beating on Filbert. All is clear, so I kill the engine and duck under the Madame's awning. A note on the door reads, "By Appointment Only." There's no sign of the Madame, so I pick the lock with a broken bobby pin I find on the floor and slip inside. The hinge squeaks so loudly I'm surprised the state bulls back on Market don't come charging.

The foyer is unlit, but thanks to a slice of daylight coming through a tear in one of the curtains, I can see it's empty. I don't blame the Madame for shutting down. If I were hiding Garvey, I'd do the same.

My eyes shimmy as they adjust to the darkness. I know the hallway to my left leads to the Madame's chamber—a small room furnished with little more than a folding table and a crystal ball. I'm glad the champ's not here to see how easily my oxfords find their way across the checkered tiles.

I'm not even at the threshold when the Madame steps out of the hallway, alone. I can barely make out the curly brown locks that spring out from under her turban or the thick lines of makeup that streak across her eyebrows and lips. I hope she's having the same trouble seeing me. My nose is healing, but my eyes still have yellow haloes hanging underneath.

"Snow . . . Jersey," she says. Her voice is soft and carries the hint of an apology.

I avoid the awkwardness.

"I let myself in," I say, nodding toward the door. Then I add, "Johalis said it was important."

"It is," she says and walks across the foyer to double-lock the door. "Go on ahead."

The hallway is pitch-black, but I inch my way toward the back room and she follows two steps behind. It's hot and grimy in here and the back window is sealed shut. I wipe the sweat from the side of my nose with my shirt cuff and hope she's got a fan going in the back. I can't imagine how in hell anybody could survive in here, but then I realize that Garvey is used to an eight-by-twelve-foot cell. For him, these are luxurious accommodations.

I'm about to walk into the room when I hear a muffled cry from the other side of the door. It's a sickening sound, like somebody struggling to breathe. Garvey? I take a step back and grab for my gun. I touch its handle but don't get any farther. Somebody yanks my arms from behind and shoves me hard against the wall.

"Hello, Snowball," he says.

It's fucking Reeger. How the hell he tracked Garvey here I'll never know.

He lets go of my arm and jabs a revolver into my neck. I keep my hands at my side, useless, as I listen to the desperate whimpers coming from the other side of the door.

Reeger reaches around my back and takes my gun from its

holster. Then he pops the cylinder and dumps the bullets on the floor. The metal slugs ping on the Madame's hard tiles and roll down the hallway, taking my hopes with them.

"C'mon on inside," Reeger says. "I'll read your fortune."

He opens the door and pushes me, then the Madame, into the room. Before following us, he tosses my gun onto the floor behind him.

The Madame's table has been pushed aside. On it a lamp burns—it's not bright but it's strong enough to cast a yellowish glow throughout the space.

The source of the whimpering sits six feet in front me, smack in the center of the room. It's Homer, strapped to a folding chair, a handkerchief wrapped around his head and under his tongue. He's been beaten up, but he's still managing to wail through his gag. The desperate groans coming from behind his bound tongue turn my stomach.

The only good news is that Garvey is nowhere to be found.

There's a goon standing behind the table with his arms crossed. I recognize his mustache; he's the guy from outside Ronnie's Luncheonette. I'm guessing he's a bull, maybe filling Connor's shoes as Reeger's new partner. He's a big guy, about six-three, with a jaw as square as a lunchbox. He's got a revolver in his shoulder holster, and I'm guessing he had it pressed against the Madame's forehead when she dialed the phone.

I look at the Madame and she looks to the floor. She tells me she's sorry. "I didn't want to do it," she says.

"Shut that whore mouth," Reeger shouts and smacks his knuckles across her face.

The Madame's leathered skin darkens and her eyes go black.

"Fuck you," she says and spits in his face.

He goes to hit her again but I grab his hand. He windmills his arm, twisting his hand from my grip.

I clench my fists at my side.

"Enough," I say.

I'm expecting the worst, but Reeger doesn't swing, he just glares into my eyes, his nostrils flaring and the scar on his cheek turning a deep crimson. His left ear is swollen and I hope that's where the champ's fist landed when it broke.

"Love your friends, do you?" Reeger says, his jaw tight.

He's scowling at me and I wonder what's coming next. I find out when he walks over to Homer and raises his revolver to my friend's left temple. Homer's eyes go wide. He starts wailing again—he's stomping his feet, and his cries sound like they're coming from a caged animal.

"You've got five seconds to tell me where Garvey is." The Sarge has a crazed look about him, as if he's itching to pull that trigger whether I answer or not. I don't know what the Madame told him, but I can see she got Garvey out of here in one piece, somehow.

"Calm down, Reeger," I say. Sweat is rolling down my forehead and into my eyes. I want to thumb it away but I'm afraid I'll set Reeger off if I move an inch. "I've got no idea where Garvey is, and that's the truth."

Reeger cocks the hammer.

Homer puts his chin to his chest and whimpers. Spit rolls off the handkerchief and puddles in his lap.

"I guess Homer came here to get his palm read?" Reeger says. "Or his pole yanked?"

Reeger has no idea how right he is. Poor Homer probably did come here to pay his way through the night—just like so many other misfits in Center City—never realizing he took a tail with him.

"I'll tell you the little I know," I say. "But you've got to put the gun down."

Reeger lets up on the hammer but keeps the gun on Homer.

"All the way down," I say as calmly as possible.

He brings the gun down, but the goon in the corner unholsters his.

"Talk," Reeger says, the revolver at his side.

"I know your boy Connor wanted Garvey's payments. At least that's what Myra Banks told me. Now Connor's dead, so you're taking over, collecting the payments instead."

Reeger's jaw goes tight and the sides of his neck turn crimson. He raises the gun to Homer's head and my friend starts yelping through his gag again. "Start telling me what I don't know, or I'm pulling the trigger," he says. Then he jams the barrel against Homer's ear and shouts at me. "Where the fuck is Garvey?"

"How the hell should I know?" I say, my voice losing the calm tone it had earlier. "He's on the run. He didn't check in with me when he left."

Reeger sizes me up.

"It's the truth," I say. "I've got no idea where he is."

I guess he believes me because he lowers his revolver. Of course, I've still got the issue of the armed goon in the corner.

"This isn't the end," Reeger says. "Garvey's got to answer to me."

"That's your business," I tell him. "But for chrissakes, let Homer breathe."

I walk over to Homer, keeping my hands in the air where Reeger can see them. I start undoing my friend's gag, but I have trouble working my sweaty fingers through the tight knot. After a few twists and tugs, I finally wrench the cloth out of his mouth.

Homer takes deep breaths. "Oh god oh god oh god," he says between gulps of air.

I wipe the back of his long neck with a dry corner of the handkerchief. Then I reach for the rope around his wrists, but Reeger grabs my arm.

"That's enough," he says.

"Christ, Reeger. His fingers are turning blue."

I reach for the ropes again and Reeger lets me undo them. He's not risking anything considering he's the one holding a gun.

Once Homer's hands are free, my friend rubs his wrists and slowly bends his fingers to bring them back to life. Then he wipes his palms on his shirt as the Madame comes over to untie his feet.

I turn back to Reeger. "As far as I'm concerned, our business is done."

I put out my hand but he leaves it hanging.

"We're done when I say we're done," he says. He's leaning so close to my face I can see the small blue veins on the sweaty bulb of his nose.

I walk out the door and pick up my gun, which is lying on the floor with its chamber open. I don't have the nerve to look for the bullets, but in the dim light coming from the table lamp, I see that one round is still lodged in the cylinder. I think of Connor's game of Russian roulette as I close the piece and wrap it safely in my palm.

"Let's go, Homer," I say.

My friend gets up—he's wobbly—and shuffles toward me. But after two steps, he wheels around and jumps Reeger, grabs his wrist, and tries to take the revolver out of his hand.

The fucking simpleton.

He's wrestling with Reeger; they're swinging the revolver in large arcs above their heads. Reeger's goon grabs at Homer, but I raise my gun and point it right at his temple.

"Don't try it," I say. "There are still a couple of shots in here."

The goon growls and lunges at me. I pull the trigger but the chamber is empty. I take two steps back and squeeze again. This time I send a bullet into the closet door. He freezes. So does Homer, who was banging Reeger's armed hand against the wall, and the Madame, who was biting the bottom of Reeger's leg.

I train my empty gun on the oaf's head and grab the revolver from his holster. I walk over to Reeger and take his, as well.

"Homer, my car's out front. Take the keys from my pocket and meet me there. Madame, go with him."

Homer does as he's told and the Madame follows, a little shaky on her feet.

"I'm leaving now," I tell Reeger as a puddle of sweat forms under the wooden handle in my palm. "Your metal will be up front."

I back out of the room but then step back in. "And Reeger, I really don't know where the fuck Garvey is."

I leave again, this time backing my way all the way down the dark hallway. When I reach the foyer, I open the chambers on both police revolvers, palm the bullets, and dump the guns on the Madame's display case. Then I trot out the door and toss the bullets into an open sewer.

The Auburn's right where I left it. Homer's behind the wheel and the engine's running. I hop into the passenger seat and Homer takes off as the Madame lets out a barrage of curses behind me.

"Cocksucking bull," she shouts as she pounds her fist on the back of my seat.

"What the hell happened?" I say. "Where's Garvey?"

"I have no fucking idea," she says. "He got out the window right before Reeger broke through the lock, goddamned scum-sucking bull."

She continues to blow off steam, cursing and punching, but once we turn onto North Redfield, fully out of Reeger's shooting range, I tune her out. I roll down the window and put a scarf across the side of my face to protect it from the sun. Then I put on the radio and change the station until I find something slow enough to calm my nerves. A hot, humid wind is blowing into the car—it's thick and stale—and nowhere in it is there a trace of my old friend Aaron Garvey.

My father's bruises are healing and he's starting to look like his old self again. His collar is starched and he's wearing a brown three-piece suit, even though he had to take a razor to the lining of the jacket's sleeve to get it past his plastered hand. He's sitting next to Johalis; the three of us are alone at the Ink Well sharing an early steak dinner. As we eat, I'm catching them up on my run-in with Reeger at Madame Curio's.

"Goddammit, I should've known it was a setup," Johalis is saying. "I shouldn't have let you go there alone."

The champ puts down his fork and knife. I'm not sure if he's too upset to eat, or if he has given up trying to cut his meat with one hand. I'd offer to help, but I know he wouldn't let me.

I pour myself a finger of Gordon's and tell them the rest of the story—how I had one bullet left in my gun, how I freed Homer. Then I tell them about Homer jumping Reeger.

"Dammit, sounds like Reeger was okay at that point," Johalis says.

I nod. "I think he believed me. But after Homer went at him, I was right back where I started."

I down my gin. It's pretty good stuff, far better than the bathtub garbage that's been floating around town lately. I grab the empty ice bucket, bring it to the bar, and refill it. It hits me that Homer has no idea of the trouble he's caused. He's back at his place in Fishtown, itching to get back here and man the door, too dull-witted to see how overmatched we are. As for the Madame, she'll have to work the street until the heat on her shop cools down.

I bring the bucket back to the table, toss three fresh cubes into my glass and drown them in Gordon's. Then I do the same for

Johalis. I don't pour for the champ—he's working on a seltzer—but I give him some fresh ice anyway.

"I have no idea where Garvey went," I say and take a slug of the fresh gin. Damn, I'm having a hard time keeping my glass full. "He could be anywhere."

"He's running," the champ says, fumbling with his fork as he tries to spear a piece of steak. "He's outmanned and outgunned."

"And outbadged," I say.

My father nods and munches on his food, his plump lower lip bouncing as he chews. The guy on the radio is talking about a near-riot at a milk and bread line in South Philly. Meals are hard to come by, and I'm proud I'm able to give my father the T-bone he's eating now.

"Garvey's not running," Johalis says, putting his fork down and sliding his plate toward the center of the table. "He's going after Reeger."

I tell him I disagree, but he stands up and paces the room, talking louder and more quickly. "From what you told me, Garvey's had it in for Reeger from the start. He won't rest until Reeger goes down, and he knows you're not going to do it."

I picture the look in Garvey's eye when he spoke about Reeger and realize Johalis is right.

"Then I've got to get to Garvey first," I say. "He doesn't stand a prayer of nailing Reeger—those bulls will shoot him on sight. I'll give him whatever dough I've got and get him the hell out of the country. It's his only shot at staying alive."

"You might be right," the champ says slowly. He's weighing his words, as if I might be tricking him into breaking the law. "Keep Garvey away from Reeger. And you stay away from him, too."

"The problem's going to be finding Garvey," Johalis says.

"I've got to try," I say.

"How are *you* going to find him?" the champ asks. "Even the police can't track him down."

He's right; half the state cops are looking for Garvey. But we've got a leg up on them.

"We know where he's heading," I say.

"I'm listening," the champ says.

When I don't answer, his eyes widen. "I just said stay away from Reeger," he says. "You're in no more shape to tangle with him than Garvey."

"How else can I find Garvey if I don't stay on Reeger?"

"Jersey's right," Johalis says to my father. "If he wants to help Garvey that badly, this is the way." He takes a swig of gin as if it will make the thought of chasing Reeger easier. "We'll stay on Reeger. Garvey's bound to show up sooner or later. When he does, we'll grab him and get him out of the country."

The champ punches his good hand on the table, then leans forward and looks me in the eye. "You're gonna get in even deeper. Son, promise me you'll stay clear of that cop."

"I'll only look for Garvey," I say.

The champ tells me I'm ducking his question, so I start to explain, again, why I have no choice, but stop when I realize he'll say that there are always options. I let it rest. He'll cave because it's the only plan we have that's worth its weight in table salt. He just needs a few days to get used to the idea. If he would drink some gin, I'd have him onboard in ten minutes.

Johalis looks at me and nods. We're on, with or without the champ. I feel better, less confused, now that we have a plan, regardless of how questionable it may be.

A slow waltz is playing on the radio and the music and liquor wash over me. My nerves calm and my spine relaxes as my father finishes his meal. I drain the bottle of Gordon's into my glass, same ice. Then I lean back, put a fresh shine on my tongue, and remember how Myra and I had once spoken of growing old together, how we'd have a home where our kids could play in the backyard. Then I picture Angela hiding her apron whenever Wallace walks through the front door, running to greet him before he even makes it to a table, fawning over him whenever he pulls out another one of those blasted books.

I take a healthy slug of Gordon's and it burns my windpipe like kerosene. Sometimes I feel as empty as that bottle on the table.

⌘

The sun is cooking New York City as I turn onto 127th Street. Two spindly boys in undershirts and suspenders are tossing a ball back and forth in the middle of the street; four pigtailed girls in checkered dresses are playing jump rope. I inch around them and pull to the curb in front of the Hy-Hat. I can already see that Calvin has gotten the club back on track. The sidewalks are swept clean. The windows gleam. And the sounds of clacking billiard balls and kids' voices spill out of the front door onto the streets of Harlem. It's hard to believe this is the same club that Reeger lit up on the Fourth of July.

I just left the doc's, where he told me for the thousandth time that I'm an albino. He also told me—again—that I have to keep using his cream, so I grease up my cheeks and ears before throwing a scarf around my neck and slipping on my dark glasses. A woman is walking up the block with a young girl, so I wait before getting out of the car. Kids have a hard time warming up to the likes of me—they haven't lived long enough to understand true ugliness.

Once they pass, I grab the bottle of King's Ransom I packed for Calvin and head over to the Hy-Hat. The joint looks the same as it did during my teen years—it's filled with local kids eating

sandwiches, dealing cards, playing chess—and I remember why
I love it, why I struggle to keep it alive. I take my glasses off to
get a better look at the old place and spot Calvin with Billy
Walker by the dummy bag. Calvin's holding up a pair of leather
training mitts, and Billy is swinging at them as if they stole his
lunch money. The teen's dark-brown neck is soaked. His back is
far more muscular than I remember—the gangly kid is finally
growing into his shoulder blades. Right now, Reeger couldn't
seem farther away.

When Billy sees me, he stops swinging. "Hey, Snowball," he
says. "When you coming back to New York?"

"Soon enough," I say. I don't tell him the day I leave the Ink
Well is the day this place goes under.

Calvin gives me a smile as he slips out of the mitts. "Hiya,
Boss," he says, smiling and exposing a row of cramped yellow
teeth. The bags under his eyes are still dark, but his pupils have
reclaimed the spirit the Baldwin plant had stolen from them.

"What about Mr. Leo?" Billy says, wiping the sweat off his
forehead with the crook of his arm. "When's he coming back?"

Calvin's face drops. It couldn't be more obvious how much he
likes his job—and how badly he needs it.

"I'm keeping him pretty busy in Philadelphia," I say.

Billy's obviously disappointed, but he doesn't respond, he just
goes back to work on the dummy bag. As he bangs away, Calvin
and I walk into the back office, which also serves as an emergency
guest room from time to time. His straw boater sits on the desk,
so I guess he's still hoping to find some paying work singing at a
local barbershop. I promise myself I'll carry him as long as I can.

Rose is out getting groceries, so we're free to talk.

"Any sign of Reeger?" I ask him.

"Not a peep," he says, shrugging. "I hope I never run into that
guy. I'm worried about the kids. And Rose."

I'd tell him Reeger wouldn't bother any of them, but I remember how hard the bastard came down on the Madame. Instead, I give him the bag with the bottle of King's Ransom and watch his mood pick back up.

"Your pay's in there, too," I tell him.

He pulls the envelope out of the bag and I can tell he feels like a charity case. "I'll find work soon," he says, his eyes averting mine.

"I hope you don't," I say. "I need you here."

His chin lifts and I hope it stays there.

I've got the Hy-Hat's rent money with me, so I open the club's safe and put the cash on a dwindling stack of dough we keep there for emergencies. I see Calvin's got a gun in there, too. He needs it to protect the kids, but I wonder if he'd have the moxie to pull the trigger should the heat come down.

"Okay, Calvin," I say, closing the safe. "All looks good."

I'm about to leave the office when he calls me back.

"Hey, Jersey," he says. Then he lowers his voice and asks me, "Have you heard from Garvey?"

I'm glad I don't have to lie. "Nope," I say. "But I hope he's still alive."

Calvin nods. "Me, too. I'll bet he didn't do nothing to that cop."

"You might be right," I say.

As I walk out through the game room, I take a good look around. All of these young kids are making friendships that will last a lifetime. I wonder if one of them will wind up hunting down his buddy to get him out of the country and save him from the electric chair.

CHAPTER 7

*I*t's two-thirty in the morning and I've got the Auburn idling on South Philip. Maple trees line the block and a lone streetlamp lights a short stretch of sidewalk.

I'm watching Reeger's house with the champ and Johalis; we're convinced Garvey is going to show up tonight. Myra called me an hour ago—she told me Garvey had tracked her down at the Canary, that he'd been hiding in the alleyway hoping she'd give him some cash. She gave him all she had—twenty bucks—but warned him that Reeger was inside the joint, half in the bag and throwing his weight around.

"All Garvey kept asking me was what time Reeger would be leaving," she said, her voice unsteady after seeing what had become of our old friend.

I told her not to worry, that Garvey wouldn't do anything stupid. But the second after I hung up the phone, I dialed Johalis. My hunch was that Garvey would head straight here to wait for the Sarge, gun in hand. Johalis had the same hunch.

I'm looking at the two-story brick rowhouse and trying to think like Garvey. Aside from crawling through a window, the only way to get into the place is through the front door. I'll bet that Reeger, being a cop, has a deadbolt on it. And I'll double-down that Garvey—being a death row inmate who broke out of Eastern State—found a way around it.

"Garvey's gotta be in there," I say. "I'm going in."

"Just wait here," my father says, drumming his fingers on the top of his thigh. "You ain't sure of nothin.'"

I knew the champ would want to stop me from breaking into the place, but the longer we wait, the sooner Reeger will get home.

Johalis pipes in from the backseat. "If Garvey knows that's Reeger's house," he says, "then he's in there."

My father's lips tighten but he keeps quiet.

"I'll be fine, Champ," I say and open my door.

Johalis does the same behind me. "I'll cover you," he says.

As I step out of the Auburn, my father grumbles that he'll keep the engine running and slides over to take my place behind the wheel. I cross the dank air of South Philip, jacketless, skirting the glow of the streetlamp and cursing myself for not paying the lamp lighter to leave the street in darkness. As I reach the sidewalk in front of Reeger's, I check my ankle holster and jacket pockets for my essentials: flashlight, gun, and brass knuckles. Check, check, and check.

Johalis is two steps behind me. I motion that I'm going to try the front entrance. I can't imagine Reeger left his place unlocked, but it's worth a try. I climb the three short steps that lead to the door as Johalis waits by the curb, under a maple tree, keeping an eye on the street.

A lamp burns to the side of the entrance—it shines on Reeger's address—so I pull my fedora low in case a nosy neighbor is having trouble sleeping. I grab the knob and give it a gentle turn. I was right—it's locked and doubled by a deadbolt. I look toward the maple tree and shake my head.

It's a corner lot, so I walk to the driveway on the side of the house. It's darker here, nearly entirely in shadow, and when I step into the blackness, my eyes shimmy. I don't want to use the flashlight; I'd prefer to remain invisible. A sliver of light from the street crosses in front of me and hits the building. I spot a window that probably leads into Reeger's sitting room—the only problem is that it's ten feet off the ground. I'm going to need a boost.

I turn toward the maple tree. "Psssst."

Johalis doesn't budge, so I call again. "Pssssssst."

This time, Johalis comes out from under the maple. The thin beam of light flickers across his white shirt.

I point toward the window and he takes a look. When I extend my hands—*how do we get up there?*—he crouches down and whispers, "Climb on my back."

I put one knee on each of his shoulders. Then he stands up slowly and lifts me into the air. We're swaying from side to side like a circus act.

"Get me closer," I whisper hoarsely.

We wobble closer to the building, and I grab hold of the window frame. As I slide the window open, I slip off Johalis's shoulders and hang from the window—the metal frame digs into my sweaty fingers and a knifing pain shoots down both my arms. I'm kicking my feet in the air, biting on my lip, trying not to scream.

Johalis catches my feet and slides his shoulders under them to relieve some of the pressure on my fingers. But when a car turns onto South Philip, we both freeze. If that's Reeger's car, we're dead. I've got a smooth tongue, but there's simply no way to explain dangling from a bull's window at two-thirty in the morning.

Headlights brighten the block as the car slowly approaches the driveway. I hold my breath, as if exhaling will make too much noise. I'm expecting to meet up with a drunken Reeger steering with his right hand and pointing a loaded thirty-eight with his left. What I get instead is a young Joe singing an old tavern song with his girlfriend. A few seconds later, they're gone.

I let out a gust of relief and tell Johalis to push me higher. I pull myself up, lean my head through Reeger's window, wriggle through the opening, and land face-down on an end table. When I get to my feet, I clutch my chin and lean out the window.

"Whistle if there's trouble," I say to Johalis, as if he wouldn't know what to do on his own.

He gives a nod and a test whistle.

I whistle back and flick on my flashlight. The house is hot and dark, and it smells of stale cigars. I shine the light around the long, narrow space. I'm in the sitting room, which is separated from the kitchen by a wide plaster archway. Beyond the kitchen is a study and, I assume, the bedroom. Behind me is the front door and a dining area. The place feels worn, as if somebody dressed it up twenty years ago but hasn't thought about it since. The chairs and curtains are threadbare—and were probably last washed when Coolidge was in office. I wonder if Reeger built this castle for a queen who never showed up or, maybe, was here and left. The only item that seems like it gets any use is the armchair next to the radio. Next to it, on a small side table, rests a stack of magazines and a drained whiskey glass.

I'm tempted to call out for Garvey, but any sound above a whisper makes me nervous. Especially after that entrance.

"Garv?" I say no louder than a kitten's mewl. "Garv?"

I shine the flashlight into the kitchen. Nothing seems out of place and I see no sign of my friend. I spot a stack of papers on the counter next to the toaster; I flip through the pile but find nothing more than a hodgepodge of dry-cleaning tickets, punched deposit slips, and paid bills. I open a large brown envelope next to the sink and find something far more suspicious: a wad of hundred dollar bills. No straight cops take home this kind of dough. I think about Calvin up at the Hy-Hat, trying to feed the kids with the thin stack of cash I send every week. And I remember Garvey, living on the streets, hiding from the cops, and getting by on the few bucks I put in his pocket. I push Garvey and Calvin from my mind when I see that the envelope also holds three bankbooks. The first two are in Reeger's name. One is good for a couple of hundred bucks, but the second holds nearly four thousand. The third belongs to a Louise Connor and tallies a couple of grand, saved mostly from deposits of a hundred bucks each. I have no idea how Reeger got this much dough, but it can't all be off Myra. I restuff the envelope and put it back where I found it.

"Garv?" I whisper again, shining the light into the bedroom. The champ was right. Garvey's not here.

I'm about to check the study when I hear Johalis whistle. I kill the flashlight and stuff it back into my jacket pocket as I scoot toward the sitting room window—but I'm still in the kitchen when I hear the whistle again. This time it's accompanied by the unmistakable sound of a key unlocking a deadbolt.

I draw my pistol and crouch in the darkest area next to the sink. The door opens and Reeger staggers into the room, buckling under the weight of his last whiskey. His hat sits crookedly atop his head; he's slurring the chorus of "Marie" and fumbling with the deadbolt as he relocks the door. He can't be more than thirty feet from me, but he's also in lala-land.

I stay in a crouch, my right knee locked as tight as a pair of rusty pliers. My foot is resting on a matchbook; I reach down and grab it, then slip it into my pocket as Reeger stumbles along a shaky path to his bedroom. If he goes straight through the kitchen, he'll never notice me. If he stops at the sink for a glass of water, I'll soon be at the morgue, wearing a toe tag.

Beads of sweat are trickling down behind my ear and I pray Johalis is on the champ's shoulders, ready to climb through the window and enter shooting.

Reeger takes off his jacket and throws it in a lump onto the armchair. Then he fists his necktie and tugs it loose, staggering to his side as if he just yanked his own leash. He trips over his foot and grabs onto an electric floor lamp—but takes the lamp with him to the floor. He lands with a crash; the glass shade shatters and the bulb lights up, shooting its glow into the kitchen and onto my colorless cheeks.

Reeger's out cold. He's lying face-up on the floor; his revolver sits in his shoulder holster and the rank smell of stale whiskey oozes out of him. This helpless lump is the badge who busted my nose—I should slip on my knucks and return the favor. But I fight the urge. Instead, I focus on the window and the frantic whistle I hear coming from the driveway below.

My knee smarts as I come out of the crouch. I limp my way through the sitting room, stepping over Reeger to get to the window. As I reach my right leg over his shins, his lids open. I don't move and neither does he. He just looks up at my shimmying green eyes with a confused expression on his face.

The seconds drag on as I lock eyes with Reeger's glassy pupils, trying to stay as still as a hat rack. I hear the Auburn's engine idling outside—freedom is less than thirty feet away. I slowly close my eyes and rest my head on my shoulder, hoping he'll follow suit. I keep my lids shut for ten seconds, and by the time I open them, Reeger's eyelids have gone slack. I don't know what they put in their whiskey at the Red Canary, but if we had it at the Ink Well we'd be millionaires.

When I get to the window, I see Reeger's police car below me—and Johalis standing on the far side of it, waving for me to get the hell out of the house. I lean out the window and lower myself onto the roof of the car. I slide down the windshield, scramble off the hood, and limp out of the driveway without looking back.

My father's at the wheel of the Auburn, leaning forward to make sure I'm in one piece. Johalis slips into the backseat and I jump into the front. My father barely waits for me to shut the door before taking off toward the center of town. He's so anxious to leave he doesn't bother to remind me that I just risked my neck for no reason. Garvey wasn't even there.

But that doesn't mean he's not here in Philly. And it doesn't mean I'm going to stop looking for him.

CHAPTER 8

*J*ohalis lights a Lucky. I pour him a splash of brown and give him a soda to chase it. The Ink Well is half-full, not bad considering we're due to close in a half-hour. Angela's waiting tables again tonight; she crosses the room carrying a tray of sandwiches for a group of clerks from City Hall. I haven't seen Wallace lately and I hope Angela can say the same.

As for Reeger, nobody has heard a peep out of him since I lulled him to sleep two nights ago. My guess is that he doesn't remember anything after his last whiskey at the Red Canary. Still, I stationed Homer at the door and made sure he's packing metal.

"It has to be dirty money," Johalis says. He's talking about the envelope of cash I found in Reeger's kitchen. He's spent the last two days calling every contact he has on the force, trying to figure out Reeger's game.

"But nobody knows where it came from," he says, snuffing his cigarette in an ashtray. "And nobody knows a Louise Connor."

"She's not Connor's wife?"

Johalis shakes his head. "Dead for years."

I thought for sure we'd find out Reeger had something going with Connor's wife. It seems like the kind of thing a corrupt cop like Reeger would pull.

Angela comes over to the bar, her tray filled with empty beer mugs. "The boys want another round."

I grab five clean mugs and bring them to the tap.

Johalis asks her, "Where's Wallace tonight?"

My face flushes, so I turn away and wipe down the cash register. Johalis is asking for me, but I wish he'd given me some warning.

"No idea," Angela tells him, shrugging. "Maybe he's home studying." She doesn't sound happy when she says it.

"Good for him," Johalis says. "He's better off there than here." His rich voice is nearly as melodious as the crooning coming from the radio. Bing Crosby is singing "I'm Through with Love," and I hope Wallace is listening, wherever he is.

I swap the filled mugs with the empties on Angela's tray and she carries them to the front room. Johalis is looking into his bourbon, swirling it in his glass. He doesn't mention the conversation with Angela, and I'm grateful.

"So we're back at square one," he says.

"I think so," I say. "Garvey's gotta be here in Philly, waiting to pounce on Reeger. He wants him bad."

"So we should stay on the bull," Johalis says.

"I don't have a choice," I say, wiping my hands dry on my apron. "I can't sit back and let Garvey fry without at least trying to help."

Johalis nods and I can tell he understands.

From the booth behind him, two silver-haired gentlemen call out for Rob Roys on the rocks. It's nearly one o'clock, so I announce last call as I grab the bottle of scotch. I mix the drinks and slide them across the bar; one of the gents comes over to get them. When he's out of earshot, I pick up my conversation with Johalis.

"We should probably keep an eye on the Canary," I say. "Reeger's always shaking down Myra for payments, and Garvey's been there, too."

Johalis nods. "All true. But I've got to warn you about some other news, and I'm not sure you're going to like it."

"Why not?" I ask.

"It's about Myra."

Oh, shit. My face goes hot and my ears feel like they're being pricked with needles. I'm not sure why I care so much—I guess I don't want to see her land in hot water, even though she seems to enjoy diving into it.

"What about her?"

"Reeger dug up some stuff," Johalis says. "He found out how she grew up, how you two were at school with Garvey. He got the story from Connor. Turns out Myra and Connor had quite a thing going."

I'm surprised that Myra had anything going with Connor, but if that's all Johalis has, I'm going to be fine.

"That's it?" I ask.

"No," he says.

I want to pour myself a finger or two of scotch, but I don't.

"According to my guy at the stationhouse, the cops think Myra played Connor and Garvey off each other. First, she told Connor she didn't want to pay Garvey, that they should keep the payments. Then she told Garvey that Connor was a troublemaker. She figured they'd go at each other and that it would end ugly. She was right. Connor's dead and Garvey was sent to the chair. So she had the twenty grand and didn't have to pay anybody. But she never counted on Reeger coming after her."

It's hard for me to picture Myra as a mastermind. Then again, it's even harder to imagine the she was altogether surprised by what went down at Lovely's.

"Is that it?" I say. "Because it doesn't change anything. I've still got to get Garvey outta here."

Johalis's wrinkled lids sag. "Think about it," he says. "You said Myra wants you to take Reeger's payments."

"I also told you I said no."

"But if my guy is right, she might be trying to pull the same number on you."

I know Johalis has a line on the street, but I'm having a hard time believing Myra is setting me up.

"I trust her," I say. "I've known her since we were kids."

"Maybe so," Johalis says. "But it's the same pattern. She wants to give you Reeger's payments. If you and Reeger take care of each other—just like Connor and Garvey did—she'll walk away scot-free. She'll have a piece of the Canary and not owe anybody a single penny."

Angela comes behind the bar with cash from table number two. She's got her hair pulled back behind her head, and I wonder if Johalis can see that the last thing he's got to worry about is how I feel about Myra Banks.

"Okay, I'll be on the lookout," I say to Johalis, just to end the conversation.

Angela opens the register, slides in the money, and stuffs the check in our bill jar.

My nose is all but healed, my eyes look better, and Wallace is out of the picture. If I'm ever going to get anywhere with Angela, now's the time.

"Maybe I'll stay clear of the Canary altogether," I say to Johalis.

He looks at me, and then at Angela, and says it's a good idea. Then he leans on the bar and finishes his drink.

It's nearly closing time, and one by one, the customers leave the joint like the last drops of vermouth from a tall-neck bottle. By one-thirty, there are four of us left: Johalis, Homer, Angela, and me.

I tell Johalis and Homer to get some sleep, that I'll see them tomorrow night.

Homer looks dejected as he puts on his cap. "Slow night tonight, Jersey," he says. "I'm sorry."

To him, "slow night" means no Reeger.

"Enjoy it while it lasts," I say.

Once he and Johalis leave, I hang my apron behind the bar. I turn to Angela. "Want some company on the walk home?"

"Sure," she says, as if our walking the streets together is as natural as the sun rising over the Schuylkill.

She hangs her apron on top of mine and we walk out into the steamy night air, no longer selling happiness but ready to experience some of our own. She lives below Doolie on Buttonwood, so we head in that direction. I'm picking up the scent of her perfume, even though it's buried under the grease and cigarette smoke that accompanies a night's work in the Ink Well kitchen.

I take the lead and snake through the humidity-filled side streets, staying in the foggy shadows just in case Reeger is on me. I'm packing my rod and knucks, but I'm hoping I won't need either one, at least not until I get Angela home. As I cross the street to avoid the glow of a streetlamp, I spot a figure behind a bush. It turns out to be nothing but a shadow cast by a clump of wires attached to a telephone pole.

Angela takes a look at my nose and says she can't even tell where I got hit. Then she asks me again if I'm worried about the hooligan who busted it.

"No," I say, trying to look as relaxed as possible. "He's moved on by now."

"You really think so?" she asks. It feels nice that she's worried about me.

"Absolutely," I say. "Nothing to worry about. If he shows up again, I'll point him out to Homer and we'll shut the door on him."

We turn onto Noble Street and pass two lovers leaning on a wrought iron fence, kissing in the shadows. I have no idea what it would take for Angela and me to land in their shoes, but I'd imagine the first step involves finding the chromosome I was shorted at birth.

Angela doesn't seem to notice the couple, but she's obviously relieved that I'm not worried about the Ink Well. "I knew you'd figure things out," she says. She smiles and her cheeks get even rounder.

I can't keep lying to her, so I change the subject. "So how are the plans for school?"

My eyes start to shimmy; I turn away from her and thumb the sweat off the side of my neck to block her view. But from the corner of my eye, I can see she's not even looking at me—she's gazing down at her heels and shaking her head.

"I'm not going any time soon," she says.

Maybe Wallace really is out of the picture. I wish I could step in and tutor her, but I wouldn't know where to start. I spent most of my year in college playing ping-pong at the Hy-Hat and rolling kegs on Ninth Avenue. The only thing I've got to offer Angela is the money in my closet, which couldn't replace her salary for more than six months. I see the frown on her face and promise myself I'll feed the box more regularly.

"How about you?" she asks. "Have you ever thought about going back to college?"

"Yep," I say, keeping my shaking eyes trained on a rowhouse mailbox as I hand her the same lie I give my father and, once in a while, myself. "All the time."

I want to tell her the stone-cold truth—that Reeger's probably tailing us right now, and that if school were in my plans I'd be attending class. But I can't stop lying. When she hears I'm thinking of going back, she shows me one of the smiles that I thought she'd reserved only for Wallace.

My pupils are still shaking as we turn onto Buttonwood, so now I turn my head toward the cracked sidewalk. Angela's telling me something about the Ink Well's cash register, but I'm not listening—I'm too busy hiding my eyes and wondering if we'll do this again tomorrow night. I have my answer when we find Wallace waiting on Doolie's front steps.

"Wallace!" Angela says. "What are you doing here? It's late."

"I have your books," he says. Then he turns to me. "Hi, Jersey."

I give him a nod, but I can't bring myself to join the conversation. I've been around long enough to know that no schoolbooks have to be read at two in the morning. I'm sure Angela knows that, too. And it's obvious she doesn't care.

I turn to leave and she doesn't call me back. Instead, she says good-night to the back of my head.

"Thanks for the company," she says. There's a lilt in her words that wasn't there back on Juniper.

"'Night," I say and walk back up Buttonwood without turning around.

The street is almost entirely in shadow and I welcome the dark; it's a place where I can be alone, where the sun can't reach me, where I can pretend I have a full set of chromosomes. I pull my fedora low on my forehead as my eyes well up with tears. I tell myself that Angela and Wallace can have each other—that she's not for me if school and books and Wallace mean so much to her. And I try to convince myself that Myra is waiting for me, that Johalis is wrong about her, that she has all the innocence and heart that Angela has. As far as I know it might even be true. But I'm not buying it.

I wipe my eyes as I reach Broad and Callowhill and then, shamefully, duck into Chester's Chicken Shack. Chester's is a taxi-dance hall, a place where Philadelphia's loneliest misfits pony up ten cents to dance with a fallen angel. Reputable it's not.

I've been here before. I met with Chester about tending his bar but wound up working at the Ink Well. The truth is I didn't need Doolie's offer to walk away from this place; I refused to spend my nights working a joint as depressing as this one. I don't miss the irony that I'm here again, paying to get inside.

When I open the door, I'm greeted by a musclehead wearing a tuxedo. I wonder if Chester thinks the doorman's tails will fool people into thinking the Chicken Shack has class or, for that matter, chicken.

"One dollar," he says, giving me the once-over. He's obviously confused at what he sees, and I don't blame him. Chester's attracts just about every misfit in Philly, but not a lot of sweaty, chapped albinos with faint yellow haloes under their eyes.

I pony up my buck and the penguin hands me three tickets: one for admission, one for a dance, and one for a beer. I'll pass on the beer. Here, I'll order nothing but Aunt Robertas. After the first one, I'll forget Angela. After the second, I'll forget me.

I walk up the stairs. Chester's is no bigger than my apartment and the air's no fresher than a high school locker room. Cab Calloway is blaring through the music box, and twenty men are crammed around the dance floor, watching a middle-aged taxi-dancer grind her hips against a short, sweaty bald guy with an iron hook for a hand. She's wearing thigh-high stockings and a corset; she looks as if she's half-dressed for a Victorian ball. Nobody in the crowd is talking; they're all just staring at the dancer. I guess they're respecting her privacy.

When I get to the bar, I order an Aunt Roberta. The tender, a big guy with a shiny face and a drooping mustache, arches a bushy eyebrow. I repeat myself and this time it's not a question. He shrugs his shoulders, pulls the absinthe, brandy, gin, vodka, and blackberry liqueur, and mixes up a beauty. Then he slides it to me with an apologetic look on his face. I take a pull and it's exactly what I expected—slightly nauseating but strong as a steam engine. I swear, they could use these things to power street lamps.

The dancer turns my way while grinding away at her partner. She looks through me, high on something. She's working hard for her tickets—she's got a stack of them in the top elastic band of her stocking. But instead of feeling better about myself, which is why I came in, I feel worse—like I'm peeking through a bedroom window at a woman grieving over her younger self. If it were payday, I'd hand her ten bucks so she could take a break for a while. If she got lucky, she'd never come back.

Myra's over at the Red Canary and I can get there before last call. She's not Angela, but it occurs to me she might be more. She'd certainly never leave me feeling as empty as I do right now. Besides, I can have her all to myself for the duration of a chilled martini—and despite what Johalis may think about her, she's never charged me one red cent for a dance. I slug down the Roberta and give my dance ticket to a college-aged Joe wearing an eye-patch under a pair of thick specs. Then I head for the door.

When I reach the stairs I bump into an overly made-up platinum blonde with gold hoop earrings. She's got that Jean Harlow look, the kind you buy at the beauty parlor.

"Got a light, sweetheart?" she asks me with a smile.

She's either one of Chester's dancers or a hooker—or both. I strike a match and light her cigarette. She leans in toward the flame and puts her hand lightly on mine as she torches her smoke. She's trying to hook me, but she might as well be selling beach oil—my mind is already out the door. I trot down the stairs and pass the musclehead. I give him the quickest of nods. *I won't be back any time soon.*

The outside air feels fresher than it did when I got here. I walk down Broad, hop in the Auburn, and head across town to the Red Canary. I don't walk through the door until three in the morning, but when I do, the joint is still going strong.

Myra just finished her last set of the night, so I wait for her in the bar area. I take the corner table next to the fire exit. From here, I can keep an eye on the entrance and still have an easy out.

If Reeger walks in, I'll sneak out the exit. If Garvey does, I'll take him to Blind Moon Alley. If they both show, I've got trouble.

The redhead is working again tonight. She must realize Myra will be joining me because she puts two chilled martinis on the table.

"You're looking a lot better," she says with a nod toward my nose. "I can see your face now."

I don't say anything because I'm not sure seeing my face is a good thing.

She puts two cocktail napkins next to the drinks. "I guess all wounds heal in time."

"Not all," I say.

Red looks confused but drops the subject. As she hustles off to the kitchen, I spot Myra sashaying across the main room. She's wearing a snug turquoise number that hugs her chest, clings to her hips, and leaves her calves exposed; her hair is pinned to the side of her head and falls in loose waves over the opposite shoulder. She takes the seat across from me; her lips look soft and wet in the glow of the table lamp. The piano player launches into "Walkin' My Baby Back Home," and I try to forget the way Angela's face lit up when she saw Wallace.

"Where were you?" Myra asks, slipping out of her heels and sliding them to the side of her chair. "You nearly missed last call."

I'd rather not bring up Chester's Chicken Shack, so I tell her I was unloading a new shipment of moon.

She takes an envelope out of her purse and hands it to me. "Take it."

"What is it?" I ask.

"Two hundred bucks. Two payments on Garvey's loan."

"I already told you I don't want it." I slide the envelope back to her and remember the look of doubt on Johalis's face when I told him I trusted her.

"Go on," she says, putting the envelope in the middle of the table. "I'm done giving it to Reeger, so you might as well have it. Give it to Garvey."

"I don't even know where the hell Garvey is."

"You'll find him eventually. Take the money."

"Just pay Reeger," I tell her. "It'll keep him off everybody's back."

"No it won't. He's all over me whether I pay him or not."

She sips her martini and looks at me over the rim of her glass. I can still see the hurt in her eyes, a lingering sadness hiding behind the adult bravado. Right now, she's the only woman who's in my corner, and all I've got to do to make her happy is pocket the damned money.

"Go on," she says. "This is what friends do. They help each other. They make each other feel good."

She lifts her stockinged foot under the table and plants it on my crotch. I tell her to stop, that I know what she's doing. She doesn't listen.

"Don't you want to help me?" she says, looking me in the eye and gently rocking her foot back and forth.

I should be saying no, but I feel my legs widen to give her more room to play. She wiggles her toes and I'm happy to report that her clubfoot has healed nicely.

The corner of her lip curls and she says, "Why don't we talk about it some more in my dressing room?"

My eyes shake but she doesn't care; she keeps gazing into them as she moves her foot in quick, small circles.

I want no part of this. If I take that money, I might as well declare war on Reeger.

Now she's rubbing me in long, slow strokes.

"Sure," I hear myself say. Then I watch as my hand slips the envelope inside my breast pocket.

I'm about to button my jacket when Reeger's mustached goon walks into the bar. A few seconds later, Reeger follows.

"Looks like I'm already on the job," I tell her, my eyes on the door.

She's savvy enough not to turn around. "Reeger?"

I nod as I watch the Sarge order a pair of drinks. The tender pours him two whiskeys.

"Raid?" she asks.

"I don't think so," I say. "But let's not wait to find out."

When Reeger and his heavy turn away, I scoot to the fire exit.

Myra slips her shoes back on and grabs our martinis. "Can't leave soldiers on the battlefield," she says and brings me the half-filled cocktails. There's a twinkle in her eye, and for a brief moment, we're back in Hoboken running from a pack of twelve-year-old bullies.

We head down the fire stairs and duck out the back exit. We scramble into the Auburn and drive back to the Ink Well, finishing what's left of our martinis. We stay off Broad and stick to deserted side streets, some of which I've never traveled before. When we reach Juniper and Vine, I pull the car into Blind Moon Alley and park it there, just in case Reeger is tailing us. But he's not.

We scoot into the safety of the Ink Well basement and take the stairs up to the bar. I turn on the radio and pour us refills. I don't bother mixing cocktails; I just plop a cube into each glass and follow with a splash of Gordon's. Doolie has a jar of paper umbrellas that he likes to put in highballs—he says it distracts people from the heat—so I throw one into each drink and slide one of the glasses to Myra.

"What's with the umbrella?" she asks me.

"Protects me from the sun."

She takes her drink to a booth opposite the bar. I follow her, but I never make it to my seat. Within seconds, our lips are locked and we're feeding the fire she started back at the Canary. This time, it catches like a gasoline bomb. I put the tablecloth on the floor and we go hot in each other's arms, right there in front of the bar, like two kids on a beach blanket after sundown. When we finish, we lay motionless, staring at the ceiling and cooling down in the breeze coming from Doolie's electric fan.

As I look up at the tin sheets between the Ink Well's beams, I'm trying to sort out my life, trying to figure out how I wound up where I'm at now—and where I'm hoping I land.

The locals are home, Philadelphia's sleeping, and I'm here at the Ink Well, ready to take on a crooked cop with an ax to grind. And as night slowly rolls into day, I picture Angela curled up in Wallace's arms, her head resting peacefully on his chest, beginning the kind of life I wish I had.

⚜

The rain patters on my parlor windows as I flip through the *Inquirer*. Garvey's still the big news. *Cop Killer Remains on the Loose.* The newspapermen have been working overtime to find anything fresh on my friend. They're still writing about the shooting at the Red Canary, and the shorter articles are covering his time at Eastern State. Of course, all I'm concerned about is the manhunt, which has now moved to Altoona. There, an unemployed railroad worker claims to have spotted Garvey sleeping among a pile of bricks at a construction site. I don't believe it. Then again, I don't not believe it, either.

I go into the kitchen, open a beer, and make myself a sandwich. I've got what's left of Doolie's turkey, so I toss some dark meat onto a couple of slices of bread and hit it with some ketchup. It's not fancy, but it'll stop my stomach from growling. I take the sandwich into the parlor, set it on my desk, and put on the radio.

Instead of a news report, I get a woman singing a sultry version of "Embraceable You." I have no idea who she's singing about, but I'm right in front of the mirror and can see it's not me.

I peel back the window shade and eyeball Ronnie's. A heavyset oaf in a black bowler and gray raincoat has been sitting on the bench all morning, an obvious standout from the beggars that loiter in front of the place hoping to find some day-old bread in Ronnie's garbage cans. The oaf has taken his hat off and walked inside; he's now eating at the counter by the window. I guess he got hungry or wanted to duck the rain. Either way, I'm sure he's one of Reeger's boys. When he looks up toward my window, no doubt waiting for Garvey's face to appear, I wave hello and blow him a kiss. And I wonder why people call me a wisenheimer.

I'm about to take my first bite of lunch when I realize the dough Myra gave me is in my closet, sitting on top of Angela's school fund. That's more than eight hundred bucks combined. I've got to get some of that cash out of here. The smart thing would be to put Myra's money in the Hy-Hat safe, but I'm not planning on driving to New York any time soon. I take a seat at the Underwood and hammer out a note to Calvin, telling him what to do with the cash and to expect more of these envelopes as Myra gives them to me. I stuff the note and the greenbacks into an envelope and scribble the Hy-Hat's address on the outside. As for Angela's shoebox, I've buried that in the closet, down below a stack of Ink Well menus that Doolie asked me to store up here.

I leave the apartment to mail the letter, but not before holstering my pistol. When I shut the door, I stick a match in the doorjamb. If it's on the floor when I return, I'm going to enter shooting.

I take the stairs to the street and spot a better option than the mailbox. A mail truck is idling on Vine Street. I wave to the driver and he leans out the side of the truck, his face red and sweaty from the heat. Wearing that uniform must be like working in a woolen sleeping bag.

He flinches when he sees my cheeks.

"You're not looking so good yourself," I say, pointing at his red, sweaty nose before handing him the envelope. He gives me a quick, strained smile and drives off with no idea what he's got in that envelope—or the problems that it's caused.

When I get back upstairs, I find my father knocking on my door, his hat in his hand. I'm sure he's here because he refuses to enter the Ink Well—unless I'm serving dinner, in which case, I might be able to get his principles to bend.

"Open up," he's shouting at the door. He's out of breath; he must have run up the stairs.

"I'm right here, Champ," I say, taking out my keys. "Calm down." I eye the doorjamb and see the matchstick is exactly where I left it.

"I'm calm," he says while tapping his foot a mile a minute.

I don't bother telling him about the envelope I just mailed. There's no point. I've already let him know I'm taking Myra's payments, and he's already given me the speech about my neck and how far out I'm sticking it for a woman I hadn't seen in years.

When we get inside, I grab my sandwich and ask him if he wants half. He waves me off.

"Johalis got some news on our friend Reeger," he says.

I'm going to either love or hate this conversation. Based on the news Johalis has been finding of late, I'm betting it's the latter.

"You remember Louise Connor?" the champ says. "The bankbook?"

"Yeah," I say. "What about her?"

"Turns out she's Connor's daughter. Nine years old. She's blind."

"Blind?" I say.

"Yeah. Reeger's been givin' money to her."

"Hmmm," I say. "So he's not having an affair with her."

"Nothin' like that," he says.

He wipes the sweat off his forehead with the crook of his elbow. When the cuff of his jacket rides up his arm, I see the cast on his hand and try to forget how it got there.

"Reeger's takin' the money for her," he's saying. "He's payin' her way at some school for the blind."

"I don't buy it," I say. "You can't tell me that Reeger's a decent Joe."

The champ shakes his head. "Maybe he's not. But he's takin' care of the kid."

I want to tell the champ that Reeger's up to something, but he's going to ask me how I can be so certain. And I won't have an answer.

He shakes his head in frustration with me.

"I told you not to take those payments, goddammit," he says. "You think you're helpin' that gal of yours, but you're not doin' any such thing."

"She's not my gal," I say, but even I know that's not the point.

"Doesn't matter," he says. "Son, you're screwin' with the police. Bad 'nough we're helpin' Garvey, but now you're takin' Reeger's money. You're givin' those boys the right to come after you."

"It's not Reeger's money," I say.

"It's not yours neither!" the champ says, banging his hat against the side of his leg. He's pacing around the room, his frustration bubbling over.

I'm still trying to swallow the news about Louise Connor. "Is Johalis sure Reeger's giving all the money to the kid?"

"Aren't you listenin' to me?" he says. "Yes, he's givin' it to a blind girl. And he's gonna come lookin' for it."

I'm not sure what to say. I just mailed Calvin two hundred bucks that was supposed to be paying a blind girl's tuition. I don't know how it happened, but I'm starting to feel like the bad guy.

CHAPTER 9

*I*t's not even seven o'clock but the one-shot drinkers have already come and gone. You could set your watch by them. They come in at five-thirty, spend a few bucks to revive their souls, and then head home at six-thirty, recharged and ready for dinner. At eight o'clock, we'll get wave two. They'll be the ones I know best—the misfits, the outcasts, the forgotten. They don't come here to avoid home. They come here to find it.

Doolie is in the kitchen. He's not cooking—no sane person would want to be stuck in that kitchen in this heat—but he's carving a ham he baked early this morning. He'll assemble a few dinner platters, which is smart. Whatever doesn't get eaten tonight will become tomorrow's lunch special.

It's Wednesday, so Angela is doing her weekly double shift. The long day has drained the bounce from her gait, but she still manages to flit over to Wallace, who's sitting alone, reading *Black No More*. I've never heard of the book, but he's got no more chance of waking up white than I do of strolling the beach with a suntan. He's nursing a whiskey sour, and I feel like sending him an Aunt Roberta, just to watch him lose his composure for a while.

For the moment, I'm not worried about Reeger stopping in for a surprise visit. I've got Johalis working the bar and Homer guarding the door. Homer's not even supposed to start until eight o'clock, but the poor bastard's so eager for another shot at Reeger that he's been coming in early and stopping by on his off-days. Personally, I don't find myself missing the Sarge all that much.

The one guy who's not here is Garvey, and frankly, if he

showed up, life would get a lot simpler. I'd fill a flask with moon, drive him to the Hy-Hat, give him whatever cash we've got in the safe, then get him out of the country. After that, I'd start passing Myra's envelopes on to Reeger, and Garvey would never be the wiser. But until I know my friend is across the border, I've got no choice but to keep taking Myra's dough. Garvey will need that money. At least Louise Connor has schoolteachers watching over her. Garvey's living on the street. Nobody could survive out there without any cash. If I don't help him, he'll wind up getting caught. And killed. And they won't screw it up this time.

Two newlyweds sit down at the corner of the bar. They tell me their names are Harold and Georgia Wilson and that they just got married at City Hall. They're looking to celebrate.

"What kind of champagne do you have?" Harold asks. He's got rich brown skin, and when he laughs, his fleshy cheeks shake. I can see why Georgia fell for him.

"Only one kind," I say, "and it's got no label." I take a look at their worn clothes—the frayed seams on the lapel of his suit, the patched tear on the shoulder of her green dress. "Tonight, it's on the house."

Harold and Georgia light up as if I told them I'd be driving them to Niagara Falls in the morning.

I fill two flutes with our house champagne and change the radio station. I'm looking for something appropriate for a newly married couple and find "All I Want Is Just One Girl." I turn it up and tell them it's in honor of them. They raise their glasses and toast each other.

We're low on absinthe, so I open the trapdoor and walk down to the sub-basement to get a fresh bottle. I see the cases that Garvey arranged into a makeshift armchair and wonder where he is now. I hope he's eating.

As I'm rummaging to find the liqueur, I hear a pop upstairs.

It's a gunshot for sure. I instinctively reach for my pistol but my apron's empty—I left my rod in the back of the cash register drawer. Fuck, fuck, fuck. I slip on my knuckles and creep up the spiral stairs. Then I crawl out of the hatch and crouch in the shadows, peeking over the bar.

Reeger's here and he's packing heat. Worse yet, he's not alone. He's got two uniformed bulls standing behind him and both are armed—the bald guy has pulled out his service revolver; the freckly one with the scar across his ear is holding a hunter's rifle. Everybody else in the joint—our staff and customers, the people I'm being paid to protect—are huddled in front of the booths, their hands in the air. That includes Doolie, the new Mr. and Mrs. Wilson, Johalis and Homer, and Wallace and Angela.

This isn't a shakedown. It's a raid and I know the drill. The gunshot was aimed at the ceiling to get everybody's attention. Now they'll pile us all into a paddy wagon and take us to the precinct to book us. I'm just not sure what game Reeger is playing. If he wanted to shove me around, he didn't need this much muscle.

Johalis sees me in the shadows and arches an eyebrow—*should I shoot?*—but I give him a slow shake of the head. The champ is right; we can't pull out a gun every time there's trouble, especially when the roughnecks are wearing badges. Look at Garvey—he did that very thing and wound up on his way to Old Smokey. Besides, one guy can't outblast three bulls, not when one of the bulls is holding a rifle and tickling the trigger with his index finger.

I look back at Johalis and motion toward Homer, who's punching his own thigh and looks as though he's ready to go off like a Roman candle. *Keep your eye on him.*

Reeger shoves Doolie against the wall; he's asking him where he keeps the moon, where he keeps the money, and where he's keeping Garvey. It hits me that Reeger is screwing with my friends because he thinks I care more about them than I do about myself. And he's right. But he's going after them with his badge and, to me, that's fighting dirty.

Homer can't swallow it any more than I can.

"Fucking Reeger scumbag," he blurts out and pushes past Johalis.

He charges at the Sarge but never makes it. The freckled bull slams him in the temple with the butt of his rifle and Homer drops to his knees, holding his head in his hands, spewing curses at Reeger.

"Motherfucking badge-sucking cockhead," Homer barks out as he holds his bruised forehead.

"Don't let him up, Parker," Reeger says.

Fuck this. I let my knucks drop into my apron pocket and pull out my cash register key. I slip it into the drawer and turn the metal as gingerly as a safecracker, trying not to make a sound. I don't need to tell Johalis what I'm doing. He pulls his gun and points it at Parker's head.

I give the key a solid twist—I'm going to cover Johalis—but the damned thing jams. I try it again, but it doesn't budge.

Johalis looks Parker dead in the eye. "Go ahead and arrest him," he says, his pistol an inch from Parker's forehead. "But you ain't gonna beat on him."

The bald cop levels his revolver at Johalis and tells him to back off.

"Go ahead and shoot," Johalis tells him, "but if you do, I'm taking your pal Parker with me."

The bull keeps his gun trained on Johalis, and Johalis keeps his on Parker.

"Let Homer get back on his feet," Johalis says, "then we can all calm down."

"Let him up," Reeger tells Parker.

Parker looks disappointed—I guess he was looking forward

to a nice, cozy bloodbath. He hands the bald bull his rifle and smacks a pair of cuffs on Homer's wrists. As Homer gets to his feet, Parker twists the metal bracelets.

Homer falls back to his knees in pain.

"Scumsucking peckerhead," he yells, spit flying out his mouth.

Johalis thumbs his gun's hammer and presses the barrel to Parker's skull. "Try it again and you'll have another eye socket."

Parker backs off and Homer gets up unassisted. He looks like a drunken dancer as he tries to find his balance with his hands cuffed behind his back. Once he steadies himself, he pulls back his sloped shoulders, raises his chin, and walks to the door. I'll hand him one thing: he's not afraid of Reeger, Parker, or their fucking paddy wagon.

The bald cop takes Johalis's pistol and tucks it behind his leather belt. I'm half-expecting him to belt Johalis to kingdom come, but he doesn't. I guess bullies know enough not to beat on dogs that bite back.

"All right, niggers," Reeger announces. "Let's get this straight. We know you're hiding Garvey so you're all going to sit in a jail cell until you tell us where he is."

Reeger looks toward the bar and I'm no longer in shadow.

"Look who it is," he said. "Garvey's buddy, Snowball."

I see the fear on Angela's face and know that I won't be able to lie my way out of this one.

Reeger tells the bulls to load the gang into the wagon so he can deal with the albino freak. They file everybody out the door, and as they do, I hear a woman crying—it's either Angela or the new Mrs. Wilson. I'm glad Myra's not here.

The Sarge comes over to the bar, his gun at his side. I'm half-afraid the look in his eyes will burn the skin on my forehead.

"What can I get you?" I ask him.

He ignores the wisecrack. "I hear you're more than a lying

two-faced albino nigger freak. Now you're a fucking banker, too. Is that right?"

He leans his hands on the bar. If he raises the one holding the gun, I'm going for his throat.

"Isn't that right?" he shouts, his voice losing control and the lines on his forehead turning red. "You're a fucking banker?"

"What do you want from me, Reeger?" I'm trying to keep my voice calm to avoid working him into any more of a lather.

He leans forward and shouts into my face, his spit spraying my cheeks. His breath smells of cheap booze. "I want Garvey," he says. "And I want my two hundred dollars."

He's punctuating his words by banging his gun against the top of the bar. If that metal goes off, it's going to blast me right through the chest. He slams it on the counter again, but this time he does it as he's walking around the bar.

"And I want interest," he says, now only two feet in front of me. "Your whole gang is going to stay locked up until I get Garvey, and my money, and the vig. They'll rot in there without food, clothes, nothing. I swear I'll cut them off, you fucking albino jigaboo freak. I scrape shit like you off my shoe every god-damned day. I'm not about to let you make a sucker out of me, you piece of lying shit fucking monster."

He rips at the *Inquirer* clipping on the wall, pulling at the tape and tearing the paper down the middle.

"I can't even look at this crap," he barks. "Your fucking face makes my stomach turn."

The headline is shredded. My face is ripped—half of it hangs forward like a flapping tongue in need of a drink. I'd rather Reeger tear the whole thing down, but I won't give him the satisfaction of knowing I care.

"There's some money in the register," I say.

"I'll take it. Now."

I reach for the punch button, wondering if it will do a better job of opening the drawer than the key. I hit it with the butt of my hand and the drawer opens to the distinctive sound of a register bell.

I look down and there's the gun, the shiny .38-caliber eraser that Johalis gave me, resting in the back compartment, its trigger so easy to pull. I'm one move away from ending this whole charade. But if I do, I'll wind up on trial for killing a cop. I'm picturing a two-seat electric chair frying Garvey and me at the same time.

I reach into the drawer and pull out all the cash that's in there. Forty bucks. Not bad for seven o'clock on a weeknight, but not enough to settle up with the Sarge. I shut the drawer and hand Reeger the bills. I'm tempted to ask for change but I keep my mouth shut.

"That's better," he says, snickering as he pockets the cash. "Now where's my two hundred bucks?"

I can't say I didn't expect to be screwed.

"That's all I've got," I say.

"You'll find more," he says with a snide chuckle.

I take off my apron and ball it up. "Fuck you, Reeger. Just take me in." I dump the apron and the brass in it on the ice machine.

"That's exactly what I plan to do, Bleachy."

He pokes his piece into my spine, and as we leave, I picture Angela sitting in a jail cell, scared, sweaty, and hungry. It's my fault she's there; I can't help but feel as if I gave her up to protect Myra. I'd do anything to turn back the clock, to relive the day when Angela saw me on the front page, the day she asked me to work the bar to keep her and Doolie safe. But time keeps moving and I've yet to figure out how to stop it.

I put my arms over my head as Reeger shoves me toward the door. The last thing I see before he shuts the lights is my face on the front page of the *Inquirer*. Proud, confident, and smiling.

And ripped in two.

CHAPTER 10

Reeger didn't cart us to our local stationhouse; I guess he figured we'd greased too many local cops to stay there for long. He brought us out to his district by the docks so his fellow bulls can book us.

The minute we got here it hit me that all of these precincts share a certain smell—a combination of perspiration, dust, and greed—and this one has got it in spades. I'm steeping in it. My shirt is plastered to the bottom of my sweaty spine, my oxfords are sticking to the floor, and my lungs are filled with that rank stationhouse air. No wonder cops spend so much time at speakeasies. They've got to wash these places off their souls.

There are eight bulls manning desks in the main room; not one appears to be in any kind of hurry. I'm waiting for the old guy—his badge reads *Thorndyke*—to get off the phone and finish my paperwork. Behind him, two young bulls are leaning back in their desk chairs eating cheesesteaks; the others are booking barflies like me. The scene will be the same later tonight, except a wave of hookers will have replaced us rumrunners.

I haven't seen my friends from the Ink Well. By the time Reeger dragged me in here, they had already been arrested and fingerprinted. I can hear them calling out from the holding pen along with other prisoners—their pleas come from the hallway in the far corner of the room. They're asking for food, water, and toilet paper. The clearest voice belongs to Johalis—it blends in about as smoothly as a baritone in a children's choir. He's asking for a shot of whiskey and I'm not so sure he's joking. It wouldn't

matter if he were asking for eternal youth—not a single bull is listening. Except Thorndyke. He's acting like he's a tough guy, but
he looks up from his typewriter every time a woman's voice calls
out from that holding pen. There's a human being hiding under
that uniform. Trust me—nobody can read a cop like a criminal.

I'm itching to get in that cell to explain things to Angela,
not to mention the new Mr. and Mrs. Wilson, who broke no law
other than celebrating their future. But now Thorndyke is on
the phone, chatting with his wife, wondering what they'll cook
for their granddaughter tonight. I suppose the good news is that
I'm no longer dealing with Reeger. The Sarge handcuffed me to
a hot water pipe outside the bathroom and then left me to chase
after a hijacker at the Race Street Pier. I thought I'd be stuck there
all night, tied to that red-hot piece of metal, but the desk sergeant passed me on to Thorndyke. Considering how the evening
started, waiting for a cop to finish his grocery list is a step up.

Thorndyke hangs up the phone, takes off his wireframe eye-
glasses, and dries the sweat off his ears with a handkerchief. Then
he puts the specs back on, reaches into his bottom drawer, and
pulls out two sheets of fresh carbon paper. He also takes out a
framed picture of a young girl and places it on the desk next to
a stained coffee mug, angled in my direction. The kid can't be
more than five. She's got a smile that's an inch bigger than her
face, along with the unmistakable white hair and pinkish eyes of
an albino. I want to tell Thorndyke she's a cute kid, but I follow
his lead and ignore the photo.

"Name?" he says.

I'm not surprised he's asking. The Sarge brought me in here as
if he'd just bagged Lovely, pushing me into a chair and shouting to
every bull in the precinct that they could finally book that piece
of albino shit, Snowball. But he never uttered my given name.

"Jersey Leo," I tell Thorndyke.

He nods and pecks at his typewriter with his two index fingers, talking as he hunts for the letters. "You're the guy who saved that albino kid, right? The one from Port Richmond?"

"So they tell me," I say.

He nods. "I know who you are," he says, his amber eyes showing no resemblance to the girl in the photo.

When he asks my race, I tell him I'm half white and half Negro— and I brace myself for a zebra joke that never comes. Instead, he asks my occupation. It's a tricky question and I handle it as delicately as I know how. I tell him I own the Hy-Hat in Harlem. He types in *social club owner* without questioning why a businessman from New York would be working the bar at a joint in Philly. I'm starting to like Thorndyke; he doesn't run with the other bulls.

He turns to face me, the springs of his chair squeaking under his weight.

"Here's the situation," he says. "Your friends are in the pen. There are ladies in there, too, and my colleagues aren't about to extend any special privileges."

"I'll take care of them," I say.

He shakes his head and points toward my report.

"You've got your own problems," he says. "According to your arrest sheet, you're in worse shape than the others. You were caught taking money for the booze."

"True," I say. "But I always buy back."

Thorndyke ignores the crack and I feel stupid for wising off to the one bull who seems like a decent Joe.

"So how long am I going to be stuck here?" I say.

He puts his elbows on the arms of his chair and leans toward me. "You can walk out of here without waiting to see a judge, and you can take your friends with you. But you've got to plead guilty and they've got to pay their fines. Yours is two hundred bucks. Theirs are a hundred each."

I had no idea it was possible to walk out tonight. Had Reeger been sitting in Thorndyke's chair, I'd be rotting in that pen for weeks.

"They don't have that kind of cash," I say.

Thorndyke nods. "I figured," he says. "So it's up to you. Scrape together eight hundred bucks and you all leave."

"If I could raise that kind of dough, I wouldn't have been working the bar."

He waves off my admission of guilt as I suspected he would.

"I know," he says. "But that's the way the system works and I can't change it. Come up with two hundred bucks and you go home. Find eight hundred and you can take the others with you. Me? I'd at least pay for the ladies. That cell is no place for them."

I force myself not to think about Angela or what she's enduring. Instead, I try to figure out how I can scratch together eight hundred bucks. I don't have that much cash at my place, so I run through the people I can call. There aren't many. I can't get the champ involved, not for this. The only person I can think of is Calvin. He can take the last of the cash from the Hy-Hat safe and bring it here first thing in the morning. It'll wipe us out, but at least it'll get my friends and me out of here.

"Can I make a phone call?" I say to Thorndyke. "Before you lock me up?"

He nods. "Smart move," he says. "But take my advice and make this call count because you may not get another. The Sarge doesn't want you paying the fine. He wants you in that cell."

I pick up the receiver, imagining the litany of troublemakers who've used this same phone to make similar calls before me. I'd like to tell Thorndyke that I'm different, that I'm here because I care about people—Garvey, Myra, Angela, the kids up in Harlem. But I'm not sure my story is all that different from anything he's heard before. I keep my mouth shut and dial the Hy-Hat.

As I wait for an answer, Thorndyke puts the photo of the young girl away. My guess is that it was his granddaughter, the finicky eater. I wish she were here; I'd tell her a few things I've learned over the years. One is to use the doc's cream. Another is to wear the dark glasses; they really help in the sun. But most important is to hit the books. She'll be much better off if she becomes another Wallace instead of another me.

❦

I wake up and the sun is streaming through the bars of my cell window, broiling the left side of my face. I feel as if I've been snuggling up to a frying pan. I don't have any of the doc's cream with me—it's not as if Reeger let me pack an overnight bag—and I'm sure that my ear is blistering.

I'm locked up on my own. Angela, Johalis, and the rest of the Ink Well crew are on the other side of the stationhouse. There's nothing in my cell other than a three-inch mattress on a concrete slab, a canvas sack they call a pillow, and a ceramic toilet with no seat. My right hip feels as though it's been welded in place. When I think of Garvey living like this for two years at Eastern State, I can understand why he's so hell-bent on icing Reeger.

A young, husky bull brings me breakfast on a chipped, grimy tray. The oatmeal is as thick, and about as tasty, as modeling clay. I skip it and eat the brown banana. Then I down the orange juice, wishing I could spike it into a screwdriver. When I put the tray on the floor of the cell, I hear Calvin in the main room asking for me. He's not a second too soon.

"In here, Calvin," I shout. The torched side of my neck burns when the skin stretches.

Nobody answers, but Calvin shows up a minute later. Judging by the way he looks, he must have left the Hy-Hat in the middle of the night and slept on the train. His greased hair sprouts awkwardly from the side of his head and his soiled shirt is wrinkled and untucked. I'm sure I look no better. And I stink. I need a shower so badly I can smell my pits without lifting my arms.

"Calvin, this counts as overtime," I say.

He looks at my face through the bars of the door and his eyes widen. The burn must be worse than I thought.

"That bad?" I ask.

He doesn't answer, so I take that as a yes.

"You got the money?" I say.

"Yeah," he says. "But we got a problem."

From where I'm standing, anything Calvin is worried about can't be that bad.

"What's the matter?" I say.

"I couldn't scrounge up eight hundred," he says. His jowls seem to droop along with the corner of his eyes in apology. "We just had the exhaust fans fixed, so we only had six hundred and sixty bucks in the safe. I can throw in forty of my own, so that gets us to seven hundred. But then we're tapped."

We're short a hundred bucks; one person will need to be left behind. A number of possibilities go through my mind. The one I like most is leaving Wallace here, but that wouldn't be fair to him or to Angela. It also wouldn't change anything. Keeping him in that cell wouldn't tan my skin, gel a hank of straight black hair off my forehead, or make me the hero Angela once thought I was.

"Take the others," I tell Calvin.

"Take who?"

"Use the six hundred to pay the fines for the gang. Leave me the extra sixty. I'll take care of myself."

I can see Calvin doesn't like what he's hearing, but it's the only fair option on the table. "You sure, Jersey?" he asks, his furry eyebrows scrunching together.

"Yep, I'm sure. But do me a favor. There's a bull up front named Thorndyke. Tell him I need to make another phone call. If he's not here, then get him when his next shifts starts. You got me? Nobody but Thorndyke."

Calvin nods. "I got it."

"Good," I say. "Because if you ask anybody else, I'll be in here forever."

My ear itches, but if I scratch it I'll make it worse. I can't help but feel that the sting is a punishment, a comeuppance for the havoc I've wreaked on my friends' lives. I'm about to ask Calvin to go back to my apartment and bring me my cream, but the sun has already radiated my neck. I don't need a medicine that heals skin; I need a potion that reverses time.

Calvin reaches through the bars and hands me his forty dollars along with the other sixty. I'm sure he's giving me every penny he's got to his name. I want to get the hell out of here, but I can't take the man's life savings.

"Don't worry about me, Calvin." I hand him back his forty bucks. "Just pay the fines for the gang and make sure everybody gets home."

He looks like he'd rather join me in the cell than leave the stationhouse.

"Go," I tell him. "They're waiting. And they're hungry. Get them to the Ink Well so Doolie can put some real food in their stomachs."

Calvin leaves and I wait for Thorndyke. I need to make one more call, and it's got to be good for a hundred and forty bucks. Again, I consider calling the champ, but he'd never understand that I've been locked up for no good reason. I need to call somebody who won't question me, somebody who doesn't get caught up in the shades of gray between crook and cop, somebody who loves me for who I am, warts and all. I think that's Myra—and I'm screwed if I'm wrong.

I lie down on the cot and block the sun from my face with the pillow. Thankfully, I fall asleep again, and by the time Thorndyke comes to get me, the moon is out. I'm guessing he started his shift at eight o'clock, but I have no sense of what time it is now. Going by the bags under his eyes, I'd say it's two in the morning.

He grimaces when he sees the burn on my face. "Sun?"

"I dozed off," I say, as if everybody grows blisters after a good night's sleep.

"Sorry about that," he says and sounds like he means it.

He steps into the glow of the ceiling fixture and I can see that he, too, has been in the sun. Unlike me, he's been left with bronze cheekbones. Maybe he was teaching his granddaughter how to fly a kite in the park. And maybe she thanked him with a kiss on the cheek, crinkling up her face when she felt his gray bristly beard on her lip. And maybe she'll grow up like every other five-year-old kid, and nobody will care that she's short a chromosome or two. And maybe if I scratch my ear, my finger won't feel like an industrial soldering iron.

Thorndyke leans on the cell door. "Your friend told me you need the telephone."

"I need a lot of things," I say. "But that's the main one right now." I gingerly touch my index finger to my ear hoping to make the itch go away.

"You already used your call," he says as he takes out his keys. "Next person you're supposed to be talking to is a judge."

He unlocks the door and pulls it open to the screech of metal against metal. Then he motions for me follow him. I do it, following his lead down the dimly lit corridor, stepping in and out of his shadow as his shoes squeak against the granite floor and his keys jingle on the hook of his belt.

"You're lucky I'm here," he says. "I'm usually working the docks."

I'm not sure what to say. "Thanks," I tell him.

He doesn't answer and I take that to mean he doesn't want anybody to know he's doing me a favor.

We get to his desk; he sits me down and points to the phone. "Make it fast," he says. His tone is edgier than it was when we were alone.

I'm about to grab the receiver when a hooker sitting across the room starts yelling at the bull typing up her paperwork. He tells her to calm down, but she's really lathered up.

"Fuck you," she barks. Her hands are cuffed to her chair so she kicks her feet up on the bull's desk, swinging her heels at him and knocking his typewriter to the floor.

Another cop comes over to help drag her to the pen. The three writhe in a sweaty dance; whenever the bulls have her down, the hooker wriggles free of their grip.

"Goddamn fucking bulls," she spits as she gyrates her body and twists herself free.

As they pull her by the arms across the room, I see that the moll is Madame Curio. Her face is soaked with sweat and covered with bruises—her right cheekbone has ballooned into a ripe tomato and her eye is nearly shut. My guess is that Reeger brought her here hoping she'd cough up some dirt on Garvey's whereabouts. Even if the Madame were the type to sing—and she's not—Reeger would have been barking up the wrong tree. The Madame doesn't have any better idea of where Garvey is than I do.

Thorndyke sees me eyeing the Madame.

"Know her?" he asks.

"Family friend," I say.

"You've got interesting friends."

"My friends have interesting bruises."

"Listen," Thorndyke says, leaning toward me and lowering

his voice. "If you start opening your mouth and making trouble, you'll never get out of here. Take my advice. Use the phone and save your fucking neck."

It's good advice. I pick up the grimy receiver, but before I dial, I ask Thorndyke how much it would cost me to pay the Madame's fine.

"No fine," he says. "She's a regular here. She's gonna have to see the judge. You're not gonna get her out of this one."

I'm sure that somewhere in this town is a bull that disagrees—I've just got to find one with empty pockets. I can't let the Madame rot in here alone.

I dial the Red Canary and wait to speak with Myra. I'll tell her where she can find the hidden key to my apartment; then I'll ask her to take a hundred and forty dollars out of Angela's shoebox and bring it me. She's the one who said friends help each other. I sure hope she meant it.

⚜

Starting with my mother, who left my father and me right after I was born, the women in my life have routinely cut out when I needed them most. I'm sure Johalis is still expecting to put Myra on that list, but he's going to be disappointed. Myra came to the stationhouse straight from the Red Canary, chewed off a piece of Thorndyke's ear, and paid my fine with her own money. I'll bet I'm the only albino bartender who's ever been sprung from this place by a hazel-eyed knockout in a lavender evening dress.

Once we were safely outside the building's steel doors, she told me she felt guilty. This was all her fault, she said. I'm sure Johalis would have agreed had he been with us, but I shrugged it off. I told her I knew what I was getting into when I took that envelope. She hugged me for absolving her of her guilt, pulling me so close I could smell the scent of her skin underneath her perfume. I could see the burden of self-hate lift from her shoulders, and her smile took the same albatross off mine. We flagged a taxi and I had the cabbie take us past Rittenhouse Square. Myra didn't care how badly I stunk—she snuggled up to me, handed me a flask of gin, and put her head on my shoulder. I cranked down the window and sucked in the hot, humid, smog-filled air, rinsing it down with a swig or two of Gordon's. The mix of smells and flavors—Myra's hair tonic, the exhaust fumes from late-night delivery trucks, the juniper-laced alcohol—somehow tasted of home.

That was last night, and Myra's still here today.

She's sitting on the couch, wearing one of my shirts with her legs folded beneath her. This is the first time I've seen her without makeup, and she looks more beautiful, and more mine, than I would have ever dreamt. I'm enjoying this and I'm not about to ruin it by speaking with Johalis. I'm also not going to look at the mirror—or out the window at Ronnie's Luncheonette.

I've got a chicken roasting in the oven; the smell is wafting through the apartment. The radio is playing Rudy Vallee, I'm pouring martinis, and Myra is telling me the lies I love to hear.

"The burn on your neck is looking better," she says. "It's just your ear now."

"Thanks," I say. "When I go by the Hy-Hat on Monday, I'll stop at the doc's and have him take a look."

I hand her a martini and we clink glasses. We don't need to talk about how we feel—the fear, the helplessness, the uncertainty. Once you've seen somebody tormented in grade school, it's easy enough to fill in the blanks.

"So things are okay now?" she asks.

"Not exactly," I say. "Doolie's shutting the Ink Well for a couple of weeks. He wants to lay low until the heat dies down.

It doesn't matter, though. I'm done there. He says he doesn't feel safe as long as I'm around. And I can't say I blame him."

I take a slug of my martini and give it a second to land before talking again.

"But getting rid of me isn't going to help," I say. "Reeger will still be hunting down Garvey, and he'll still be nailing the Ink Well to do it. I've got to find Garvey before Reeger does. I'll give him all the cash I've got—including whatever you give me in your envelopes—then I'll get him the hell out of the country. I'll tell the cops he died. Reeger won't believe me, but he'll have no proof otherwise. Then I'll start passing your envelopes on to Reeger and everybody will be happy. It's still the only way I can see getting out of this."

"It might work," she says. "But if it does, promise me you'll be the one giving Reeger the money. I'm done dealing with him. I'm tired of getting pushed around."

She should only know how I feel.

"Fine," I say. "Just stay the hell out of his way until I find Garvey. That means disappearing from the Canary for a while. You're no safer there than I am. Reeger'll come down on you as hard as he's hammering me."

"Where else can I go?"

I don't have an answer. The Ink Well sure isn't safe. And Madame Curio's is no longer a secret.

I shrug my shoulders.

"Maybe you're already there," I say and wave my hand at my parlor.

Myra doesn't say anything but she looks relieved, as if she no longer has to fake being the beautiful woman that she is.

"I can't hide forever," she says.

"Neither can I," I say.

I sit next to her on the sofa and neither one of us speaks as we finish our martinis, content to enjoy the comfort of each other's company in silence. When dinner is ready, we saddle up to the counter, eat chicken and green beans, and chat about the old days as we listen to the radio. Then I take out the orange sherbet I'd brought up from the Ink Well and set aside for Angela. I fill two bowls, give one to Myra, and lead her back into the parlor. She's too beautiful at twilight to miss, so I raise the window shade and let the evening do its work. The glittering pink and blue light coming from Ronnie's sign wraps her in a lavender halo.

"Maybe it's time," she says. Her almond-shaped eyes are wide open, sparkling like a flute of bubbly.

"Time for what?"

"To take off," she says. "To disappear. Maybe it's time for the two of us to run off to Hollywood. Leave this mess behind us."

I'm stunned that she still remembers. And I can see she's serious. My ears turn as hot as andirons. I figured the day would come she'd walk away from the Canary, but I never expected that she'd still want to leave with me.

"We could do it," she says, her voice is now gushing with the childlike excitement she was robbed of back at Elementary School Four. I'm trying to keep a level head but her energy is intoxicating, her buzz infectious. "We'll just go. You don't have to find Garvey. Let your friends track him down. They can pass him the money. Screw Reeger."

I think it out. There's nothing stopping me. All I'd need is a few days. I'd have to square things at the Hy-Hat on Monday; I'd also have to tell the champ and Johalis that I'm leaving. Johalis will have a few comments, but I'll dodge them. Every mutated cell in my body is pushing me to put Myra in the Auburn, drive west, and never look back.

She's leaning forward in her chair, staring at me as she waits for an answer.

I'm wondering where we'll get the money. To leave here. To get there. To live.

She's hanging on my answer—her eyes firing like spark plugs. "How's Thursday?" I say.

She lunges at me and plants her lips on mine. The kiss comes with the kind of reckless passion reserved for school dances and wedding nights. She swirls her tongue around mine and then traces it up my white jawline and along the rim of my blistered ear. Then she pulls away, looks me in the eye, arches her back, and lifts my shirt over her shoulders. The flickering lights accent her light-brown shoulders and small, rose-tipped breasts. I open my arms and we lock our bodies into each other as we fall to the floor, giddy from the roar of an ocean that's three thousand miles away. I want to swallow her up, carry her back to sixth grade so we can take the whole ride again and do it right this time. I kiss her lips, her tan forehead, the smooth skin behind her ears. I think of the abuse she took, how she cried at the hands of her classmates, her neighbors, all of the co-stars and bit players of her adolescence. And I remember how I did the same. I pull her close and promise myself I won't let it happen again to either one of us.

We roll, tumble, moan, ache, and kiss like the kids we never had a chance to be. And when we're done, we lie on our backs, breathing heavily, staring at those gleaming pink and blue lights as they streak across the ceiling's broken plaster beams. Myra palms her hair off her damp forehead and curls her body up against mine. The open window lets in an evening breeze—the first I've felt in a long time—and it cools my sweaty neck. Maybe it's me, but I swear it smells of saltwater.

CHAPTER 11

Doc Anders is looking at the rim of my ear, which now resembles the inside of a pomegranate—purplish-red with prickly whiteheads and watery blisters. But I'm not worried about what the doc has to say, not when I'm about to run away with the woman who's been saying she loved me for twelve years.

The only loose end I have to tie up is at the Hy-Hat. I'm not looking forward to it. I've got to tell Calvin that his stint has ended. I've never cut anybody's pay before, but if I leave Philly the champ will surely come back to New York—and I can't afford to pay two managers, not without a weekly check of my own. Now that I think about it, maybe Doolie will hire Calvin to fill my spot behind the bar at the Ink Well. I'll suggest it, but that's all I can do. It's not as if Doolie's turning to me for recommendations.

The doc dabs some ointment onto my ear with a white cotton cloth and asks me about my father's hand.

"You know the champ," I say. "He can't wait until that cast comes off."

I'm speaking the truth, but I just left my father and he didn't say a word about the cast. All we spoke about were my plans to head west with Myra in the morning.

"He'll have his hand back soon," the doc says. "Only a few more weeks and he'll be good as new."

We're sitting in the doc's office because he knows I can't stomach his examination room. Lying on that metal table makes me feel like a freak, like some kind of science experiment gone wrong. It's worse when his nurse is there. She takes notes on my blotches and blisters as if she's looking at a skeleton in a bio lab—except this skeleton has a beating heart and exceptionally thin skin.

The doc tables the cloth and slides his spectacles down his nose.

"You're not using the cream enough," he says, eyeing me over his horn-rimmed frames.

"I only skipped one day," I lie. "The cops locked me up and I fell asleep right in the rays of the sun. What was I supposed to do?"

"You could've tried staying out of jail in the first place."

Of course he's right, but I let it slide.

"It burns like a bastard, doc."

I'm not sure he's listening but that's usually the case when I chat with him. He turns away from me, mutters to himself, and rummages through his cabinet. Then he clucks his tongue and leaves the room. When he comes back, he's got a box of teabags in his hand.

"Wet these and use them to soak the burn," he says. "Every morning."

I tell him I'll do it, even though I know I won't. I'm leaving with Myra this week—I'm not about to put off the beaches of the Pacific because I'm dabbing a teabag on an ear that will be pale, white, and albino until the end of time.

The doc looks at my eyes. "They're shaking," he says.

"I'm used to it."

He nods. "Nystagmus."

I've heard the word before. It's a fancy term that medical people use for shaking eyes. It might as well mean *fucking albino*.

The doc walks over to his cabinet, pulls out a small tube, and hands it to me. It's the same stuff he gave me the last time, or damn close. I slip it into my pocket.

"How's that young lady you were chasing after?" he asks.

He's talking about Angela and I'm not sure what to tell him.

Every time I'm here, I'm talking about a different woman that I love and how she almost loves me back. I'm not about to say that I've fallen back in love with my sixth-grade crush—and that she's hiding in my apartment until we skip town on a crooked cop. He'd have every right to open my chart and check off "idiot." But he's not the one with the blistered face. And he's not the one who made plans to run off with that classmate so many lonely years ago.

"She's fine," I tell him, which I'm assuming is the truth.

His eyebrows arch in surprise. "Glad to hear it," he says.

I'm glad he doesn't follow up with anything other than his standard medical advice—use the emollient and the eyedrops, stay out of the sun, and wear the dark glasses—because my half-truths are getting closer and closer to half-lies. He writes a prescription for more cream, as if I'll ever reach the bottom of the tube he just handed me.

Once I say so long to the doc, I step out of his office and into the blazing sun. I pop my fedora on my head, wrap my scarf around my jaws, don my dark glasses, and walk up the shady side of 87th Street. The Auburn is hot as hell, so I crank down all the windows before taking off for the Hy-Hat.

It's a short ride but I take it slowly, avoiding sunny streets, and practicing my conversation with Calvin. *I've got to let you go. I'm giving your job back to my father. Good luck at the barbershop.*

A group of teens are playing punchball on 127th Street, so I wait for them to finish a rundown before easing past them. I park in front of a fire hydrant and walk up the block. The front room of the Hy-Hat is empty, but I figured today would be slow. Normal people can't wait to be outside on days like this. Me, I'm standing by the curb, the scarf blocking the summer rays from hitting my face, as I keep rehearsing the words I'll use to tell Calvin I can't afford to pay him any longer. Maybe I should start by suggesting he tend bar at the Ink Well.

I open the door to the club, lose the dark glasses, and take a look at the room where the champ broke the one tool of his trade, his hand. The place is quiet and empty. The dummy bag hangs limply. The pool tables sit idly. There's something depressing about a game room without kids—it reminds me of a smile without teeth.

A cry comes from the kitchen, a primitive call for help. It sounds like a woman. I draw my gun and scurry around the ping-pong tables, staying on my toes and avoiding spilled peanuts and a rogue cue ball. Then I position myself outside the kitchen door, waiting to hear the gravelly evil of Reeger's voice. But I don't hear the Sarge. All I hear is that agonizing wail.

I enter quickly, pistol first. Broken plates and open cans of food litter the floor. Calvin is stretched out on the ground, his right leg bent beneath him. His wife Rose is leaning over him, her palms pressed up against his chest, her fingers soaked with blood. When she moves her hands, I see the bullet hole. It's in Calvin's throat—blood is squirting out of his neck and Rose is pushing harder on the wound, trying to stop the hemorrhage. She keeps rearranging her hands, hoping to stumble upon a magic position that will stop the bleeding—but she's not finding it. She looks up at me and starts to speak but no words come out. Black mascara runs down her cheeks and a trail of saliva oozes off her round bottom lip.

"Calvin," I hear myself shout. I feel as if this can't be real, that if I walk outside and re-enter, Calvin will once again be working the dummy bag with Billy Walker. I fall to my knees over him; I can feel Rose's shoulders shaking as she sobs. I roll my scarf into a makeshift pillow and slide it under Calvin's head.

He tries to speak but no words come out, only a gurgling sound.

"I'll call Doc Anders," I tell Rose and race to the phone in the office. I get the doc on the line and tell him what's going on. He says he'll be here in a few minutes, but even that seems too long for Calvin to hold on.

I dash back to the kitchen and find Rose hunched over Calvin, her head bent, her attention darting back and forth from Calvin's eyes to his chest.

My friend's blood has splattered onto nearly everything in the room. It speckles the sink and the refrigerator; it's pooling under my knees. I pick up a crumpled napkin from the floor and wipe a sweaty red streak from his forehead. Then I look him in the eye and make sure he's staring back at me. The dark bags under his lids are swelling and I'm afraid this is the last time we'll speak.

"Hang in there, Calvin," I say and grab his hand. "We don't want you going anywhere just yet."

He squeezes my hand so I know he can hear me. I turn to the door hoping to see Doc Anders, but Calvin squeezes my hand again. This time he doesn't let up. He wants my attention and I know why.

"Reeger?" I ask him.

He blinks his eyes and I take that as a yes. My guess is that Reeger showed up looking for Garvey. He probably started throwing his weight around and Calvin didn't take too kindly to being bullied. I'll never know exactly what happened here, but the facts are unimportant. I promise myself that if Calvin dies I'll take care of Rose. And Reeger.

"I'll give the Sarge your regards," I say to Calvin.

He gives my hand another squeeze—he likes the idea—but the sound of screeching tires interrupts our conversation. The doc comes running into the club; his nurse is with him. They strap a contraption that looks like a gas mask over Calvin's mouth and slip a stretcher under his body. They're calling out medical phrases to each other and I have no idea what they're saying. I feel helpless and stupid. These two can save Calvin's life; all I can do is promise to drop a hammer on a badge. The champ has been right about a number of things—one of them is that throwing a gas bomb at a fire only makes the flames bigger.

Doc Anders works on Calvin as Rose sits silently, twisting the fingers of one hand in the palm of the other. I can see her mind racing through her past with Calvin—and her future without him.

The doc and his nurse strap Calvin to the stretcher, lift him off the floor, and carry him out of the kitchen and through the game room to the front door. But I know the look of defeat and the doc has it etched around his sagging eyes and across his taut lips. It's too late. Calvin is dead.

I was supposed to be heading west with Myra today but spent the morning at Laurel Hill Cemetery. The sun beat down on Calvin's open grave, frying the burnt grass around the ditch to a yellow brown. I found shelter in the shade of an oak tree as the priest delivered his eulogy, telling us that Calvin had left us for a better place. As ugly as Philly can turn, I couldn't stomach hearing that death was an attractive alternative, and I bet that Calvin would agree with me. Rose wept openly as she looked down at the petal-covered coffin. Doolie stood by her side as he said good-bye to his childhood friend. Three Negro men were there—three-quarters of Calvin's quartet— their heads bowed, their eyes shut in prayer. I leaned against the oak tree, my hat pulled low to stop the sun from broiling my skin—and to hide the shamed look on my face. Everybody there blamed me for Calvin's death and I couldn't disagree.

After the burial, Doolie opened the Ink Well so Calvin's friends would have a place to grieve, and even though nobody invited me, I came. I felt I owed it to Calvin. I can still feel the regulars staring at me. Angela hasn't even said hello.

Doolie's behind the bar. Homer is also here—Doolie likes having him on staff to man the door. Rose is sitting across from Wallace at table one, staring into the cigarette smoke that swirls in front of her face, its trail as wispy as the memories she'll now be carrying. Her hair, which is normally wet with pomade and combed down over her forehead, is pointing straight up toward the heavens. There are also some faces I don't know, most likely Calvin's friends or family. They're eating lunch at the other tables—the place is full, but for all the wrong reasons.

Out of respect, Doolie turned the radio off and unplugged the music box. He's got the electric fan buzzing, but it's not strong enough to beat the heat. Nor is it loud enough to drown out the clanging noises coming from the construction crew on Vine Street. Despite the racket, everybody is speaking in hushed whispers. Grief has already knocked us down and it's still throwing punches. This is a solemn time for the Ink Well, and it's killing me that I can't mourn Calvin's death with the others, that I feel responsible for his death and for his family's pain. I no longer feel comfortable in the place I called home— even to say good-bye.

The champ is with me and I appreciate the support. We chose a booth in the back of the joint so as to not to interfere with the other mourners. I've got a bourbon in front of me and the champ is working his way through a double seltzer on the rocks. I recognize his blue jacket and maroon necktie; it's the same combo he used to wear when he represented the Colored Merchants Association in Harlem back before the market crashed. I can see that one of the brass buttons has been replaced—it doesn't quite match the others. Beads of sweat dot his chin as he urges me to stick to my plan and run away with Myra. I guess Johalis hasn't been spreading any of those stationhouse rumors because my father is really singing Myra's praises.

I tell him my plans haven't changed—but that I'm post-poning them a week or two so I can settle my score with Reeger.

"What's that gonna get you aside from the 'lectric chair?"

"I can't walk away from this, Champ," I say, nodding my head toward the mourners in the front room. "I owe it to Calvin. It's my fault he's dead."

"Your fault? What'd you do? You gave the man a paycheck. Yeah, he was at the Hy-Hat, but that's 'cause you gave him a job."

I want to believe him, but when I glance over his shoulder at the locals who are looking at me—the troublemaker who put their friend in Reeger's crosshairs—a blanket of guilt dampens my spirit. "He died because he was working for me, Champ."

"I know it," my father says. "But you couldn't have stopped it. Reeger was lookin' for Garvey, plain and simple."

"So?"

"So Reeger's comin' down on anyone and anything around Garvey, including you."

I sip my bourbon and think about it. Garvey was pushed into gunning down Connor—and now Reeger wants a pint of Gar-vey's blood. The champ is right.

"Why do you think I been helpin' you?" my father says. "You got caught up in Garvey's mess. He didn't get caught up in yours." He reaches out with his casted hand and pats my forearm with his calloused fingertips.

"Leave town with Myra," he says. "Go tomorrow. Let Reeger and Garvey settle this. You're not part of it, Son."

I look at his plastered hand, his mismatched brass button, the scar over his eye. The man has his dignity and has always fought for mine. He wouldn't tell me to walk away from a battle that was justified. I'll always wonder how he's able to see so clearly between right and wrong, and why it's always been so difficult for me, his own flesh and blood.

"Okay, Champ," I say. "You win. I'll leave tomorrow."

We sit and nurse our drinks, staying a while out of respect for Calvin. But there's no longer anything here for me. The magic of the joint was never in what you were doing, but how you were doing it. And right now, I'm doing it alone.

I tell the champ to go on ahead, that I'll settle our tab and meet up with him later. I walk up to the bar and put a few bucks down. That damned newspaper still hangs on the back wall—except now it's been taped back together. I can't imagine it will stay there for long.

Doolie comes over and slides my money back at me. "Thanks for showing up," he says.

I tell him I appreciate all he's done for me and I leave the cash where it is. Then I wait until Angela's in the kitchen before crossing the dining room to leave. I have no idea if she would have said good-bye, but I'm sparing myself the blow of getting an answer I don't want.

As I walk out, the only person who looks my way is Homer. He stops me just as I reach the door.

"You need help with anything, you just call," he says and shakes my hand, his eyes focused somewhere over my head.

I tell him he hasn't heard the last of me, but I'm lying. I'll be leaving tomorrow morning with Myra, straining to spot a better future somewhere on the horizon.

I step out of the dim light of the Ink Well onto Juniper. The construction crew around the corner is going full steam ahead; it sounds as though the workers are filling a hole with cannonballs. The noise is a refreshing change from the hushed tones inside the Ink Well.

As I cross the street and head to the florist, I take off my fedora and let the rays singe my face. For one brief moment, I'm not hiding. The doc's cream is in my pocket but I leave it there.

Myra knows me for who I am and I'm not going to let go of her. I'll bring her flowers tonight and we'll leave this place for good in the morning. This is my chance and I'm taking it. The sun broils my cheeks; it burns my skin with the sting of truth. And freedom.

⟣⟢

I stroll up the stairs carrying a box of roses. I'm leaning on my father's words—*You got caught up in Garvey's mess*—but I still can't help but feel responsible for Calvin's death. I look at the flowers in my hand and remind myself I'm not just another guilty conscience seeking absolution. I'm not a cheating philanderer bringing flowers to an unsuspecting dame, nor am I a two-timing widower placing them on my dead wife's grave. And I'm certainly not Lovely, who makes a habit of dropping full bouquets on the bleeding, mutilated bodies of the penny-ante crooks foolish enough to double-cross him. All I am is an everyday Joe letting my old classmate know that I'm done swallowing the taunts and jeers I've spent my lifetime choking down—and that I'm ready to prove it.

A discarded *Inquirer* sits at the top of the stairs in front of my apartment. I'll bet Garvey is still on the front page, but it doesn't matter anymore, at least not to me. I kick the paper aside, pull out my key, and check the doorjamb. The matchstick is on the floor. Either Myra left the apartment, which she said she wouldn't do, or Reeger's boys paid her a visit while I was at the Ink Well. That damned construction crew. Reeger could have shot up my entire place and I wouldn't have heard a sound over the ruckus. I toss the roses on the hallway floor, draw my gun, and slowly turn the doorknob. When I see the door isn't locked, I cock the pistol's hammer.

I step into the parlor an arm's length behind my gun. Everything seems to be in order. Then I hear a sickening wail coming from the bedroom. I'm sure it's Myra. This is all too reminiscent of what just happened at the Hy-Hat, and I'm hoping, praying, that I won't relive the same outcome here. Please, not with Myra.

I stand to the side of the doorway and listen again. It's quiet, except for the whimpering. I don't know if it's safer to wait or to burst into the room, so I push open the door and rush inside, ready to put a bullet into anybody other than Myra. I scan the room in a panic. The place is ransacked. There's a hole in the wall. The window is broken. But Myra's alone.

"Jeeersey," she's moaning.

She's sitting on the bed—her plaid dress is ripped and hanging off her shoulder. Her eyes are puffy; mucus trails from her nose and glazes her upper lip. She's got my sheet tied around her foot and she's clutching it as if she's afraid it will crumble if she lets go. The linen is stained with blood; it looks as if it's been used to package meat at the butcher shop. I rush over to check her foot but she hugs my waist and presses her head against my stomach.

"Jesus Christ," I say. "Are you all right?"

I'm still trying to get a look at her foot but she won't let go of me. She's squeezing so tightly she's cutting off my breath. Saliva and tears are coming right through my shirt and wetting my stomach.

"They broke it," she says through sobs. "My foot. I couldn't tell them where Garvey is, so they smashed it."

"Oh god, I'm so sorry, Myra." My shame rushes back at me as my father's words echo into the distance.

"Jeeersey," she's sobbing.

She leans over and heaves as if she's going to vomit. Then she lets out a piercing cry and I'm not sure if it's from the pain or because those scumbags knocked her back to the schoolyard.

"Don't worry," I tell her. "We'll fix it."

My brain is racing, but I don't have many options. The only way to help Myra—and stop Reeger from getting at her again—is to bring her to Doc Anders. But I can't get her all the way to New York in this shape—and it would take the doc hours to get here. My only other choice is to call Johalis. He's no fan of Myra's, but he's at his best under pressure and might know a local doctor who can keep his mouth shut.

I run into the kitchen and dial Johalis's number, hoping he's home. He picks up on the third ring.

"Yeah?"

Oh, those golden pipes. I run through the situation and he tells me to meet him at the back entrance of Philadelphia General in Blockley. I don't ask questions.

"We'll be there," I tell him.

When I get back to the bedroom, Myra's still moaning; her mouth is open, but only guttural sounds are coming out.

I stand where she can see me without having to turn her head.

"We've got to get downstairs," I tell her.

She nods.

"I'll be your crutch," I say.

She nods again, and through her sobs she says, "It'll never be the same again."

I'm worried that she's talking about us.

"Your foot will be fine," I tell her, even though I haven't looked under that ball of cloth.

I help her off the bed, slowly. When she gets to her feet, she leans on me and we inch toward the stairs. She's got her right knee in the air and hops forward on her left foot, yelping every time it lands. This isn't going to work.

When we reach the hallway, I pick her up and carry her in my arms. I make my way around the bouquet of roses and avoid the newspaper whose headline I now see is announcing a renewed effort in the hunt for Garvey. Myra puts her left hand around my neck, her right arm around my shoulder, and keeps her right knee resting on the crook of my arm. It's slow going—I take the stairs one at a time—but eventually, I get her out of the building and into the Auburn.

Myra leans back in the passenger seat and rests her right foot on a pillow as I hightail it over to Philadelphia General, checking the mirrors for a shadow. Through it all, she sits silently in the passenger seat beside me, her silky hair hanging in front of her face—sweaty, ragged, and limp.

I swing the Auburn around the back of the hospital and Johalis is right where he said he'd be: by the back entrance off University. The sun has set but the lamps have yet to be lit. I'm thankful for the cover.

I walk around the car and help Myra get out. She puts her arms around my neck and looks at me through teary eyes.

"I hate them," she says as I pick her up again.

Johalis comes over. The afternoon heat hasn't lifted and his cheeks are glazed with perspiration. I'm grateful he's helping and not asking any questions—of me or of Myra.

"We can go in here," he says. "There's a doc waiting upstairs."

I carry Myra through the double doors. The place has that medicinal odor—half grade-school cafeteria, half science lab—that I now recognize as the scent of late hours and broken lives. When we reach the third floor, a doctor is walking the hall. He's about the champ's age; he's got a shock of curly black hair piled on his head, two days' growth on his cheeks, and a look of concern in his dark eyes. A white lab coat is draped over his full, round stomach. On the pocket, a name tag reads *Dr. Dailey*.

He shakes Johalis's hand and then turns to me. "You, umm, must be Jersey." He speaks slowly, like a gramophone that needs to be wound.

"I am," I say. I'm about to tell him Myra's name but decide to keep it off the paperwork, just in case Reeger comes calling. "This is Betty Blake. She was in a car accident off Market."

Dailey gives me a look that says he knows I'm lying.

Myra is leaning on Johalis and lets out a low groan. Her pain is palpable.

"Let's get her into room three-eleven," Dailey says.

Myra puts her free arm around my shoulder and the three of us hobble into the room. Once she's sitting on the bed, Dailey walks Johalis and me to the door.

"I'll take it from here," he says.

I want to tell Myra I love her but stop myself because I don't want Johalis to hear me. As I turn to leave, Myra shouts out to me.

"Promise me we're still leaving."

She's cried her voice raw and sounds more like a chain-smoking sailor than a nightclub singer.

"Promise," she insists.

I bite my lip, hard, to stop my eyes from welling up.

"Nothing can stop us," I tell her, but I'm afraid we both know our moment is flittering away. She forces her trembling lips into a smile and I try to do the same.

When Johalis and I walk out into the hall, I shut the door behind us. I can tell Dailey has begun examining Myra's foot because her howls penetrate the wall. The screams cut through me like a surgeon's knife.

This is it, I tell myself. I've had years of tomorrows taken away from me and I'm not going to let my calendar get any shorter. I don't care what Johalis thinks of Myra, and I don't care what the champ says about Reeger. To hell with the cops—and to hell with the fucking electric chair. I'm going to settle this score with Reeger. And when I serve him his bullet, I'm going to make sure he knows it's from Myra's old classmate, the albino freak the kids used to call Snowball.

CHAPTER 12

*D*ark clouds are rolling over Eastern State and I wonder if the inmates see enough sky to notice. Me, I welcome the shadows. At least I won't have to walk the prison grounds with a scarf wrapped around my cheeks.

I'm here for Madame Curio. According to Thorndyke, she'll be stuck inside this granite fortress, locked up alongside gangsters and killers, until she appears in court a few weeks from now. I'd bet my bottom tube of skin cream there's a law against holding the Madame here—she's yet to be found guilty of anything—but there was a gas explosion at the women's detention center, which is all Reeger needed to push her paperwork through the broken system.

A gust of hot, humid air blows down Fairmount Avenue—a storm is coming—and I hold my fedora to my head as I get out of the Auburn. The place is no cozier than when I came to visit Garvey. When I reach the main entrance, an old-timer named Driscoll puts me through the standard drill. I can see his heart isn't in it; he frisks me for metal but doesn't comment on the flask in my back pocket.

He walks me toward cellblock five, telling me how much fun he had when Capone was here in '29, how he's the one who helped the boss sneak in the desk, the cushy mattress, the oriental rugs, and the telephone. When I ask him if he could do the same for the Madame, he drops the patter and calls me a wisenheimer. I don't let on that I was serious.

The visitor center is a big square room with cavernous ceilings, long tables, and barred windows. It smells like a locker room and has four large fans that buzz loudly as they blow the rancid air in circles. There must be fifty people in here. It's not hard to spot the inmates—their faces are nearly as colorless as mine, their expressions as gray as their state-issued coveralls. This entire block of prisoners was bussed from the detention center, and they're all probably guilty of the same crime: they won't sing.

Unlike Milmo and Flanagan, who wanted to squeeze every bit of life out of Garvey's last meal, the guards in this block are relaxed and quiet. Maybe they figure it would be bad form to hammer women, or maybe they wait until the outsiders are home, listening to the radio and tucking their kids into bed, before taking out their nightsticks. Either way, the guards must know they're not at risk. There's a watchman at the end of the rotunda who'll shut the entire cellblock down if things get out of hand. Yes, the women outnumber the guards, but the odds are stacked in the other direction.

Driscoll tells me to sit at the center table, that the Madame will be out shortly. I take off my hat and wipe my forehead as a pair of twin boys race across the room to hug a skinny woman in state grays. It seems that their dad, despite his wife being locked away in a stone fortress, has more of a home life than I do. I can only hope he appreciates it.

Ten feet behind him, at the table near the end of the cellblock, a woman dressed like a secretary and wearing wireframe glasses is whispering to a bleached blonde inmate who's got a cigar planted between her painted lips. The secretary's got her mouth to Blondie's ear and her left hand underneath the table. Her elbow is working overtime. The blonde is staring up at the clock as if it's going to explode when the little hand hits the stroke of twelve—which, by the looks of things, could be any second now. It's nothing I haven't seen at Madame Curio's, but even the Madame shuts the door during business hours.

The steel corridor door opens and the Madame steps into the room, handcuffed and escorted by a strapping guard with a nightstick in his hand. If we were back in New York, I could grease a palm and get her the hell out of here. But these aren't my streets and I haven't been pouring booze here long enough to saddle up to any rogue bulls. The Madame must know a few politicians who could free her—after all, she makes a living by yanking power from those who wield it—but she's too smart to merge those two worlds. And so are they.

The guard undoes the Madame's cuffs and she walks over to my table. The bruise on her cheek is fading. She's not wearing her turban, and her copper-colored hair springs from her head in tight curls. Her eyes are round, wide-eyed, like a young girl's. Without her bracelets and kerchief, she looks more like Little Orphan Annie than the busiest hooker in Center City. It's almost as if her moxie was in her makeup, that there was no way to remove one without taking the other. Seeing her like this makes me realize she's got parents somewhere, probably crying over the loss of their daughter.

"Jersey Leo," she says, taking the seat opposite me. "You in the newspaper lately?"

I hand her the flask I've got in my pocket.

"Check tomorrow's obituary," I say.

She screws the cap off the flask and takes a hearty slug. If she's hoping the booze is going to give her the spunk she needs to get through a stay at Eastern State, she'd better hit it again. And she'd better do it now because last call comes when visiting hours end.

"Thanks," she says, the glow of the booze slowly replacing the missing rouge on her cheeks.

She's waiting for me to say something but the words aren't coming to me. I'm hoping she's got some skinny on Reeger—she survives in the darkest corners of the city, maybe she knows how I can get at him—but first I owe her an apology.

"So why'd you come?" she says. Her words are nearly gobbled up in the din around us. "Miss me?"

"No," I say. "I just wanted to tell you I'm sorry about all this."

"You should be," she says. "I was fine until you pulled me into your shit. You owe me, and you owe me big time."

I feel my face drop. So much for the champ's absolution.

"And don't start the poor-me garbage," she says. "Just get me the fuck out of here."

I curse myself for opening my mouth during those long, lonely nights on Filbert Street. "I'm trying," I tell her. "But they told me you had to go through the system, that you were a repeat offender. Prostitution."

She shakes her head. "Fucking Reeger. That bull hit me with everything he had. It's all bogus."

I'm about to tell her that I've got receipts that prove otherwise, but a wave of shame rolls over her eyes. This is the real Madame—not the one that claims she grew up a gypsy in the circus, but the young pigtailed girl who dreamed of doing something grand with her life. It hits me that the Madame and I aren't all that different. For all of her gyrating, cursing, kicking, and spitting, she's a mouse hiding inside a lion's suit.

"Your friend Garvey's got an angel looking out for him," she says to me. "Reeger and his boys busted into my place right after he left."

"I know," I say. "I was there."

"Not then," she says with a smirk. "Garvey came back again. I gave him some food and sent him out on the road." She takes another slug of hooch and wipes the shine from her lips with the back of her hand.

"Figures," I say. "I think he's looking for Reeger."

"Well, he shouldn't have a tough time. Reeger's out for him, too."

"Yeah, but he probably wants to get Reeger alone."

She shakes her head. "He's crazy. Why doesn't he just get the hell out of here?"

"He needs money."

"Then fucking give it to him," she says. She takes another hit from the flask, but it's a smaller sip this time. "This whole thing has brought me nothing but trouble."

"Same here," I say. "I've got a lady in the hospital and a body in the morgue."

Her eyebrows scrunch into her version of a question mark. I'm sure she's trying to get her arms around the idea that I've got a woman who isn't charging me by the hour.

I lower my voice and tell her about Myra. And Calvin. And the Ink Well. What I don't mention is the party I've got planned for Reeger. But she knows the rules of the street, the rules we play by. The Sarge is picking off my friends one at a time. The only move I've got is to bring him down.

"You're talking about a fucking bull," she says.

I give the Madame a subtle nod, as if the guards will hear me if I nod too loudly.

"I know," I say. "Any idea where I can find him? Before Garvey does? I want him all to myself."

"You're as crazy as your friend," she says.

When I don't answer, she sizes me up: my shimmying green eyes, my yellow hair, my white skin. I can see she's afraid to help me any more than she already has. I can also see that I'm the only one here for her.

"Some pool hall," she says. "Garvey was planning on nailing Reeger there. But that's all I know."

My mind races back to the matchbook I palmed at Reeger's. It came from a pool hall, but I can't remember the name.

"I'll find it," I say.

"Good," she says before taking a sip from the flask. "Now how 'bout getting me out of here?"

She puts her elbows on the table and leans toward me. If I did the same, our lips would lock. "I'll make it worth your while," she says in a husky voice.

I don't want to turn her down, not like this, not while she's selling her last shred of femininity. But I've got Myra waiting at Philly General, her foot blasted into a million pieces, and I'd like to bring her something worth more than the old me.

"I've got Johalis greasing some bulls," I say. "Sooner or later, we'll spring you. And you won't owe me anything in return."

"Nothing?" she says.

My eyes are shimmying and I don't give a damn. "Not anymore," I say.

The Madame leans back and takes another shot of booze. I've gotten what I need but I stay anyway, listening as she tells me of her plans to stop drinking, to quit hooking. But visiting hour only lasts sixty minutes and we soon eat them up.

A guard barks out that it's time to leave. I say good-bye to the Madame and promise her that she'll see daylight soon. Right after I find Reeger.

⌖

I'm cruising along the Schuylkill with the windows open, cooling off, letting the misty rain soothe my broiled ear. I've got Reeger's matchbook in my pocket. It's from Bobby Lewis's joint, a billiard parlor over by the Delaware. Lewis is a shark, one of the best, but his place is tucked away in a section of town that most working stiffs are too scared to visit, and most bulls won't go without backup. I've spent the morning trying to connect Reeger to the place. A rogue bull and a pool shark? It doesn't fit, not in any way that helps me.

I pull into the hospital parking lot and walk in through the main entrance. I'm wearing dark glasses and have my handkerchief wrapping my jaws; the sun has already branded my exposed cheeks. A busty brunette is working the reception desk. When she sees me, a look of confusion crosses her face. I guess she thinks I'm here to be cured.

"I'm here for a woman named Betty Blake," I say, holding up my box of flowers to show I'm a visitor and not a patient.

"One hour limit, no exceptions," she says, still eyeing my raw cheeks with that bewildered look. She'd fit in nicely with the guards at Eastern State.

"I know the rules," I say.

I take off my glasses and shove the handkerchief into my pocket. Then I skip up three flights of stairs with a bounce in my step that only comes from knowing you're making somebody's day. Halfway down the hall, I pass a young Joe with a bouquet of flowers in one hand and a towheaded girl in the other. I wonder if the guy knows how good he's got it, how much other people would give to be walking in his shoes.

When I reach Room 311, I find Myra in bed, lying on her back with three pillows under her head. She's half asleep; her hair is fanned out behind her on the white linen. A plaster cast covers her right leg from the knee down.

She gives me a drugged smile.

"The doctor says I'll be out in a week," she says. Her speech is as thick as buttermilk and her lids as heavy as wet velvet. My money says the laudanum has got her floating somewhere north of Mars and southwest of Pluto.

Her head rolls in my direction. "We're still running away, right?" she says.

I'd put her in the Auburn and drive to the train station right now, but she deserves to come back down to earth before recommitting to riding shotgun with me.

"As soon as you're back on your feet," I say. "For now, you've got to rest up."

She was asleep before I made it to the period.

I put the roses in a water pitcher on the windowsill and slide them to a corner where she'll be sure to see them. I write a note— *To my prom queen of Elementary School Four*—and put it on the *Inquirer* beside her. The headlines are shouting about a protest at City Hall and I'm relieved Garvey has finally dropped off the front page.

I shut the lights and leave the room. In the hallway, I look for Johalis's friend, Dr. Dailey. He's walking the hallway with a clipboard in his hand.

"So how's she's doing, Doc?" I ask him. "Betty Blake? Room three-eleven?"

Dailey nods and says he remembers me. I guess he doesn't have a lot of patients with busted feet and albino visitors.

"Your friend doesn't know this," he says in his slow, halting rhythm. "But we ran into a few, umm, complications during the surgery."

My stomach rolls; I feel as if the doc is dangling me from the rooftop. I'm hanging onto his words, and the slow pace of his speech, the way he pauses between words, is unbearable.

"I'm afraid several of the small bones were shattered," he says. "We did our best, but we were unable to repair all of them."

"What does that mean?"

"I don't know yet," Dailey says. "I'm hoping she'll be able to walk on the foot, but it's too early to tell. If she does, she'll probably have a limp, or she'll need a cane. Maybe both."

"But she may not be able to walk at all?"

Dailey looks at me and gives me the first clear answer I've ever shaken out of him. "That's correct," he says.

I picture Myra, pint-sized, in Hoboken, a look of humiliation stamped on her face as she crosses the schoolyard with that blasted boot on her foot. Then I think of how she'll crumble if she gets the news that she'll be limping her way through life again, that the few years she had of walking without a boot, a cane, or a crutch have come to an end.

I want to be there when the doctor tells her all this. I want to console her. I want to touch her skin, stroke her hair, and wrap my arms around her. I want to tell her everything will be swell and know that I can back it up. I want her to believe in me, the albino from Hoboken who was a hero for a day.

And I want to kiss her tear-stained cheeks until that beautiful, broken foot becomes whole again.

⚜

The neon *Billiards* sign stopped glowing over an hour ago. The hustlers have come and gone, as has the rain. Bobby Lewis's is a two-story joint; it's at the intersection of Fitzwater and the grift. The roads are dark, wet, and empty—Fitzwater might as well be in total blackness. The only streetlamp around here is behind me; there's also a light burning in the building's side window, but it isn't strong enough to reach the walkway. I can't imagine who would still be inside the place; maybe one last sucker still has a buck to lose.

I'm behind the wheel of the Auburn, parked halfway up the block. The champ, Johalis, and Homer are with me; they insisted on coming along in case I run into Reeger's triggermen. The champ is still hoping I can cut a deal with Reeger, that I can give him Myra's payments in exchange for his calling off the witch-hunt. I don't blame him for pushing me to walk away from this—he doesn't want to see me wind up in Garvey's state-issued slippers—but Reeger will never go for that deal. Besides, the champ isn't the one who just left his heart soaking in laudanum in Room 311. If he were, he'd have come up with a plan similar to mine: jam a gun into Reeger's mouth and see what happens next.

"The place must be emptied out by now," I say. There's a quiver in my voice and I hope the champ doesn't hear it.

"Maybe it is," Johalis says. "But maybe not."

Johalis is nearly as jumpy as I am. He already tried the front door, which was locked, and then peeked through the side window but couldn't get a good look inside. He also checked the back door but found it blocked by a garbage truck—left there either by a lazy custodian or a corrupt cop who doesn't like snoops. My gut says it's the latter.

"There's got to be a way inside," I say.

The champ tells me to wait to be sure there are no stragglers left, but I scramble out of the Auburn before he can finish.

I trot across Fitzwater, my feet keeping time with my pounding heart as the champ curses and gets out of the car behind me. Once I'm on the far side of the street, I turn around and see the champ and Johalis running to cover the front of the joint and Homer taking the wheel of the car. Johalis motions that I should go around back and try the rear entrance again. The champ doesn't look happy.

I creep down the side of the building toward the back alley. When I get there, I find an abandoned path even darker than the side street—the lamps back here stopped burning hours ago and my albino eyes aren't helping the situation. I can barely make out the silhouettes of the brick apartment building on my right and the back of Lewis's place on my left. The garbage truck is over-flowing with rubbish and blocking the pool hall door. What I can't see of the trash I can smell. The heat is cooking the debris; the alley stinks of rotting fruit and stale beer.

Somebody doesn't want any late-night visitors.

Johalis told me about the garbage, but he didn't tell me about the transom above the door. It's sitting six feet over the truck, wide open. The only thing missing is a sign that says *Enter Here*. I climb up on the truck and plant my feet on its hood. A rat crawls over my right oxford and I shake it off. As I reach for the transom, I hear voices coming from inside. They could be paying customers, but it seems awfully late for a nine-ball tournament.

I wriggle my head and shoulders through the window, then push myself a little farther into the space. If Reeger's here, I hope he doesn't find me now, halfway into the building, squirming through this narrow opening with my arms pinned to my sides. I look down and see that somebody has taken the precaution of blocking the inside of the doorway with a white cushiony sofa, which would have been a smart move assuming a bartender with more moxie than brains wasn't crawling through the transom. I push the rest of my body through the window and drop onto the sofa, landing on the soft seat. It couldn't have gone more smoothly had they blocked the door with a giant marshmallow.

I draw my gun and inch down the hallway toward the main room. Somebody's barking out a chain of curses, and once I get close, I'm sure I've found my man.

My anxiety is seeping out of my palms, drenching the gun's wooden handle. I'm itching to put Reeger in my crosshairs, to hear him beg for his life, to hear him plead for mercy as he swears to never touch Myra or any of my friends again. But I can't make a move until I know exactly what's waiting for me.

I'm an arm's length from the entrance to the poolroom. The air is as wet and thick as engine oil—and as quiet as Calvin's funeral. There are no clacking billiard balls, no music, no voices, no anything. All I hear are the soles of Reeger's shoes squeaking against the tiled floor. My heart is pounding out a drum solo that would make Teddy Brown jealous.

"You think you can strong-arm me?" Reeger says, breaking the silence. I can practically hear the arrogant smirk cross his face. "Big deal. You found some papers."

His words hang in the air until another voice responds.

"They're proof." A soft whistle accompanies the words. That's Garvey. He and Reeger must be alone because if the Sarge had any muscle with him, Garvey would be dead.

My mind's racing too fast to come up with a solid plan—and if I screw up, I'll wind up on the lam with Garvey.

"What are you going to do?" Reeger says to Garvey. "Kill me too?"

There's a moment of quiet before Garvey answers.

"Yep."

That does it. I break into the room, my gun in front of me. Garvey is behind the pool table across from the manager's office; Reeger's in front of the office doorway, right next to a ceiling-high trophy case. They're each pointing a pistol at the other but look toward me when they hear they've got company.

"Put down the gun, Reeger," I say, extending my pistol in front of me, my elbows locked. "You too, Garv."

"Snowball?" Garvey says. He looks dumbfounded, as if I'd died and he were looking at my ghost.

"What, you're surprised?" Reeger asks him. "This fucking freak is always showing up where he doesn't belong. It started the day he was born."

I hear Garvey cock the hammer. For a split second, we're back at Elementary School Four and Garvey is taking on the blood-crazed teachers again.

"Gun down, Garv," I say, keeping my pistol trained on Reeger.

I can't see shit, but I make my way across the room, winding around the tables, my pistol leading the way, until only one table separates me from Reeger. The sole lamp that shines is the clock with Lewis's smiling face on it. It's three-twenty. Anybody with a life worth living is asleep.

"I said put the rods down."

Garvey doesn't lower his gun, which I now see is my snub-nose. He's got it trained, along with his eyes, on Reeger. With his free hand, he raises a handful of files.

"I got it, Snow," he says.

I have no idea what he's talking about and I'm not about to ask questions now. I take another step toward Reeger. My heart charges its way up my throat, and my mouth tastes sour.

"Drop the revolver, Sarge."

Reeger doesn't budge. I cock the hammer but he still doesn't move. Neither does Garvey. We're frozen, locked in a three-man standoff. My eyes are dancing and a bead of sweat rolls down between my shoulder blades. A poster of Bobby Lewis hangs on the wall behind Reeger—it reads *Shoot for the Moon*. I feel as if he's talking to me.

Reeger moves first. He takes a step back toward the manager's office and hides his body behind the trophy case. I no longer have a clean shot.

"Go ahead and shoot, Snowfreak," he says. "But you better kill me, 'cause if you don't, I'll fuck you over like there's no tomorrow. You'll spend your life in the slammer, curled up in solitary wishing you could shit the warden's cock out of your bloody albino ass. And your boy here will be right next to you, sitting in a barber's chair with cables connected to his fucking head, getting fried like a fucking egg sunny side up. So either shoot that gun and kill me, or make like a nice freak and get your bleached girlie balls the fuck out of my sight."

I'm grinding my teeth, itching to pull the trigger and stop his mouth from moving. But that's what he wants me to do. He wants me to shoot because he figures I'll miss him. The second after I fire he'll jump out and nail one of us, maybe both.

"You're a lost cause, a goddamned fucking freak of nature," he's saying, taunting me with the names I've heard since grade school. "Do people like you have balls or are they powder puffs?"

His plan is working. My fingers are so sweaty the trigger feels as if it's been greased. Sweat is running down my lids and into my eyes, stinging my pupils and blurring my vision even more. My temples are pounding, building up a pressure in my forehead that won't get released until I pull this fucking trigger. But I can't get a bead on him.

All of a sudden something crashes behind me. I wheel around and see that the champ has broken through the front door. He and Johalis are coming at us, telling us to stay calm. The champ has his hands extended in front of his chest and keeps repeating that he and Johalis are unarmed.

Reeger's hands are sticking out from the side of the trophy case; he's got his gun leveled at Garvey. My knees are shaking so I lean on a pool table to steady them—but I keep my pistol pointed toward the Sarge, waiting for him to peek his head out.

"Let's all put the guns down and talk this out," my father says.

"Yeah, Reeger, let's talk," Garvey says. "Tell them about your little enterprise. How you fucked me over."

Reeger starts saying something about loan sharks, about how they're the scum of the earth, about how he doesn't care what happens to them or their albino freak friends. My heart is still hammering at my rib cage like a prisoner banging on prison bars. I'm out of breath—I feel as if I've been running for hours even though I've barely moved since I got here. I take two steps to my left to get a better angle on Reeger. He's now got both feet in front of the trophy case and his hands extended a couple more inches. I've got him in my sights. I'm sure I can plug him. I can settle the score for Calvin and for Myra in one shot. I can serve justice. All I've got to do is squeeze the trigger—but I can't bring myself to do it, not if he's not pointing his gun at me. I feel like I'm gunning down an unarmed man.

"Tell them the story, Reeger," Garvey is yelling. "Tell him how you fucked me over. How you fucked Myra over. How you fuck *everybody* over."

Reeger barks back and the two of them are shouting over each other. Johalis and my father are telling us to table our rods, but Reeger and Garvey aren't listening—they're still going at it, arguing over who's right, who's wrong, who helped Myra, who hurt her, who's a crook, and who's a loan shark.

Their voices echo throughout the billiard parlor, but their words don't matter. I've got my pistol trained on Reeger as I picture Garvey at Elementary School Four, fighting off those twisted teachers. I think of the cast on the champ's hand, the cotton stuffing that was packed up my nose, and the Madame rotting in jail, bruised and broken. I think of Calvin, his hand squeezing mine, his eyes pleading for justice. And I think of Myra, a prisoner at Philadelphia General, her foot shattered back into 1919.

Nobody is going to stop Reeger unless I do.

I tighten my grip. I aim the gun. But Reeger fires.

The bullet hits Garvey square in the forehead. My friend drops to the ground like a sack of old schoolbooks.

"No!" Johalis shouts and runs over to my fallen friend.

I do the same, my ears ringing from the blast and my heart banging on the back of my throat like a battering ram. I'm on my knees and looking down at Garvey. He's staring up at the ceiling, his eyes open and glazed, a round, red hole above his left eye marking the spot the state had reserved for a live electrode.

I turn and see Reeger leveling his gun at my father. I'm not about to let him take the champ. I brace my hands atop a pool table and train my rod on the Sarge's chest. I'm going to pull this fucking trigger before he does. I'm going to pull it for Calvin, for Myra, for anybody who ever expected me to be a hero—especially Garvey, who's lying on the floor, feet crossed, arms outstretched, a halo of blood spreading out beneath his skull.

"Put the gun down," the champ is telling Reeger. He's got both hands in the air, trying to calm the Sarge.

Reeger cocks the hammer. The fucking bull is aiming his service revolver at a man whose only weapons are an outdated suit and a three-pound plaster cast.

I shut my eyes when I squeeze the trigger. The jolt goes up my arm and down my gut—I feel it down to my balls. Reeger slumps to the ground, his head leaning against the bottom shelf of trophies, a round bloodstain spreading across the chest of his white shirt. I can smell his insides from here.

"Oh Lord, Jersey," my father says, running over to Reeger. "It coulda been you, it coulda been you, it coulda been you," he keeps repeating as he lays Reeger down flat and smacks his face, trying to revive him.

I'm on my knees, shaking. I'm nauseous. I'm freezing. I'm telling myself I had no choice. Reeger killed Garvey and would have killed the champ. Still, I can't shake the idea that I just killed the man a blind girl depends on.

My father comes over and kneels next to me; he puts his casted hand on my back and pats the back of my neck as I choke out sobs.

Johalis is still hunched over Garvey—his eyes are darting from the champ and me to Reeger, then to Garvey. He grabs the snubnose from Garvey's hand, springs up, and swaps it with the pistol I'm holding. Then he picks up the folders on the floor next to Garvey.

"What are you doin'?" my father asks, but we both know the answer.

I want to tell Johalis not to bother saving me, but instead of speaking, I heave. A mouthful of vomit lands on my lap. I run into the bathroom, kick open a stall door, and hurl the rest of my guilt into the bowl. By the time I'm done, Johalis and the champ are standing behind me. Johalis reaches around me, flushes the bowl, and gives me a flask of whiskey to rinse my mouth.

"You okay?" he says as he wipes down the stall door and toilet handle.

I couldn't be further from okay but I tell him I'm fine.

"Then let's get outta here," he says. "And don't touch anything."

We hurry through the pool hall as Johalis scrambles through the place trying to wipe every surface we may have touched. He gets the pool tables and doorknobs; he even runs to the back entrance to clean the frame of the transom and the wooden arms of the white sofa. When he comes back to the poolroom, we wind our way through the grid of tables, step over Garvey, and leave by the busted front door, hopscotching through a kaleido-scope of broken glass shards.

The air outside is no fresher than the dank air inside. I take big gulps of it as Homer speeds the Auburn up to the curb. Johalis and the champ scramble into the car, then I do the same, even though the sixth-grader in me is dying to go back inside, turn back the clock, and say thank you to Garvey one last time.

⊰⊱

I'm hiding out with my father, Johalis, and Homer in the only place I knew would be safe: the Ink Well. It's still closed; nobody has been here since Calvin's funeral. We sped here in the Auburn and the four of us snuck in through Blind Moon Alley.

We're in the front of the joint, sitting at Wallace's usual table.

I have no idea where Wallace is tonight, but I'm fairly certain he hasn't gunned down a bull and gone underground to duck a murder charge. Wherever he is, I'm hoping that Angela is with him—and I'm glad that she's far, far away from this.

I've spent the last ten minutes going through our options. The problem is we have no idea if the cops are after us. Yes, Johalis cleaned up the scene, but who knows what he left behind. I've got the radio on, braced to hear an all-points bulletin mentioning my name. Instead, I'm getting Gene Austin crooning "A Faded Summer Love."

"Why would anybody question it?" Johalis asks. "Garvey and Reeger were out for each other."

"True," I say. I don't bring up the missing file or the idea that some other rogue bull might be looking for it.

I go behind the bar and pour myself a double shot of whiskey, no ice. I'm in my old spot, the place I stood serving moon the night the pay phone rang and disrupted my peace. The joint hasn't changed—the muted lighting, the soft radio, the glittering glass bottles are all still here—but the guilt hanging over me has me thinking only one thing: I'm the one the state should be frying. I take a gulp of booze; my throat's raw from vomiting, and the whiskey burns going down. With a little luck, it'll be strong enough to wipe my conscience clean.

"Maybe nobody will dig too deeply," I say, trying to convince myself along with the others. "They'll want to believe Reeger took down Garvey. They'll make him a hero."

I bring the whiskey bottle to the table and the champ pours himself two fat fingers.

"We killed a cop," he says. "They're gonna care."

He shoots down the brown and tightens his jaw when it lands. We're finally having a drink together, but we're doing it for all the wrong reasons.

Homer gets up from his seat. "So what now, Jersey?" he says. The poor simpleton still thinks I've got answers. He's nervously smacking his cap against the side of his thigh as he waits for me to speak.

"I guess we sit here and hope the cops buy it," I say.

"What if they don't?" he says.

Homer's worried for me—but he has no idea how deeply he's been sucked into this, too. I killed the cop, but he drove the car.

"Then we run," I say. "Same as Garvey."

"Garvey's dead," my father says.

There's no way to respond, so I don't. I go to the kitchen to get us some food. Doolie cleaned out the icebox before shuttering the place, but I find a dozen eggs and some bread and make us an early breakfast. It's not much, but it'll get us through sunrise.

When I bring the food to the table, Johalis is smoking a Lucky and looking through the folders Garvey found at the pool hall. He's sorting through notes scribbled on cocktail napkins, newspaper margins, and ledger sheets.

"Jesus Christ," he says, arranging the torn pages as if he's doing a jigsaw puzzle. The wrinkles around his eyes look deeper than before. I try to convince myself it's the lighting.

"Doesn't matter what you got there," the champ says. "We're guilty. And we're on the run."

"We may be running from more people than you think," Johalis says. "It looks as though Reeger was in deep with some pretty crooked bastards."

Homer walks around behind Johalis to look over his shoulder. "Jersey knew he was crooked," he says.

"But he didn't know the half of it," Johalis says. Then he looks up toward me. "Did you know Reeger was in business with Lovely?"

Again, I have no answer. But it doesn't matter, because he's not expecting one.

"Lovely's name is in here. So is Garvey's. And Myra's. These numbers add up to a hell of a lot more than what you saw in those bankbooks. This is no small-time operation. There's over a hundred thousand here, easy."

My father turns to me. "Maybe we can show that to the police. Nobody can blame us for gunnin' down a dirty cop."

I shake my head. "Champ, I'm not going to walk into a police station and tell them I gunned down a bull, even if he was dirty."

"I s'pose not," the champs says. He gets up and paces the room.

Homer's still smacking his cap against his leg. "He had it coming," he says. His tone is angry, as if he wants to find Reeger and kill him again.

"It doesn't matter if he was crooked as an ice hook," I tell him. "We just gotta hope nobody pins that murder on us."

"Who says they won't?" the champ asks.

"Who says they will?" I answer.

Johalis pours himself a shot of booze.

"Either way, I'm going to look into this," he says, putting the papers back in the folder before downing the whiskey.

"Nobody on that list is gonna speak to you," I say with a shake of my head. "Even the ones who are alive."

"Don't worry," Johalis says. "I've got a buddy at the station-house. He'll shoot straight with me."

Johalis didn't give me a name and I'm not about to ask. But he must know the bull pretty well, because snooping around a stationhouse and asking about a crooked cop is like trying to dig a garden spade into marble.

"Great," I say. "When you speak with him, ask him what the hell we've gotta do to get the Madame out of the pen."

"I'm trying," Johalis says.

"Then try harder," I say. I hear the edge in my voice and apologize to Johalis. I'm frazzled, but it's not his fault.

"I just wanna get her out," I say.

"Try keeping yourself out first," my father says.

An emergency report interrupts Duke Ellington on the radio. The announcer says there was a shooting at Bobby Lewis's Billiard Parlor on Fitzwater, and that escaped convict Aaron Garvey was killed by police sergeant Jack Reeger. Garvey, the voice says, had been hiding in the back room of the billiard parlor, surviving on food left in the kitchen, when Reeger stumbled upon him. Reeger tried to bring Garvey to justice, but a fight broke out and the fugitive shot Reeger in his left lung. As he lay dying, the heroic policeman managed to unholster his revolver and get off one last shot, hitting the hunted man in his forehead and killing him instantly. The sergeant, the voice says, will be promoted posthumously; a ceremony will be held on Saturday in Rittenhouse Square.

I'm digging my fingernails into my palms as the announcer continues. He's now reading a message from the chief of police telling the citizens of Philadelphia that the streets are again safe. I'm holding my breath until the report ends, hoping there's no mention of my name. Finally, when the announcer finishes and Bing Crosby starts singing "I Surrender, Dear," my fingers go limp and I exhale.

"I think we're clean," I say.

"We're free?" Homer says. I don't answer, but he raises his glass and downs whatever's in it. If my glass weren't already empty, I'd do the same.

"We ain't free," the champ says, "'Cause we're not sure of nothin.'"

"No, we're not," I say. "But we don't have to stay here. Let's go home. If anybody runs into trouble, call the others."

"Jersey's right," Johalis says. "Anything beats hiding out here." He takes a pull on his Lucky and snuffs it in the ashtray. "I'll do some digging and let you know what I find."

The champ sees he's outnumbered. "I guess we have no choice," he says, shaking his head. "I'll stay one more night with Johalis and go back to New York in the morning."

"Good idea," I say. "I'll stay here in Philly for a while."

Neither Johalis nor the champ is surprised. They know I'll be here until Myra leaves the hospital—even if I have to carry her out on my back.

We shake hands and head out of the joint the same way we came in: with our heads down and our guards up. I tell the champ we'll talk in the morning before he leaves for the Hy-Hat.

Then I sneak over to the main entrance and creep upstairs to my apartment. Once I'm inside, I lock the door and go to the window. I can't help myself. I pull the shade and take a peek at Vine Street—if any bulls are tailing me, I want to know.

The rising sun is turning the sky a soft shade of orange. A row of pigeons stands at attention along the gutter of the building across the street. And down below, sitting on the bench in front of Ronnie's, is Reeger's mustached friend, his eyes trained up at my place.

CHAPTER 13

Myra's half-asleep in her wheelchair, her plastered right leg extended in front of her as I push her into the hospital's sun room. A strong metal fan sends a cool breeze across the space as I wheel her to the window. She looks far less glamorous than she did at the Red Canary. Spilled food stains her hospital gown; a roadmap of bloody lines crosses the whites of her eyes. I'm finally with the real Myra, and as far as I'm concerned, she outshines any lipsticked, spotlighted kewpie doll at the Canary, including the one she used to be.

"It feels good to be out of bed," she tells me, her words thick from a morning dose of laudanum. I'm happy she'll be off the stuff in a couple of days.

"I'll be better soon," she says.

There's no need to tell her she might not make it all the way back up the hill. There's also no point in spilling the story about Garvey or Reeger. I sit next to her, keeping my face and hands in the shade as she soaks up the luscious afternoon sun.

A heavyset nurse with a white dress, white hat, and sturdy calves brings in lunch. I help Myra eat, cutting her sandwich into small, bite-size pieces, putting them in her mouth, and making sure she chews before swallowing. When Myra finishes her meal, I wash her hands with a damp cloth and rub cream on her fingers. Then I brush her hair off her forehead and wheel her back to Room 311 where she can get some sleep.

Two fresh-faced nurses are waiting to put her into bed. Both are wearing all-white uniforms, right down to their ivory shoes.

"We're running away," Myra tells them, a lopsided smile on her lips. "Shhh. It's a secret. Just me and Snowball."

She looks at me as if I'm Ramon Novarro and I feel my face flush. I motion to the nurses that my friend is drugged and loopy.

I give Myra a kiss on the forehead and tell her I'll be back tomorrow. Then I walk out of the hospital and onto the streets of Blockley, wondering why I felt I needed to make an excuse when Myra said we were running away. I guess I didn't think anybody would believe that Myra would take up with the likes of me. Maybe even I don't believe it; maybe Johalis's warning is still tossing and turning in the back of my mind, making me restless and unable to sleep. But I do know one thing for sure. I'm three blocks from the hospital and my heart is still back in Room 311, kissing Myra's forehead.

I get in the Auburn just as Rudy Vallee launches into "That's When I Learned to Love You." The breeze dries the sweat in my hair and cools my neck. I picture Myra and me on the sands of the Pacific. I've got my pants rolled up; Myra's wiggling her toes in the sand and the surf bathes her unmarked feet. We wrap ourselves in each other's arms and tumble on the beach, the blazing sun tanning my bronzed back.

I turn onto Jupiter and park a half-block from Vine as the sky fades from light blue to dusky orange. I walk to my place with an eye out for Reeger's buddy, but instead of trouble, I find Doolie lighting the lamp outside the Ink Well. The joint is once again open for business. I'm not surprised; he must have heard the radio reports. If Reeger and Garvey are dead, so are his problems.

"Jersey," he says with a smile. Somehow, his hair looks grayer, and his shoulders more slumped, than I remember. I can see he's tired of all the craziness, and I don't blame him. "You're still in town," he says.

"For now," I say, wondering if Myra and I will ever really leave for good, if I'll ever watch this chapter of my life fade in the rear-view mirror.

"I'm sorry things didn't work out here," he says. "But I hope you know that nobody's kicking you out of Philly."

"I do know that," I say, even though there's no longer any need for me to stay. The Ink Well couldn't be safer.

He opens the door. "Shot of moon?"

I don't want to say yes—I'd be walking in a failure—but I've needed a belt ever since I left Myra at the hospital. I follow him into the joint.

Angela is waiting tables in the front room; she's in a black dress with a frilly white apron tied across her waist. She's chatting with Wallace, who's sitting at his table with an open book in front of him. I'm not upset, not any longer, but watching Angela hang on Wallace's words makes me wish I'd listened to the champ and finished college. I'd sure rather be in Wallace's educated shoes than where I am now: unskilled, out of work, and waiting for my lover's foot to heal so we can run to the other side of the country and try growing up again.

I walk over and say hello. Angela greets me with a kiss on the cheek; Wallace shakes my hand. They seem relaxed and I'm assuming that's because Reeger's gone. I wonder how they'd react if they knew I was the one who erased him.

"It's good to see you," Angela says.

"Sure is," Wallace says, nodding.

They're saying hello, but all three of us know their words mean good-bye. I wish them well and excuse myself to join Doolie at the bar. As I head to the counter, I can't help but steal a glance at the booth where Myra and I resumed the journey we'd started back in grade school.

Doolie pours me a splash of moon. I down it and my spine softens.

"I guess you heard the news about Garvey and Reeger," I say, curious to hear what he's picked up on the street.

"Yep," he says, tightening his lips and shaking his head. "Sorry 'bout your friend."

I nod. "He caused you a lot of trouble," I say. "But he wasn't as bad as the papers are saying."

"Probably not," Doolie says. "But he wasn't no saint, either. From what I hear, he was planning to shoot Reeger then turn the gun on himself. He was gonna go out in a blaze of glory. Crazy."

"Hadn't heard that," I say, wondering where in hell the *Inquirer* got that one.

Doolie pours me another, this time with an iced seltzer chaser. I take the drink but there's little point in lingering—the moon has already outlasted the conversation. We clink glasses, then I gulp the shot and shake Doolie's hand. Over his shoulder, I see my face staring back at me—the ripped, taped, forgotten hero.

"Thanks, Doolie," I say, pretending everything is as jake as it was when I started working here.

I turn to leave but stop and say good-bye to Wallace. The book in front of him is called *The Beautiful and the Damned*. It might as well be called *Myra and Me*.

"Any good?" I ask Wallace, nodding toward the book.

"Wonderful," he says.

He starts talking about the story—he tells me it's a morality tale about love and greed and corruption—and I wonder if there's anything in there I haven't seen firsthand. I'm not about to admit to him, or myself, that I'd never pick up a book that thick, regardless of what it's about.

Wallace hands it to me. "Just finished it. It's all yours."

"Really?" Part of me wants to shove it back at him. The other part wants the book.

"Thanks," I say, taking it but fighting the urge to look inside. I'll take a peek at the first couple of pages later. If Wallace can find it so damned interesting, maybe I can, too.

Angela is looking at us as though she's watching Einstein and Freud swap notes. I want to believe she's proud of me for seeking knowledge, but I'm sure she's prouder of Wallace for sharing his.

I'm about to ask her if she's still planning on going back to school but I don't want to embarrass her. I thank Wallace again for the book and say a final farewell. The truth is I'm going to miss the joint. In here, I was one of the gang. On the street, I'm one of a kind.

I walk out the door, leaving Angela and my long-forgotten hope for the two of us behind me.

As I walk up the stairs to my apartment, I flip through the novel. The book looks wordy and dense, but I'm determined to enjoy it. I don't put it down until I step inside my apartment. When I do, I'm staring down the barrel of a Colt thirty-eight special.

"Evening, Snowball."

It's Reeger's mustached friend. He's wearing a threadbare white shirt under a pair of brown suspenders. He's got wide, round sweat stains under his arms and on his chest; he looks more like a railroad laborer than a dead bull's muscle.

"You can drop the rod," I say.

"I can but I won't," he says, chuckling as though I couldn't keep up with a brain as sharp as his. His breath reeks; he's either been drinking hack moonshine or high-caliber dog piss. "Now turn around and walk out the door like a good little freak."

I'd like to bang the smile off his face, but my knucks are in the nightstand by my bed and my gun is strapped to my ankle.

"Where we going?" I say.

"To say hello to Mister Lovely."

Oh, fuck. That's about the worst answer I could have gotten. Lovely doesn't talk to people. He mutilates them.

"Why me?" I ask, as if I didn't know Lovely was in business with Reeger and wants to even the score.

"I have no idea," the goon says and smiles again. "But I'm glad it's you and not me."

He pushes me out the door and his wristwatch scrapes my blistered ear. It stings, but I wouldn't let this guy see me wince if I were laying face-down on Doolie's griddle. I walk two paces in front of him, grateful that he's either too stupid or too drunk to think of patting me down. He shadows me, his Colt in his hand and his jacket draped over it.

He tells me to walk toward Vine, so that's what I do. On the way, we pass a young guy sauntering into the Ink Well; he's wearing a white shirt with a stiff collar and he's got black garters on his arms. He must be the new bartender. I hope he knows how good he's got it compared to his predecessor.

"Where are we going?" I say again.

The goon lets out another one of those creepy chuckles. When we get to his Studebaker, he throws me inside and won't let me open a window. I'm baking in the passenger seat, smelling the liquor that oozes from his pores, wondering if I should try reaching for my gun. I don't. Even if I could shoot my way out of this, Lovely would find me. Maybe not today or tomorrow—but soon enough.

As we cross Market and head toward the water, I realize we're going back to Bobby Lewis's. I remind myself that as far as Lovely or anybody else is concerned I've never been there, I've never seen the back alley, and I don't know a thing about any missing folder.

The thug turns onto Fitzwater and I see Lovely's Packard town car parked out front, a chauffeur reading the paper in the front seat. We park behind it and my chaperone pulls me out of the car by the shoulder. Bobby Lewis's is closed—it's still a crime scene—but we step around the police barricade and walk through the front door, which has been replaced by a couple of wooden boards. I don't dare say it to the goon, but using the door is a far cry easier than wriggling through the transom window.

The place is empty and has a ghostly feel to it. Spilled blood stains the raw wooden floor. So do two chalk lines, one of which outlines the silhouette of Aaron Garvey. I wonder where his body is now—I'm betting the bulls buried him in an unmarked grave to avoid the glare of photographers' bulbs. There's nothing I can do to give him the graceful exit he deserved. I wish there were a way to let him know that I settled with Reeger, especially now that I'm going to pay the price for doing it.

"In there," the goon says as he points his chin toward the manager's office. Outside the room, two muscleheads stand guard. They're each wearing herringbone suits and look about as relaxed as the cue sticks on the wall rack next to them.

The goon's about to step on the chalk outline of Garvey's head so I push him out of the way. He wheels around and points the Colt at my forehead, his lips twisted into an ugly scowl. Behind him, the muscleheads reach inside their jackets and pull out their own revolvers. If anybody fires, I'll land right where Garvey died.

"Show some fucking respect," I say to the goon.

My eyes shimmy and he looks at them strangely, as if he's staring at a hypnotist's pendulum. I'm itching to grab my pistol and put a slug between his bushy eyebrows, but he's pressing his Colt against my chest and the muscleheads have their hands on their rods. My ankle never seemed farther away.

"Get in there," the goon says and nods toward the business office.

I do what I always do when somebody's got a loaded thirty-eight pointed at me: I follow instructions.

On the way in, I pass the muscleheads.

"What's the matter?" I say. "Never saw an albino before?"

They don't answer; they just stare straight ahead. Either Lovely told them to act like brainless robots or they came up with the idea on their own.

The goon pushes me into a cramped room that smells of furniture wax and tobacco. The space holds four file cabinets and an oversized oak roll-top desk; a fully stocked bar runs across the back wall. An old skinny guy wearing a starched white shirt, black pants, and burgundy vest sits at the desk, hunched over a foot-high stack of folders, a bottle of whiskey, and a Smith & Wesson revolver. Next to the gun sits a coffee can filled with fleshy body parts swimming in some kind of alcohol. They look like pig knuckles soaking in brine, except they're human. One floater is definitely a thumb—it's so preserved I can make out the knuckle and fingernail. Another looks like a testicle.

This must be Lovely—the man the papers are still calling Otto Gorsky. He's got to be ninety. His head is bobbing like a buoy on the ocean; his hands rock up and down as if they're holding yo-yos. I could probably snap his wrist with one hand, but that coffee can is keeping me in check. Those scraps are a reminder that his goons are ready to carve me up on his say-so. And I'm betting they can't wait for that say-so.

He looks up and greets me as if we were long-lost friends and haven't seen each other since first grade. His dark eyes crackle with life behind their wrinkled, sunken lids.

"Snowball," he wheezes. His fleshy jowls hang loosely and his lips cry out for the doc's ointment—they're as wrinkled as dried prunes, cracked, peeling, and at the corners, bleeding. He shakes my hand and his fingers are stiff, bending only at the second knuckle. He points to a chair opposite him, and I sit down. My knees are shaking nearly as badly as his shoulders. If he has me dismembered, I hope it's after I'm dead.

He stares at my yellow hair, my colorless cheeks, my eyes. Then he says, "You really are one ugly motherfucker."

"My mother doesn't think so," I say.

"Funny man," he says. "But you don't know your mother. I've heard the story."

I don't say anything, but the guy has done his homework. My mother skipped out on the champ and me right after I was born.

"You were raised by your nigger father," he says, shaking his head, either out of pity, disgust, or necessity.

My fists tighten so hard I feel the tension rise up through my forearms. I want to grab Lovely's shaking head and bounce it against the desk until he either starts calling my father "the champ" or his skull smashes like a melon. Or both.

"Am I right?" Lovely says. "White mother, nigger father?"

I don't answer. I *refuse* to answer.

"That's why you are what you are," he says. His voice gives out when he gets to the end of long sentences—the power in his body is a far cry from his power on the street. "They say that the niggers, they make the albinos when they fuck the white women."

My hands are balled into fists; my toes are curled into knots. "That's not why I'm albino, you stupid fuck," I say, surprised by the menacing tone in my own voice.

Lovely acts hurt, as if nobody has ever called him stupid before. He turns to his muscle. "How 'bout the balls on this kid?" he wheezes. "Charlie, put the gun away and shut the door."

I now know the goon's name, not that I plan on having an occasion to use it.

Lovely pulls two juice glasses out of the desk drawer with his rickety hands. He nearly drops them both, but I know better than to ask if he needs help. Once he sets the glasses down, he pours us each a shot of brown, spilling nearly as much as he serves.

Charlie comes over and wipes the spill with his handkerchief.

He doesn't say a word—he just blots it up and returns to his post behind me.

"Here," Lovely says, pushing one of the glasses toward me. "This is the best I've got. It's pretty decent."

I pick up the shot, raise it to my lips, and wait for Lovely to join me—I'm not about to drink without him—but he can't get his hand to his lips. He winds up lowering his head to meet the booze in front of his chest. Once he does, I down the brown. I have no idea what the hell he just poured from that bottle, but it's some of the smoothest whiskey I've had since I left New York.

I put my empty glass back down on the desk.

"Okay, Mister Lovely," I say, careful not to wince as I spit out that twisted name. "Are you going to tell me what this is about?"

I'm trying to wipe my palms on my pants leg without looking awkward, even though I doubt Lovely would be offended at bad manners.

"You sent for me," I say. "And I'm here."

"Yes, yes. You're here now," Lovely says. "But I'm more curious about the other morning."

My stomach flips but I try not to react. I don't know how the fuck Lovely knows I was here, but he wouldn't be asking me if he had any doubts. It hits me that if he knows this much about me, he could have a goon picking up the champ right now. Or visiting Myra. If I get out of here with anything resembling a life, the first thing I'm going to do is check on the two of them.

"Yeah, I was here," I tell him because there's no point in lying. If he asks, I'll say that I watched as Garvey pulled the trigger. But Lovely doesn't come at me with a question. He just smiles, his wrinkly white face creasing like a crumpled newspaper.

"You got to watch the bastard go down?"

I'm not sure if he means Reeger or Garvey. "Which bastard?"

"Reeger," he says. "You watched him get it, you lucky son of a bitch?"

If Lovely is glad Reeger's dead, I really don't know why I'm here. My thoughts keep going back to the champ and Myra. And Johalis. I hope they're clear of this.

"I thought you were in business with Reeger," I say, wondering how else Charlie the goon jumped from one boss to the other.

"In business with Reeger? That two-faced scumsucker was moving in on my loans, taking over the payments." Lovely is getting worked up, and the more agitated he gets, the more he seems to shake. "He didn't only take the money, he'd hike up the vig. And he was coming down on my muscle, too, throwing them behind bars. I never saw one cop take on so many triggermen. I had a fucking contract on his head, and nobody was able to put him down, until you and your friend Garvey came along."

He stops and pulls out a small bottle of pills from his vest pocket. He can't get it open, so Charlie comes over, unscrews the cap, and plucks a single pill. He puts it on Lovely's tongue and pours him a finger of whiskey. Then he helps the old man drink it so he can wash the medicine down.

"I never said I put down Reeger," I say as he finishes his shot.

He ignores me and tells Charlie to pour two more shots of brown. I'm starting to wonder if this stuff is regular booze or Lovely's magic serum. It could be both.

Lovely talks to me but his eyes are on Charlie, he's watching him pour the booze. "The only problem is that the papers are going to make Reeger a fucking saint for catching an escaped convict," he says. "If you could've made it look like he was fucking some boy, maybe raping a nun, now that would've really been something."

Lovely does his best to drink his shot, but half of it lands on his chin. Charlie comes over and wipes Lovely's face with a fresh handkerchief, then goes back to his post behind me. Lovely's shoulders relax as the booze does its work.

A smile crosses the old man's face. "Did he moan? Scream in agony? Beg for his life?" he asks as he gazes up at the painted tin on the ceiling. He looks like a kid waiting to hear his favorite bedtime story. When his lips stretch, I spot a glint of gold in a row of shiny white teeth. I wonder how many local Joes landed in the poorhouse so he could flash that thousand-dollar smile, so he could live in luxury until the doctors pull a sheet over his remains and the evil in his soul is finally snuffed out for good.

"He didn't suffer," I say, giving Reeger an ounce of dignity for no reason other than to stop Lovely's gloating. "Garvey got him clean. Reeger never knew what hit him."

Lovely looks disappointed. "That's too bad," he says, before leaning forward and looking me in the eye. "But I still owe you. Name your price."

I've heard Lovely can be quite generous with those who help him, but I don't trust him any more than I trusted Reeger, I don't care how old and feeble he is. This is the same bastard who lends working stiffs money and chops off their thumbs when they don't pay, who enjoys pissing on the corpses of legit businessmen when they refuse to partner with him. He doesn't just hand out money. If I take what he's offering, I'll be working for him, on his payroll, until his dying day—and it's clear that he's figured out a way to live long past his expiration date. I came in here afraid to get on his bad side. Now I'm scared of leaving on his good one.

"You don't owe me," I say. "I didn't stop Reeger, Garvey did."

"But you were with Garvey, right? You did it together? Or am I mistaken?"

He's not that far off the mark. The guy's got more sources than Eliot Ness.

"Yeah," I say. "Garvey was an old friend."

"That settles it." He licks the corners of his lips, and even I'm grateful that they've finally gotten some moisture. "I owe you. You've been running around with one of my singers, right? Maybe I can help you there."

"You mean Myra?" I say. "She's more than your singer, she's your partner. It cost her twenty grand for the privilege, and it cost Garvey his life."

He gives a chuckle. "You seem to think everybody is my partner. That's humorous. No, she's a singer, no more. I've got a million Myras. They pay me so they can act like owners, get some time on the stage, throw their weight around. And I protect them. It's square."

I hate to admit it, but it fits. Myra didn't buy a piece of the Red Canary; she bought a piece of the spotlight she'd spent her whole life seeking—and she paid for it with twenty thousand of Garvey's greenbacks. For her, it was worth it.

Lovely leans forward and steadies his arm on top of the desk. "How about I give Myra her money back, no strings attached?" he says. "As a favor to you, of course."

It's nothing to sneeze at. If Myra got back the twenty large, we'd be set for a long, long time. But I think of the champ, how he managed to keep his dignity by avoiding deals like this one. I look at Lovely, the old, demented man ready to pave my road out of here. Then I picture him calling me for a return favor while I'm sitting on a beach in Santa Monica.

I shake my head. "You don't owe me."

His face turns mean. "You think you're too good for me, you fucking pasty albino piece of shit?" His black eyes are sizzling. "I wipe my ass with freaks like you."

I can't see Charlie, but I'm sure he's reaching either for his thirty-eight or a scalpel. I stand up, put my right foot on the chair, and cross my arms over my knee. My ankle is now only twenty inches from my trigger finger. If this gets ugly, I might get a shot or two off before I visit Garvey.

"Listen to me," I say. "This has nothing to do with being too good for you. It's got to do with honesty. I don't want to take your dough because I didn't earn it." I sound like my father and I'm proud of it. I wish the champ were here to see me in action.

Lovely calms down and I can only hope Charlie is doing the same. The old man leans back and nods as if he understands, but his mood is no more reliable than the stock market.

"Maybe that teen center of yours could use a few bucks," he says.

He sure knows a lot about my life, which at last count is the eleventh advantage he has over me.

"The club has plenty of money," I say.

It's the biggest lie I've told in years. There's a soup kitchen on every other corner in Harlem. There's no way the Hy-Hat is going to be able to survive. I've got to throw out something more believable.

"But I don't run the place, my father does," I say, as if the champ would ever be interested in Lovely's dirty money. "I'll ask him."

Lovely bobs his head in agreement. "That's better," he says.

I take my foot off the chair and start to make my exit, but he's not finished.

"One more thing," he says.

"Yeah?" I say, turning back to face him. I'm two feet from the office door.

"There's the matter of the missing folder."

Oh, shit. I picture Johalis sifting through the assortment of receipts, marked-up cocktail napkins, and handwritten memos. Of course Lovely would want those records. There are probably a dozen killers in town who'd like to get their hands on them.

"What folder?" I ask him.

"The one that was here and now isn't," he says. "The one that has Reeger's records. The one you took."

Charlie's shadow engulfs me, and the muzzle of his gun kisses my neck. I was so close to getting out of here. Now I'm envisioning my funeral and wonder if Myra will be there. I picture Angela and Wallace sitting in the back row as my father curses me for not taking his advice and walking away from these mobsters.

"I didn't take any folder," I say. "And you should know that, because I don't know a thing about Reeger's business. Remember? I thought you guys were in this mess together."

Lovely grabs the top of his trousers in his rickety hands and lifts his leg to cross it over the other. Then he tries to brush some lint off the cuff of his shirt and misses by six inches. He doesn't seem to notice how badly his body is betraying him, and I'm not about to tell him. It's obvious that Charlie isn't bringing it up, either.

"Now you listen to me," he says through a raspy cough. "I was never partners with that scumbag. And I need that folder. It's got names, dates, the details of my loans—at least the ones that Reeger muscled in on. I thought you had it, but you say you don't. Okay. How do you suggest I find it?"

I shrug. "Are you sure it's not in here? Or at Reeger's house?"

Lovely stares at me, his shoulders are bobbing, but his eyes are locked on mine. I think he's trying to determine whether or not I'm lying, so I force out a smile and try to look relaxed. Then my eyes start shimmying and he turns away, disgusted. Nystagmus to the rescue.

"Get out of here," the old man says. "But if I find out you're lying about that folder," he says, "I'll send you off to the morgue one piece at a time."

He extends his hand and I do the same. It's a handshake in

reverse—I actually stop his hand from moving when I grip it. Then I thank him because I can't think of what else to say.

When I walk out the door, Charlie the Mustache follows. I put two and two together and come up with this: Lovely is Charlie's new boss—and Charlie's new boss is a lot smarter, and a lot more dangerous, than Reeger ever dreamt of becoming.

I step out of the pool hall and into the evening air a free man. I palm the sweat from my forehead, put on my fedora, and walk west, leaving Charlie to figure out how the hell I fit into this puzzle. I'm sure Lovely is wondering the same thing.

I wish I had an answer for them.

CHAPTER 14

*I*t's been a week since I left Lovely wallowing in his whiskey and depravity. Since then, I've spent every day in Room 311 at Philadelphia General, sitting in an orange armchair the nurses dragged in from the sun room especially for me, watching Myra's cheeks regain their color as bacon and eggs replaced the laudanum on her breakfast tray.

She now knows about Garvey and Reeger. I didn't mention my conversation with Lovely about her supposed partnership in the Canary; she already knows how little she got for her money and doesn't need to hear me say it. I also didn't let on that Lovely wanted to give me her twenty large. She wouldn't understand why I walked away from the offer; I'm sure she'd see it as a pair of one-way tickets to Hollywood. Me, I saw it as an invitation to join the swindlers in Lovely's coffee can—one body part at a time.

Myra returned to life on Thursday morning, singing "Bye Bye Blues" along with the radio, her head on her pillow, her eyes as clear as her voice. I should have been happy, but all I felt was the guilt of knowing the doctor was about to snuff her new spark with his prognosis. I should have told her myself—I could've lessened the blow—but I couldn't bring myself to say the words I knew would hurt her so deeply.

When Dr. Dailey arrived later that afternoon, he had no such qualms. He stood at the foot of the bed, his stomach protruding beyond the reaches of his lab coat, and gave a short lecture on the anatomy of the human foot—specifically, the third metatarsal and what happens when it breaks in four places. Then he took out Myra's X-rays and began talking about her arch and how it affects her gait.

I held my breath when Myra's upper lip started quivering.

"What are you trying to tell me?" she said. She had her hand in front of her mouth, her fingers splayed in front of her lips as if she feared the bad news might hit her in the face. I wanted to reach out and steady them, but there was no shielding her from this.

"I'm not certain," he said. "But your gait will probably not be the same as it was. It's likely you'll walk with a limp."

Myra's face fell into her hands as she sobbed uncontrollably. Her hair hung down and blocked the sides of her face like curtains in front of a private dressing room. I stroked the smooth skin behind her neck and told her that a damaged metatarsal didn't change anything, but I knew the truth. In grammar school, that blasted shoe chafed more than her ankle; it scraped her soul. And those kinds of wounds don't heal. Ever.

We walked out of the hospital about an hour after our meeting with Dailey. Myra refused my help. She made her way to the Auburn on a pair of wooden crutches, her wrapped foot swinging beneath her like a plaster pendulum. I brought her back to my place, poured two chilled martinis, and cooked some spaghetti. Then I planned our trip to California.

All we needed to leave, I told her, was a thousand bucks. I tried to look like I believed we'd make it, that we could both find work and save our money, but there are precious few jobs to be had in Philly. Yesterday, a shoemaker's help-wanted sign sparked a line that stretched a full mile to City Hall. I thought about getting on it myself, but I know as little about shoemaking as I do about sunbathing.

After dinner, we came to the Red Canary for Myra's set and we're still here now. I'm at the same table, the one in the corner near the fire exit, which is now permanently reserved for Myra and me. I wonder if a private table and free drinks are the kind of perks that Lovely gave Myra in exchange for her twenty large. I could ask him—I know he's here, I saw his white-walled Packard outside—but I'd be crazy to start up with him again. The odds of seeing Lovely and walking out the door are slim. As far as I know, the odds of doing it twice have never been tested.

It's nearly midnight and the joint is still filling up. Four suits are leaning on the bar, singing along to a Cole Porter tune the piano player is banging out in the dining room. A couple of flappers are behind them, dancing and sipping shots of moon. Everybody at the bar has shiny faces and glassy eyes; I'm guessing their mood lifted about one second after they heard Reeger left for the pearly gates and took his weekly raids with him.

Myra finished her set a few minutes ago—she closed by sitting on the piano and singing "Blue Is the Night," her hobbled foot dangling just below the reach of the spotlight. She made her way to the dressing room when the lights went down, hoping the rummies would be too busy applauding to notice she was wearing a cast the size of a birdcage. I feel for her, even though that cast will come off in a few weeks.

Red puts a couple of martinis on the table as I watch Myra limp her way over, swinging on her crutches, avoiding the stares coming from the dining room. I'm surprised to see that she's got a smile on her face. Her cheeks are as round as cue balls.

"I've got good news," she says.

At this point, any news that doesn't involve somebody getting killed is good to me.

"Feeling better?" I say, nodding toward her foot.

The smile leaves her face. "Not really."

She sits down and extends her leg under the table. Then she leans forward and says with a twinkle, "We can go to California."

"Great," I say, as if we haven't been through this before. "As soon as we have the money."

"We have it," she says. Then she looks around to make sure nobody can hear us. She doesn't have to worry; the singing voices at the piano are loud enough to drown us out. "Lovely gave me back my twenty thousand."

Fucking Lovely. I should've realized that he'd pull something like this. Myra's looking at me; her eyes are as wide as a kid's on Christmas morning. I've got two choices: owe Lovely a favor, or tell Myra she has to give her new doll back to Santa.

"Myra," I begin, but stop in mid-sentence. She's looking at me and holding her breath, and I don't have the strength to watch her cry again, not after seeing her view that X-ray.

"What's wrong?" she says. I can tell she's afraid of what she's about to hear.

"Myra," I say again, "Lovely's not giving that money to you. He's giving it to me. He wants me in his circle. You can't take it."

She looks confused. And beautiful.

"What do you mean, giving it to *you*?"

"He offered me the dough. He said it was payment for killing Reeger, and I told him I didn't want it. I know all about that heartless bastard and I don't want to owe him one red cent. I'll wind up being his gun for hire. I won't do it."

Myra's not saying anything, but her stoic look is betrayed by a quivering lip—as well as a single tear that rolls down her cheek. I'm sure she doesn't want to believe me, but I'm making too much sense to be ignored.

"Why else would he give you your money back?" I say.

"He said it's a second chance," she says. "Who cares what he wants from you? You'll be so far away, he'll never find you."

"I don't care what he said," I say. "You can't take that money. It's not a chance to do things right. It's a chance to make the same mistake again. You owed Garvey, then Reeger, and now you'd owe Lovely. And there's no place in the world far enough away to duck him."

Myra takes a long slug of her martini. I know when somebody wants a drink to hurt, and this qualifies.

"There's good news here," I say. "Even without the twenty large, you're still out of debt. You don't have to pay Garvey and you don't have to pay Reeger."

I think of Johalis telling me how Myra used suckers like me to wipe away her debts, and it fits. But I didn't pull that trigger at Bobby Lewis's for her—not entirely, anyway. I pulled it for Garvey and Calvin. And me.

"All you're losing is twenty large," I tell her. "I know it's a ton of dough, but it was never yours anyway. You can live without it. *We* can live without it."

"But we can't live without it in L.A.," she says.

Her tears are putting a shine on her rouged cheeks, which are glimmering like wet stones. I nearly cry myself; my throat closes and the backs of my eyes burn. I want to help her. I want to be the hero that she wants me to be. But if we take Lovely's money, I won't be the hero *I* want to be.

Her hand is on the table; I put mine on top of it.

"I promise we'll get to Hollywood," I say. "I'll figure something out."

I want to believe my own words, but I can't even imagine how I'll scratch up the dough to get us on the train. Every possibility—hijacking comes to mind—is nearly as bad as working for Lovely.

"I *will* get the money," I say again, trying to sound more confident the second time around.

Myra's sobbing, and all I need to do to lift her pain is tell her that I'm okay with owing Lovely. But I can't do it. Instead, I sit there, my hand on hers, listening to the piano player bang out "My Future Just Passed," wondering if he's playing it for me.

⚜

I'm with Johalis at his place on Ludlow, my shoulders still wet from the afternoon rain. He pours me a finger of whiskey and we raise a glass to Madame Curio, who walked out of Eastern State this morning. She deserves a shot herself; she was locked up in that hellhole for nearly two weeks. Now she's free, but springing her cost plenty. I had to pay Johalis's bull two hundred bucks to lose the Madame's file in a pile of dead inmates' dental records.

"To the Madame," I say before downing the whiskey.

The brown sends a wave of calm through my chest and I feel I've earned it. I promised the Madame I'd get her out of the pen and I delivered. Not that it matters anymore, but I had to dip into Angela's shoebox to do it. That Zealandia box now holds all the money I've got to my name—three hundred and forty bucks. The Hy-Hat safe is empty; the champ can't even meet the rent. At the rate I'm going, the most exotic place I'll be taking Myra is a bread line on Market Street.

"All's well that ends well," Johalis says before going into his kitchen to get some ice.

I sit on Johalis's sofa and take a look over the folder that Garvey found at the pool hall. As I flip through the papers, a trumpet student blares out a scale upstairs. I ignore the screechy exercises as best I can, focusing instead on the pile of notes and paystubs. Lovely's name pops up on three cocktail napkins, a roadmap, and two ledger sheets. In each instance, a number is written next to his name. And every one of the numbers is preceded by a dollar sign.

Johalis comes back in with a bucket of ice in his hand. "Why would Lovely care so much about the folder?" he says. "He's got half the city's cops in his pocket."

"Maybe he's worried about the other half," I say. "Or maybe he really is out to destroy Reeger. I'm telling you, I'm surprised we haven't caught him at Laurel Hill, pissing on the guy's grave."

The trumpet is now blowing a sour version of "The Star-Spangled Banner."

"I ran it by my boys at the precinct," Johalis says. "From what we put together, Reeger wasn't a loan shark. He muscled in on loan sharks, took over their payments, told them that if they didn't like it, they could spend a few years in the slammer. It worked, because he was ripping off sharks and crooks. Nobody was going to complain. And Reeger isn't the only bull in that folder. Connor's in there. Others, too. But Reeger was the head of the ring."

I look down at the folder. Johalis is right—a lot of these names belong to other cops. They were the muscle that swung Reeger's hammer.

"What am I supposed to do with this file?" I say. "I can't bury it."

"Why not?" Johalis says, concern peeking out from the lines on his face.

"Because every news report is saying Reeger was a hero for killing Garvey. I can't let the world think that."

"Let it be," Johalis says. "Just be happy Reeger got what he had coming."

It's good advice, assuming all I wanted to do was save my own skin. But I owe it to Garvey to clear his name. Besides, greed never dies with the greedy. The cops in this folder will follow Reeger's lead, and if I don't stop them, there will be other Garveys and other Myras. I have to do something with this file; I just don't know what yet.

I walk to the door and shake Johalis's hand. "Thanks," I tell him. "I owe you one."

"No, you don't," he says. "I owed your father and I still do. If it hadn't been for him, I'd be sipping shine with Reeger right now."

I think of the champ and the lineup of friends he's got waiting to help him. The man gains respect simply by respecting himself. I wonder if I'll ever be able to do the same.

"Thanks just the same," I tell Johalis. "You owed my father, but you helped me."

Johalis nods. "Any time you need me, just call."

I hope I never have to take him up on that offer.

I step out onto Ludlow. The sun is beating down on the wet, shiny street; the air is as moist and heavy as a used washrag. I put my dark glasses on and tug the straw brim of my fedora down low. I walk to the corner as the trumpet blares "Me and My Shadow" behind me. I get in the Auburn, start the engine, and drive home. I doubt Lovely's boys are following me, but I stick to side streets and back roads anyway.

By the time I get home, Myra has already left for the Red Canary. The place feels empty without her. I remind myself that this is how I lived—alone—until a few weeks ago. I guess I'm no different than an inmate coming out of solitary at the pen. Just because I came out of it alive doesn't mean I want to go back.

I put on the radio and sit at the Underwood. I type out a one-sentence letter: *The attached folder was pulled from the hands of Sergeant Reeger as he lay dying at Bobby Lewis's pool hall.* I don't sign my name. I just stuff the letter into an envelope along with the folder, then address the envelope to the *Inquirer*. If anyone at the paper looks into this file, they'll surely uncover the crooked bulls hiding inside. If they don't, at least I'll know I tried.

Before I head out the door, I reach into Angela's shoebox, pull out twenty bucks, and grab another envelope. This one I address to the champ at the Hy-Hat. We're not only behind on the rent; he needs money for a new icebox motor. I know we can't afford to keep the Hy-Hat open any longer—not without me pouring drinks somewhere—but it pains me to shut it down. The club is my getaway: the kids there are free of guns, free of moon, and free of the Reegers and Lovelys of the world. And this is when they need us the most—the longer the bread lines, the shorter their cash. If we close down, they'll have nobody to take them in. They'll wind up working the city's speakeasies, just like I did.

I'm not about to desert them again, not after driving off with the champ and Garvey and leaving Billy Walker holding the bag. Luckily, the kid is as sharp as he is strong; he handed the bulls a pile of malarkey and walked out of the precinct as clean as a pile of starched linens. But that doesn't mean I had a right to put him in that position.

I put a stamp on both envelopes and leave my place.

The sun is setting and the shadows of the trees stretch across Juniper. I check Ronnie's Luncheonette and see nothing but an empty bench out front. The place is free of hoodlums, just like I am. I have to admit the evenings in Philadelphia are much more enjoyable when nobody is looking to send a bullet through my skull.

I drop the envelopes in the mailbox and walk up Juniper to Enrico's flower shop. If I hurry, I can pick up some roses for Myra and still catch her set at the Canary tonight.

The young salesgirl at Enrico's knows me. I'm not surprised; I'm sure there aren't many locals plunking down two-fifty for bouquets nowadays.

"The usual?" she asks. She's got shiny brown hair and the same expression of innocence I see on the faces of the kids at the Hy-Hat. It's the look of a young teen who's ready to take big bites out of the world but hasn't yet found out the world bites back.

"Sure thing," I say. My eyes start shimmying, so I turn away and pretend to examine a row of potted plants.

It doesn't take her as long to assemble the bouquet as it does for my eyes to calm down, so when she hands me the box, I look down at my oxfords. I hand her three bucks and tell her to keep the fifty cents change—as if I've got it to spread around.

I leave Enrico's with the box under my arm and a spring in

my step. I'm free of Reeger and in love with Myra. As the champ promised me so many years ago, I won't be spending the rest of my life alone.

When I reach the corner, I take out my car keys—but see that I won't be getting to the Red Canary any time soon.

The Auburn is gone.

❈

I lay the flowers on the kitchen table. Then I grab a bottle of Gordon's, splash a triple-shot over three ice cubes, and stir the booze with my finger.

If I don't find the Auburn, Myra and I will never get out of here. As it was, we needed a thousand bucks to leave for California. I figured we'd raise about four hundred of it by driving to New York and selling the car before getting on the train. Without that cash, we're down to a few hundred bucks and haven't even gotten a foot out of the door yet.

I'm glad Myra's at the Canary because I don't want her to see me flummoxed. I have no idea how to find the Auburn—and I've yet to come up with a way to scratch together the extra dough. If Myra wants to circle a date for our getaway, she's going to need a calendar as thick as the yellow pages.

I've got one move left, but I don't want to make it. I could call Lovely. He'd have the Auburn back under my pale ass in the time it takes him to lop off a grifter's thumb. But calling him would be as bad as taking his money. I refuse to leave Philly with any loose ends—or loose cannons—behind me.

I put on the radio. Cab Calloway is playing "Nobody's Sweetheart" and I'm glad it no longer applies to me. I'm in front of the mirror, and for first time since my nose was broken, I take a good, long look at myself. I can't say I like what I see.

I pour another gin—a double—then take a slug. Leaning back on the couch, the booze goes to work and I welcome the peace that arrives as reality fades. I drift away from my plan to find the Auburn and, instead, land on a beach in Santa Monica, where I'm watching Myra slip out of her swimsuit as the sun toasts my chest and the turquoise water laps at her feet.

We're rolling in the sand when the telephone in the hallway rings, yanking me back to Philly. My head throbs and my neck aches, and I curse Mr. Gordon for filling the bottle that landed in my kitchen.

I wipe the sweaty sleep from my eyes as I walk to the phone. It's three in the morning and Myra's still not here. I'm guessing she'll be on the other end of the receiver, but when I pick it up, I hear Homer's voice instead. He's talking fast and in a hushed whisper.

"Jersey, I know it's late but you gotta hear this."

He must be working the graveyard shift at the docks. I give it a fifty-fifty chance that he's back in trouble with the street bulls guarding the pier.

"I'm listening," I say.

There's a long pause. I picture him staring up at the ceiling, searching for the words that can explain his arrest.

"It's Myra," he says. Then he stops talking again.

The rims of my eyes get hot. My tongue goes dry and my heart sinks to my balls.

"What about her, Homer?" I say. My saliva is as thick as paste. "What?"

"She's here at the docks," he says. "And she's about to get in trouble, big fuckin' trouble."

I'm praying Homer is overreacting, but he can't be, not at three in the morning.

"What's going on?" My temples are pounding so hard I'm surprised Homer can't hear them.

"There's a shipment of whiskey idling offshore. I was supposed to sign these containers off to nobody but Otto Gorsky, y'know, Mr. Lovely. But Myra's telling me to sign them off to her."

I breathe a sigh of relief. My simple friend means well, but he doesn't know the deal.

"Lovely is Myra's boss," I say. "She's probably buying the hooch for the bar."

"No," Homer says. "She's not buying the booze, she's selling it. And it's a ton more than any bar needs. She wants me to sign off so a boat can leave with the hooch. It smells funny, Jersey. I'm telling you, she's crossing Lovely. And if I sign, I'm a dead man."

Homer could be right.

He could also be wrong.

I run through the reasons Myra would be on the docks selling hooch that was earmarked for Lovely. It can't be for the money, because she doesn't have to pay off Reeger, not anymore. Besides, if she needed cash, she would've just kept Lovely's twenty grand. There's only one scheme that makes sense—and I'm ashamed of myself for even considering it.

"Homer, how did Myra get down there?" I ask him.

"What do you mean?"

"How'd she get to the docks?"

"How the fuck should I know?"

He's not making this easy. "Homer, is there a car around?"

"I don't see one. But she can't drive anyway, she's got a busted foot."

I've seen people with crutches drive—it's far from impossible. All it takes is a little coordination and a lot of determination.

"You sure you don't see any car?"

"Nope, no car," he says. "Jersey, what's going on?"

The sweat on my neck goes cold as the pieces continue to come together. Myra's been playing me all along. She's selling

Lovely's booze for one last big score before leaving Philly. And she's doing it from behind the wheel of the Auburn, which means I'm no longer part of the ride.

Johalis was right; this whole mess boils down to her. She set Connor and Garvey up, then she did the same to Reeger and me. This is her last move and it's a beauty. She'll sell the booze, take the cash, go off to California without me, and leave me here, alone, to deal with Lovely.

I palm the sweat from my temples as I realize what it is that Myra sees in my red, blistered skin and fluttering green eyes. It's the same thing the Madame sees when she stares into her crystal ball.

She sees nothing at all.

CHAPTER 15

*T*here's a thick fog hanging over Penn's Landing, but it doesn't slow me down. I know my way around the piers—I've been here a few dozen times over the years, usually picking up booze from rumrunners who don't have connections at the New York harbor. I wish I were in one of those old trucks right now. Instead, I'm riding in the back of a taxi, hoping to find out that everybody around me is wrong about Myra. The odds aren't in my favor.

I tell the driver to kill the lights and creep up King Street to the wharf. This is the darkest area of the landing and that's no accident. Carpenter's Wharf channels so much booze it might as well have a tap at the end of it.

I can't see much from this distance, but I can make out the silhouette of a schooner at the end of the pier. It makes sense—bootleggers like Lovely often hire fishing boats to get the booze from rumrunners waiting out in the Atlantic, just beyond the jurisdiction of the Coast Guard. But I don't see the workers that are normally on hand to take the whiskey off the schooner and load it into the trucks. And I don't see the trucks.

"Let me out here, driver," I say.

The cabbie pulls over and I hand him a sawbuck. Then I tell him to make a U-turn and keep the lights off until he's back on Dock Street.

Getting out of the cab, I check for my snubnose. It's right where I put it—in my shoulder holster, pressed up against my chest. I follow the trolley rails toward the end of the pier, dwarfed by the shipping containers that surround me. The landing smells about as fresh as a junkyard—giving off a steady whiff of damp weeds and spilled oil. The only sounds that break the nighttime air are my oxfords hitting the wooden path, and the river beneath me, splashing against itself.

The fog is wet and heavy. I take off my fedora and wipe the mist from my forehead with the sleeve of my jacket. Then I put my fedora back on and tug its straw brim over my eyes. I don't know why I bother. If anybody spots an albino walking the Philly docks at three in the morning, they're going to remember—hat or no hat.

I'm halfway down the pier and there's still no sign of Homer, Myra, Lovely, or anybody.

I'm about a hundred yards from the schooner when I spy an Auburn parked in front of an empty loading dock. It's got to be mine, unless there are two Auburns with the same line of rusty bullet holes across the back.

The last thing I need is to be accused of stealing my own car, so I take a glance over my shoulder before pulling open the driver's door. It swings freely—the lock has been jimmied—and I see a screwdriver jammed into the ignition keyhole. I can't help but feel as though my car has been violated.

I reach under the seats and unearth nothing more than a ball of gunky dust. But then I check the visor and find an envelope with a stack of hundreds as thick as my thumb. I don't have to count it to know how much is there. It's twenty grand. And it belongs to Lovely.

As I stuff the dough into my breast pocket, I spot a shoebox under the dash. My eyes have failed me before, but they're not letting me down now. That's a Zealandia box and I'll bet there aren't any shoes inside of it. It's the box from my closet, the one holding the last of my cash, the one I had earmarked for Angela. I guess it wasn't enough for Myra to steal only my heart.

Two lights shine at the end of the pier. They look like a pair of flashlights, so I stay close to the containers in case I can be spotted in this fog. Then I creep toward the glow.

When I get about sixty feet away, I can hear Myra's voice. I move closer and spot her leaning on a pair of crutches that are tucked under her armpits. A guy in a fisherman's cap is holding both flashlights; he's pointing them at Myra's hands as she counts through a wad of bills.

I step out of the shadows and stand squarely in front of her.

"I hope that includes the price of selling me out," I say.

"Jersey," she says and gives a smile. If I didn't know better, I'd think she was happy to see me. But I do know better.

The captain shines one of the lights in my face. He looks spooked, as if I were the ghost of his dead quartermaster.

"Who the fuck are you?" he says.

"I'm the sucker," I say. My eyes are shimmying to beat the band, but I keep them trained on Myra. "There's always one. This time it's me."

"You're one of those circus freaks," he says, pointing both flashlights at me. "You're one of those albinos."

"I'm that, too," I say. "But right now, sucker fits best."

Myra's hair hangs over her left eye, but her right one carries a mix of guilt and shame.

"Okay, we're done," the captain says to Myra and turns off both flashlights. We'd be in total blackness if it weren't for the fog light on the schooner.

The deal's done and the captain walks back to his boat. Myra doesn't stop him and neither do I. As far as I'm concerned, he can take Lovely's booze all the way to the Pacific and fill my reservation on the beach. Right now, I'm only concerned with Myra—and the skinny that Johalis sang into my deaf ears.

"You set all this up from the start," I say. "Connor and Garvey.

Reeger and me. And now you're ripping off Lovely. Who were you going to pin this one on? Let me guess. That circus freak with yellow hair and green eyes."

She looks wounded. Her eyes moisten and she shakes her head. "I took the money so we could go to Hollywood," she says, pushing the hair off her face. "Together."

She's trying to stay balanced on the crutches and I fight the urge to help her.

"I guess you were going to come back for me, after stealing my car and my money," I say.

"I was," she says and looks at me with those glistening almond-shaped eyes. "I swear."

Something happens to a man's heart when he knows the woman he loves is lying to him. It becomes so raw it feels every pain it's ever been dealt, every injustice it's ever experienced. I'm looking at Myra, but all I'm seeing are the things I'll never have: a day of sunbathing in Santa Monica; a childhood worth reliving; the mother who left a month after I was born.

"Bullshit," I say. "You played me. You counted on me nailing Reeger, but you figured I'd get the chair. You would have been free and clear."

"It's not true," she says, a damp shine glistening on her cheeks. "You have it all wrong."

The schooner's engine revs as the captain readies to pull it away from the wharf.

She tries to step toward me but is hampered by her crutches. "It's not too late," she says. "I've got the money. Let's go. We can leave right now." She holds up the captain's dough to show me our future, but she might as well be promising me a trip to Lovely's operating table.

"What's your angle this time, Myra? Set me up against Lovely? I'll pass."

Her eyes go wide. She must realize she'll be left to deal with Lovely on her own; she can't be upset that I'm not going with her.

Suddenly, I hear footsteps behind me. A lot of them. When I turn around, I see Homer running toward us, his cap scrunched in his hand. Six bulls follow him; they're carrying flashlights and nightsticks.

Homer is yelling out to me. "Jersey, I got the cops."

It doesn't take an Einstein to figure out that once Homer realized Myra was running out on me, he broke his code of silence and sang like a canary.

My suspicions are confirmed when Homer points at the schooner and tells the bulls it's the boat with the booze.

Four cops make their way onto the schooner. The other two walk over to me with their nightsticks ready. When the taller bull steps through the fog, I see it's the one from the stationhouse, Thorndyke. He looks disillusioned, as if he expected more from an upstanding albino bartender.

"Is this the guy selling the whiskey?" he asks Homer. His glasses are covered with the dew from the foggy air.

"No," Homer says. But he doesn't say anything else. I guess he can't bring himself to finger Myra now that he sees me standing with her.

"Her?" Thorndyke says with a look of surprise.

Myra looks desperate. She's boxed and she knows it. If the cops take her in, they'll nail her with plenty. If they let her go, then Lovely will catch up with her and take a couple of her fingers to make up for the double-cross. There was only one way her plan could succeed: she had to get out of here tonight.

"It wasn't me," she says to Thorndyke. "I know how it looks but it wasn't me." She's talking fast, in short bursts like machine-gun fire.

"Who was it then?" Thorndyke asks.

Myra's looking to her right and left as if she wants to find somebody to pin it on. But there's nobody there.

She looks at Thorndyke and says, "Aaron Garvey."

Thorndyke raises an eyebrow. "Aaron Garvey is dead."

"I know," Myra says. "But he made the deal before he died. He was buying alcohol for the Red Canary. He wanted me to buy it for him, but I wouldn't do it. I came here to call the deal off." She holds up the dough and shows it to Thorndyke. "See? I still have the money. Ask Jersey, he knows."

She looks at me, her eyes pleading with me to back her up.

Thorndyke and his buddy are next to her, waiting for me to say something.

Homer is beside them, doing the same.

Myra looks at me, "Jersey, please."

I picture her as a girl of twelve, the braids in her hair, the hurt in her eyes—and the look of hope that filled her face when we talked about Hollywood. I want to believe that girl is still in Myra, somewhere.

But then I picture Garvey, the guy who stood up for me all those years, the guy who deserved to die with a hell of a lot more dignity than he did.

"It's not so," I say.

Thorndyke looks to the floor. I can see he's disappointed; I guess he doesn't want to book a woman on a bootlegging charge.

"Homer's right," I say. "Myra's running this booze."

Thorndyke pulls the handcuffs from his belt and panic invades Myra's expression. Her eyes are jerking from the bulls to me, then to the glinting steel in Thorndyke's hands.

I can't look at her as I fill in the rest of the blanks for Thorndyke. "Lovely made the deal but she stepped in. She was supposed to pick up the booze but sold it to the guy in that schooner. I won't bother telling you all she took from me."

When I turn back toward Myra, she's got a gun in her hand and it's pointed at my chest. I have no idea where she had it hidden, probably holstered on the side of her crutch. She can't be more than eight feet away from me—which is far too close for her to miss. If she squeezes the trigger, I'll be dead before the gun cools. But she'd be crazy to do it. To get out of here alive, she'd have to keep shooting while running to the Auburn on crutches.

It's starting to rain and the shower mixes with her tears. I want to take out my handkerchief and blot the anguish from her face. I want to kiss her until it's yesterday.

When she speaks, her voice is weak and shaky. "I only did it because I didn't believe you'd come away with me. You were never gonna get the money, not if you kept pouring it into that precious club of yours."

Part of me believes her, at least the part about my coming up short on dough. Had I put the Hy-Hat aside and worried about us—and had I somehow managed to come up with the cash—our ride together might have lasted a while longer. But it's too late for us now. And it's too late for Myra. Once the bullies broke her spirit, she was never able to mend it again.

From the corner of my eye, I see Thorndyke inching his revolver out of its holster.

"Put the gun down, Myra," I say, knowing how bloody this scene could get. "Even if you kill me, you'll never get out of here alive."

Her tears—or maybe the raindrops—are turning her eye makeup into thick black streaks. As they run down her face, she looks like some sort of almond-eyed ghoul.

"Just turn around and start walking," she says.

I don't budge, mostly because I know she's ready to put a slug between my shoulder blades.

Then she adds, "We're leaving right now."

If she's thinking we can walk to the Auburn and drive off to California, she's crazier than I thought. Even if I wanted to go with her, the bulls would nail her in the back before she hobbled her way to the shipping containers.

"It won't work, Myra," I say, nodding toward Thorndyke and his partner, who have their revolvers trained on her.

"Lower the gun, lady," Thorndyke says.

"Listen to him, Myra," I say. I lock my eyes with hers, afraid she'll get rattled if she keeps looking over at Thorndyke and his partner. "It's over."

She looks at me, still crying. Her upper lip is quivering as the downpour continues to paint shiny black bars on her tan cheeks. Her hair is soaked and flat; the rain is running off the rim of my fedora.

"I said lower the gun," Thorndyke says, more loudly this time.

I see Homer standing in the rainfall behind Thorndyke, his mouth hanging slightly open. I hope he doesn't do anything stupid, anything that would stop Myra from dropping the rod.

"What are my chances?" she asks me.

I'm assuming she means the odds she'll walk away clean. "We'll find you a good lawyer," I say.

"A lawyer can't stop Lovely from making minced meat out of me."

"I'll handle him," I tell her.

The smirk on her face says she doesn't believe me.

"I promise," I say.

"Drop the gun *now*," Thorndyke says and cocks the hammer.

Myra looks me in my eyes. "I did love you," she says. Then she aims the gun at me and pulls the trigger.

A split-second after she fires, a second shot rings out and hits her in the left cheek. She drops to the ground, her crutches bouncing on the wet ground beside her.

"Myra!" I shout, my voice swallowed up by the empty darkness around me.

I run to her but there's nothing I can do. She's motionless—blood is flowing down the side of her face, tinting the puddle of rain beneath her. Her plastered foot is twisted awkwardly beneath her.

Thorndyke drops to his knees and holds his head in his hands as the downpour soaks the back of his uniform. His eyes are shut and his lips pulled tight; he looks as though he just got hit himself. I wonder if Myra is the only person he's ever killed. Either way, he must be coming to grips with the same thought I am. Myra never aimed to hit me—the bullet sailed eight feet over my head. She only pulled the trigger because she knew that once she did the bulls would put an end to her troubles. And she was right, I suppose.

Homer comes over to me, his drenched cap pulled low on his sloped forehead, his lips turned downward. He puts a hand on my shoulder and I try not to break down, but the grief pours out of me as powerfully as the river beneath us rushes toward the ocean.

I don't try to explain to Homer why I'm sobbing. Nobody—not him, not Thorndyke, not even the champ—can understand what Myra meant to me. When she died, the light went out at both ends of my tunnel.

She was one of the few bright spots of my childhood.

And the only glimmer of hope for my future.

CHAPTER 16

I load my suitcase into the back of the Auburn. A cloud drifts in front of the morning sun, so I take off the scarf I've got wrapped around my jaw and toss it into the backseat.

I said my final good-byes to Myra a week ago. There were no services, no priests, no crying friends, no family. Not even her father showed up. In the end, she had nobody but me. I bought a plot at Laurel Hill and had her buried there; I placed a bouquet of roses on her grave and stayed until it started to rain. I knelt in front of the stone marker, the rain spitting on the top of my fedora, and the moist, freshly broken earth dampening the knees of my pants. I told her I thought I might have loved her, and that I'd have had her buried in Hollywood if I'd had the money. I couldn't help but wonder if things would have been different had we made it there, but I'm better off having never found out. The only thing more dangerous than spending your life with a woman who doesn't love you is spending it with one who'd set you up for the electric chair.

When I got up, I brushed off my pants, and walked to the Auburn, ignoring the warm drizzle. I started the engine and drove past the cemetery gates, knowing I'd never return.

A mile up Ridge, I passed a newsboy hawking the *Inquirer*. He held it high over his head and shouted the headline: *Records Uncover Police Sergeant's Web of Deceit, Garvey Case Revisited*. I pulled to the curb and called the kid over. The article was a beauty—it took over the front page and even had a picture of Garvey standing in front of Elementary School Four holding a baseball bat across his shoulders. Somebody must have done some serious digging for that one. I bought five copies, gave the kid a buck, and told him to keep the change. Then I sat in the car—right there on the side of Ridge—and read every word, wishing Garvey were with me to see the justice he'd served.

I've got one of those copies with me now as I pay one last visit to the Ink Well. Doolie is never here before noon on a weekday, so I let myself in with my spare key. The place is empty, hot, and stuffy. I can practically smell the dust that's settling on the memory of the albino bartender with the busted nose.

I've got the Zealandia shoebox under my arm and I put it exactly where I'd planned: on top of the ice machine, not far from where Angela's apron hangs. On it, I leave a note that tells Angela to use the money to chase her dream out of the Ink Well and into the classroom. I hope she listens.

Next to the ice machine, that blasted issue of the *Inquirer* still hangs on the wall. There's my face, scarred by the rips that Reeger left in it. I take it down, crumple it up, and toss it in the trash. Then I grab a roll of tape by the cash register and replace it with last week's paper. Hopefully, the locals who sit here trying to forget their workdays will learn a lesson about judging a man before knowing him.

As I step out from behind the bar, I picture Myra sitting on the end stool, a frosted martini glass between her polished fingernails, a litany of sweet lies coming from her painted lips. I remember the nights we spent right here, how young and free and happy I felt when we were alone. I want to feel that way again; I want to be in love again. It occurs to me that I miss myself as much as I miss Myra.

I walk to the door and take a look around the joint. Garvey stares back at me from behind the bar, a smile on his young face, and I wish him good-night before turning out the lights.

An orange sun is shining on Juniper when I get in the Auburn. I've got one more stop before heading back to New York—I want to find Lovely and return his twenty grand. I start the engine and head toward Fitzwater, making my way through the streets that seemed so sinister when Reeger was prowling them. I pass Washington—which is only a mile from Bobby Lewis's—when the radio announces that Otto Gorsky, the man the locals call Mr. Lovely, died last night from an unnamed disease. They refer to Lovely as a friend of the Philadelphia police, but they don't mention that half the force is as crooked as the Schuylkill. I picture the old man dying inside his mansion and wonder if his hired goons carved him like a turkey as he took his final breaths—or if he spent those last few moments sitting in an armchair, sipping cognac, wishing he'd lived a life he could be proud of. I promise myself I won't wind up in either one of those positions.

I lower the visor, slip on my dark glasses, and make a U-turn toward Northeast Philly. I'm tempted to bring the dough to the Hy-Hat, but not everything the champ has spent a lifetime preaching has been lost on me. If I can't return the cash to Lovely, I can put it where it belongs. I turn off Richmond, wind through a few side streets, and pull to the curb in front of 86 Fuller. It's a small, two-story brick rowhouse; I'm surprised to see Rose working in the garden so early in the morning. I picture Calvin coming home from the graveyard shift at the Baldwin factory and Rose waiting for him here, tending to her plants, just like she's doing now. Neither realized how soon their world would come crumbling down.

I reach into Lovely's envelope, pull out half the cash, and put my glasses on the seat beside me. As I walk up the path, Rose is on her knees, tying up a batch of dried branches. She probably hasn't done much out here since Calvin died and wants to clean it up before we roll into autumn.

"Hiya, Rose." My eyes shimmy but I don't bother turning away.

She looks up but continues working. She's not wearing any makeup and looks older than I remember—the pain of losing Calvin is still etched around her eyes. Her gloved hands are dirty; her smock is stained by grass and dirt.

"Jersey," she says. She has a vacant stare, the kind of look somebody gets when they're going through the motions of life but not really living it. She gives me a smile—from her lips, not her heart.

"Did you see the papers?" I say.

"Sure did," she says, gathering another bundle of branches. "I guess the truth had to come out sooner or later."

"Reeger had some scam going," I say. "Eventually, it came tumbling down. These things always do."

Rose stops working for a moment and her face sags.

"I'm glad that cop is dead," she says. She seems to be listening to her own words, as if they're coming from somebody else. I'm sure she never expected to be saying them herself. "I hope it was slow and painful."

"Well, Calvin helped," I say. "He didn't die in vain."

I'll never admit the truth: Calvin's death was a waste; it was the whimsy of a rogue bull with an agenda to fill and a wake of bodies behind him.

She shrugs. "I suppose so."

She gets back on her knees and starts plucking some weeds from the dirt.

"Calvin left you this," I say and hand her the cash. "I found it in the safe at the Hy-Hat."

Her eyes scrunch together; she doesn't believe me. "Calvin didn't have this kind of money," she says.

"I think he'd been putting it aside from his pay at the plant. He told me to give it to you if anything ever happened to him."

She shoves the cash in the pocket of her garden smock. Then she looks down and puts her face in her hands. She doesn't cry but her shoulders bob and her elbows shake.

"It can't get me Calvin back."

I feel guilty, as if I'm trying to buy her absolution with Lovely's blood money. But nobody can save Calvin now, and he would have wanted me to take care of her. This is the best I can do.

"He wanted you to have it," I say, swallowing the grief that's rattling the cage inside of me.

"Thank you," she says.

There's nothing left to say and we reach an awkward silence. It's clear she wants to be alone, so I tell her that I've got to leave. But I add that I'll visit the next time I'm in town.

"I'll be here," she says as she takes out a pair of pruning shears and goes to work on a shrub.

I wish her well and walk back to the Auburn. When I leave, I pull away slowly, and give one more wave from the driver's seat even though she's not looking my way. Then I turn on the radio. Connie Boswell is crooning "I'm All Dressed up with a Broken Heart." I know how she feels, and I bet Rose does, too.

It starts to rain, so I put on the wipers. It's a sun shower; it shouldn't last long. I've still got ten large in the envelope and I know where it's going to go. I drive into Overbrook and pull up on Malverne in front of the building marked *Pennsylvania Institution for the Instruction of the Blind*, a towering stone structure that sits at the top of a grass field. Three arches mark its main entrance.

I tug on my fedora and raise my lapels before hopping out of the Auburn. It's a light, steady rain; I trot across the manicured lawn and duck under the center arch, where I pull out a handkerchief and wipe my face dry. Then I shake the water from my oxfords and walk through one of the building's tall oak doors. The tiled lobby has a vaulted ceiling and an elaborate, gilded chandelier, but nobody is there to see it. Judging by the distant piano and singing voices, all the teachers and students are in an auditorium on the other side of the building.

I scan the lobby and spot a door with the words *Director's Office* written in gold across a beveled window. That's my man. I walk over and tap lightly on the glass; when nobody answers, I slip into the room and shut the door behind me. The place is dead quiet. Across the room, there's a desk with a nameplate that reads *Robert Sullivan, Director*, so I take out the rest of Lovely's money, grab a pen, and write a short message on the outside of the envelope: *For Louise Connor.* I leave it on the desk and trust that Mr. Sullivan will see it gets put to good use.

When I make my way out of the building, the rain has stopped, the sun is still shining, and the smell of wet grass fills the air. I walk back across the lawn and take off my fedora, letting the sun toast my damp skin for a few brief, glorious seconds.

Then I get behind the wheel of the Auburn, toss my hat on the seat beside me, and start the engine. There's nothing left for me in Philly. But that doesn't mean I have nowhere to go.

It's barely noon when I pull into Harlem. The sun shines down on 127th Street, and a cool breeze blows through the Auburn's open window. The doc's cream protects my face, and my dark glasses are doing the same for my eyes.

As I drive up 127th, I spot a delivery truck in front of the Hy-Hat. Something is out of whack. Three guys in overalls have pulled a new icebox off a truck and are wheeling it into the alleyway that leads to the service entrance. A dozen other boxes sit next to the truck; I can only assume they're also on their way into the joint.

I park across the street and walk into the club. The place is busy—four girls are playing ping-pong and a couple of boys are outside the kitchen licking ice cream cones—but the front of the game room has been cleared out. Fats Waller is coming through the radio and Billy Walker is pounding the dummy bag in the corner. The champ's got his jacket off and his sleeves rolled up as he barks out combinations.

"Left, right, left, uppercut," he shouts and Billy responds with a lightning-fast combination to the dummy bag.

"Hey, Champ," I call out.

His eyes light up when he sees me—they always have—and I hope he can tell that mine do the same when I see him. He gives me a wave and my lips stretch into a smile. His hand is free of the plaster cast that had been driving him crazy and racking me with guilt for the past two months.

"Sorry about Myra," he says as he walks over to me.

My father knows Myra died but he has no idea she set me up. I plan on leaving it that way—for the champ and for Myra.

"Thanks," I say. "But I'm doing okay."

He sizes me up and sees I'm speaking the truth.

"Hey, did you hear about this?" I say. I hold up the *Inquirer* with Garvey on the front page. My father never learned to read, but he can see Garvey's young, smiling face. I read him the headline.

"Yep, heard all about it," he says, nodding and taking the paper. "I'm gonna hang it up," he says. "Right over there."

He points toward the wall by the punching bag, about six feet from where he spends most of his time.

"Garvey would like that," I say and the champ nods again, more slowly this time.

One of the delivery guys pokes his head into the room and asks where we want the icebox. My father points toward the kitchen.

"What's going on, Champ?" I say. "We're fixing up the joint?"

My father gives me a smile. "We sure are. New pool tables, too." Then he nods toward the open area. "And a boxing ring."

"With what?" I say, cursing myself for giving away all of Lovely's cash.

"With the twenty-five large," he says.

Two more delivery guys trudge into the place carrying long boxes that I'm assuming hold the corners of the ring. The short guy with the beard wants to know where they should set up.

"Right over there," the champ tells them, pointing to the empty area by the dummy bag.

As the workers lay down the boxes, I turn and face the door so they can't hear me.

"What twenty-five large?" I ask the champ.

"The twenty-five large I found on my desk," he says and flashes me a sly smile.

I know my father, and he thinks I sent him the money. But I also know me, and I'm sure I didn't. I'm dead broke—I left the last of the cash on Sullivan's desk for Louise Connor.

"When did you find it?" I say.

His eyes narrow. I can see his wheels turning, trying to figure out if I'm covering up or not.

"Yesterday mornin'," he says slowly.

I may not have given the club the money, but I know who did. Lovely. It fits perfectly. He lived long enough to see the *Inquirer*—to see that Reeger died in disgrace—and credited me for it. He knew I wouldn't take the money, so he sent it here.

The champ's looking me over, the glint gone from his eyes. "That money ain't yours?"

His lower lip is hanging down as he waits for an explanation. He doesn't want anything that came through the law-breaking hands of Lovely, or Reeger, or any other crook. And I'm not about to argue with him because his convictions have put him in the shoes I wish I were wearing. He once told me that blood-stained money soils the soul and he was right.

But that particular pile of cash is stained with Lovely's blood, and Lovely is dead.

"It's mine," I tell him. "I didn't want you to know. I've been saving for years. I'm here, Champ, and I'm staying this time."

My father gives me a smile that could light a movie marquee. He wraps his beefy arms around me and squeezes so hard I feel my ribs bend.

"C'mon into the kitchen," he says. "They hadda unplug the old icebox. We gotta eat some of that stuff before it melts."

We go into the kitchen, grab a container of strawberry ice cream, and bring it outside where an early autumn breeze is cooling the Harlem streets. The champ brushes off a spot on the front steps of the club and sits himself down. I do the same, right next to him, in the shade.

I've got *The Beautiful and the Damned* under my arm, and I'm ready to start the next chapter. I can get as much out of it as anybody can—maybe more—and now that I'm free of the dirt that's been clinging to me for years, I will.

Inside, the workmen are stringing ropes around the boxing ring that the champ and I will use to teach the local kids hard work and discipline—the very things it took me a lifetime to learn.

My father holds the ice cream and we take turns dipping into the carton, one spoonful at a time, as we listen to the clackety-clack of paddles hitting ping-pong balls.

We're a long way from Santa Monica.

But we're close enough for me.

ACKNOWLEDGMENTS

*W*e meet again—this time in the basement of a Philadelphia brownstone. I'm glad you came. Rudy Vallee's on the radio and Doolie's pouring one last round of martinis. Let's close the place.

And while we're at it, let's toast a few special people.

Dan Mayer at Seventh Street Books did more than bring this novel to press. He rolled up his sleeves, grabbed some shinola, and polished its pages. And my agent Elizabeth Evans had the foresight to know he was the guy to do it. Here's to both of them.

There are others. Alex Jackson helped me find my way to Blind Moon Alley. Lee Martin deserves a nod, as does Dr. Dave Page, who assisted as I mended Jersey's broken nose. I'll also raise a glass to Larry and Jeff Trepel for adjusting the timing on Jersey's Auburn, not to mention the other cars that rolled through these pages.

Cheers.

The music has stopped and our glasses are empty, so it's time I head home to my wife, partner, first reader, and biggest fan,

Ouisie. She believed in Jersey, believed in me, and keeps me believing in myself. For that, I offer a humble thank-you and a bottomless heart.

Farewell for now. I hope to see you again for Jersey's next adventure. You know where to find me: I'll be at the bar with the rest of the gang, waiting to pour you a shot of moon.

ABOUT THE AUTHOR

*J*ohn Florio is a freelance writer whose work has appeared in print, on the web, and on television. He is the author of the Jersey Leo crime novels (*Sugar Pop Moon* and *Blind Moon Alley*) and *One Punch from the Promised Land: Leon Spinks, Michael Spinks, and the Myth of the Heavyweight Title*. He lives in Brooklyn, New York, with his wife, Ousie Shapiro. Visit him at johnfloriowriter.com.